Siren's Last Song

A SAPPHIC FANTASY

ASHLEIGH MARTIN

MARTIAN & CO PUBLISHING

MARTIAN & CO.
2026
PUBLISHING

For all the Black girls, gays, and theys that love fantasy.

Content Warning

While Siren's Last Song does contain romance, the novel primarily focuses on Avarie's grief about the death of her sibling. This may be difficult for some readers to experience. Please note additional content warnings below.

- Death of a sibling (off the page)
- Viewing of body (on the page)
- Interspecies prejudice

An updated list of all content warnings are available on the author's website.

"Siren's Last Song"

Drown her, drown her. Watch her go.
Down, down to the waters below.

Impostor, impostor. Seek her out.
Find her quick, ignore all doubt.

Drown her, drown her. Return where
    sirens lie.
If you don't, land dwellers may die.

Anonymous, excerpt from *Siren's Last Song* by L.H. Sirene

Aalto lingers by the entrance of his chambers, searching for a sign, for anything to alleviate the disquiet chiseled into his bones. Something doesn't feel right, he just can't quite put his fin on it.

He fiddles with the moon ring on his right hand. Another ring, symbolizing a more serious commitment, will soon encircle his marriage finger. Aalto longs for simpler days—rollicking around the palace with Avarie and Mairya without a care in the world . . . He thinks about Mai. He loves her, but he isn't foolish enough to believe their union is grounded solely in reciprocated feelings. Most betrothals aren't. Nevertheless, loving her was more than easy because of her kindness and encouragement in the moments of his screaming self-doubt. Something that he doesn't dare share with his family. He is the king-to-be. He can't share his fears with *anyone*. But Mai's private, listening ear makes his impending responsibilities feel all the lighter.

And being with her meant he didn't have to venture outside of Merelani for a bride—for reasons Aalto can't name, he feels a calling to stay close to home.

Everything will change after today.

A flash of movement catches his eye just as he is about to shut the door. He floats across the Grand Foyer to see a figure with scintillant purple scales swimming to the surface.

His heart drops, and what some may label as 'hereditary anger,' pulses in his chest.

"Good Goddess. What the hell is she doing?"

But he already knows.

Every guard in service to the palace is too busy with the coming ceremony to notice anything awry. Now is the perfect time for mischief.

He flies out the door and slams it shut, feeling a sense of foreboding finality.

She's a flighty contradiction. Avarie. A storm of curiosity and unease. He doesn't know how she does it—dethroning her fear for courage and vice versa. All he can do is accept that Avarie is skittishly turbulent.

A stubborn cough lodges in his throat. He fails to clear it. What is stuck there—an illness? Or ceremonial jitters?

A song?

Aalto prays for nothing of the sort.

It must be his imagination, though the dread brewing in his stomach screams otherwise. Perhaps it's some sort of solidarity with his chronically anxious twin. He worries for her, but that emotion cannot surpass his love. Nothing in this world will be more important than the sun to his moon.

Aalto hopes that one day Avarie can remove the heavy armor of anxiety with as much ease as he does.

For the thousandth time, he focuses on what he *can* control—another attempt at rescuing Avarie from harm. Whether from outside forces or the critical gaze of their father, it doesn't matter. Aalto will always rush to his twin's side for as long as he lives.

Chapter One

In the name of stubborn curiosity, and with a determined shimmy, Avarie bypasses the barrier concealing her watery home from poachers. The magical dome, which was invisible to outsiders, bends to her frame and allows her to drift past the outskirts of Merelani. Avarie throws a look over her shoulder, her locs spinning in a flurry as she verifies that the barrier is resealing.

A quick glimmer from the enchanted dome confirms its closure, the sight of it soothing Avarie. Her teeth sink into her bottom lip as she continues swimming to the surface. "It's fine. I've done this a million times."

Well . . . She's dreamed of this moment a million times.

Avarie knows humans like the back of her translucent fin. *Sorta*. It's perfectly safe to breach the surface at this time of day. *Probably.*

It would be a different story altogether if her father were to catch her outside of Merelani . . . He might not ground her— she's far too old for that—but Bruinen's disapproving scowl could make her *reconsider* going to the surface.

For a while, at least.

The human world is compelling to her, possessing her to ignore every rule her kind have, unspoken or otherwise. And the Denizian shoreline is so close that Avarie can already visualize its gritty sand in her hands.

Avarie breaches the surface, flicking her long, shimmering tail as her body bobs to the sea's dance. She remains where she is, about three mer-tails away from the pier, shoulders exposed to the open air and eyes zeroing in on the sand decorating the shore. In the distance, there's a group of docked ships. They appear so small from her vantage point, making her wonder their true size should they come closer.

"Bruinen would really lose it if I snuck ashore."

Despite her fears, the elusive world above the Merelani Sea still manages to send a ripple of curiosity through Avarie. With every fiber of her being—from the tip of her loc'd head, down to her webbed, fan-like tail—Avarie longs to know what it's like to live in their world.

Is it as wonderful as her books claim it to be?

Avarie has an idea in her mind about the human world. An inkling, really, derived solely from all the land-dweller books she's devoured. Her taste for all literature is insatiable, but human books are so much more seasoned, and numerous in quantity. Humans publish books prolifically. Merpeople? She's lucky to read one new book a year. It's also impossible to ignore the differences in writing—merpeople vehemently condemn humans while a small fraction of human authors craft stories of unity.

Well . . . There's this one human author lauding tales of harmony between their species.

A salty-sweet scent swells into Avarie's nose as she inhales, recentering her focus on the surrounding beauty. The water's rhythm is calm, her tail only needing to sway a little to keep her upper half above the water. Today will be a perfect day, she declares. One impossible to omit from memory.

Overhead, there's a cloudless sky. The swiftly awakening sun smiles down on her, drying the water droplets that speckle her exposed, brown skin. If the sky were an exquisite canvas, the sun would be the focal point drawing the viewer in and making them yearn to know the painting's meaning. The sun glimmers so intimately atop the water that it makes Avarie wonder if the Mother of the Sea also has some stake in the bright star.

Avarie continues observing the vacant shore. Just one innocent touch of the gritty sand is all she desires. That, and maybe a new book.

Crrkh!

Terror squeezes the air from her lungs, her bravery vanishing just as quickly as it arrived. Avarie ducks below the surface, eyes closed and shoulders trembling. She curls into a ball, ignoring the absurdity of the position, as if whatever made the noise will not see her in the crystal-clear sea.

"Father's going to be so mad—why couldn't I just follow the rules?"

Crrkh!

Avarie's tremors begin to cease.

Crrkh!

Her eyes pop open. Something about the repetitive noise does not seem human. "What is that sound?"

As per usual, curiosity usurps her fear. Avarie tentatively peeks above the water, only allowing her eyes and forehead to be visible.

A sheepish laugh leaves her mouth as she stares at the pier, noticing how the aged wooden planks groan against each other, creating an unpleasant and earsplitting noise. Although the worry is beginning to dissipate from her body, Avarie is reminded that the mere action of exposing her face to the open air is risky.

And breaching the shore is far worse.

It's foolish—*forbidden* to venture ashore. Merpeople experience excruciating pain when they fully flop onto dry land; their scales begin to shed one at time, like an agonizing sort of molting. The miserable sensation is carved deeply into their flesh, like a harpoon spearing an unsuspecting sea creature. It's cruel, really, to be punished for curiosity. Not to mention, there's an even worse outcome. If poachers were present, they would ensure Avarie never returns to the palace alive.

That thought alone gives Avarie pause. She fidgets with the sun-shaped jewelry on her right ring finger. She flicks the ring and watches the sun jewel spin on its small metal axis. It dances in the light like her scales. It is true that there hasn't been a poacher attack in two years. But all of Merelani knows that rising to the surface, as Avarie is foolishly doing now, can lead to casualty.

It certainly doesn't help that mermaids are often mistaken for sirens—those so-called sinkers of ships and killers of men. Although sirens were misunderstood themselves. The way humans think all sea creatures with long tails are alike is beyond insulting. Avarie has yet to meet a siren, but the stories she grew up with depict those groups of women as fierce protectors of the sea. They were warriors, not feral monsters bent on the unjust destruction of human life. Only cruelty could inspire a siren's vengeance.

Avarie cannot imagine stealing a human life when even plucking dead leaves from her garden's plants causes her pain. But despite knowing she could be mistaken for a siren, curiosity clings to Avarie's heart. It makes her want to resist the rules and ignore the insurmountable danger that could await her.

Just one touch . . .

Avarie deliberates as close to the shore as she can be without harming herself.

The warm sand looks enticing to her.

Avarie squints into the distance, eyeing a particular spot on the shore. There seems to be something embedded in the ground. Suddenly, as if to entice her further, a strong gust of wind blows the concealing sand away and reveals a book, its pages now flitting back and forth in the breeze.

Is this one she's yet to read? Or better yet, something from her favorite author, L.H. Sirene?

Can she be quick enough to flop ashore, grab it, and retreat back into the sea without anyone noticing? Or will the instant pain of leaving the water's safety prevent her from grabbing the book entirely?

With stubborn determination, and perhaps a little stupidity, Avarie makes her choice, the potential of an unread book serving as the final motivator. She double-checks the coast for humans. Satisfied by her solitude, Avarie inches forward. She slides her body to the thinnest part of the shore, fingers digging into the damp sand. The dry sand farther along sings to her; it looks as warm and as inviting as she remembers from childhood. Now, if she can just stomach the pain of losing a scale, the abandoned novel will no longer be out of her reach.

Just a few more inches . . .

Without warning, strong hands grasp her by the tail and yank her back into the deep. Her locs and arms plume upward into a straight line as the rest of her body is dragged in the opposite direction.

Chapter Two

Cries of protest croak from Avarie's throat as she is dragged back to safety, back to the concealing confines of the Merelani Sea. Mild anger heats her cheeks. She glares downward, knowing with certainty who she will see—Aalto. Her annoying and overprotective twin. Merelani's future heir.

"Let me go!" Avarie shouts while wiggling like a common eel.

"I can't. Not while you're being an idiot," Aalto says. His deep voice sounds serious, albeit with an edge of humor. "I knew you'd be out here. Of all days?"

Avarie's typically soft voice rises an octave. "If there ever was a time, why not when the focus is all on you, brother?" She winces from the change in pitch, a sure giveaway for when she's pulling an excuse out of her tail.

"I want you back at the palace, Avarie. At once. There's no time for games today. Daylight signals humans to roam freely, and their kind is not to be trusted." Serious Aalto returns, a frown eclipsing his face and making the scar on his lip curl at a comical angle. Avarie swallows down an amused laugh. She hates when Aalto acts like King Bruinen—all seriousness and no fun. But she knew from the beginning that he would become like their father. It's the consequence of being the firstborn.

Avarie rolls her eyes, though a small part of her knows Aalto is right. There will be no warning when a poacher attempts to capture her, just a split second she's not in control of. She's better off reading the multitudes of enchanted, waterproof books already stocked in her chambers.

Aalto continues the chiding speech that Avarie never asked to hear. "You've already lost one scale to dry land, sister, are you trying to lose the rest to poachers? Or did you want to get mistaken for a siren this time?"

Avarie remembers the first and only time she ever stole a moment on land. It was eight years ago, and the experience had clung to her mind like a barnacle to a boat. The instant she sat on land, her tail erupted into an invisible, arduous fire that left her squirming and screeching at the top of her lungs. She desperately clawed her way back into the sea, but not before a scale popped off. Goddess, that short-lived adventure hurt. She had only wanted to see the place where all her favorite books had come from, but all she got out of it was a pale, discolored spot on her right hip; it's a stark contrast to the rest of her luminescent purple scales. Still, she'd give almost anything to roll in that gritty sand once more.

But not today.

Today belongs to Aalto. It's his coronation. Not a time for Avarie to bend unsaid rules. Everything must go as planned when he accepts the throne.

Avarie's lips lock stubbornly shut, which, to her annoyance, prompts Aalto to continue speaking. "You don't find it silly to awaken every morning hoping that your favorite author will, by some stroke of enchanted luck, be sitting at the pier waiting for you? Why trade your safety for a glimpse of a human girl? I'm beginning to think you have a little crush."

Aalto's mischievous smile burns all her remaining patience away.

"You're a nuisance. A menace to Merelani. You know that, right?" She glares at her brother, but her frown eventually wavers and twists into a grin.

Aalto reaches forward and starts shaking her fin, knowing good and well that it will send her into a ticklish fit. "Mind you, I'm your favorite nuisance," he says.

Avarie flicks him away with her tail and laughs. "It's truly beyond concerning that they're letting you become king."

Aalto rolls his eyes, "Oh, so *you* want to rule instead, sister?"

Her mouth crumples into a genuine frown. "I swear on the Sea Goddess that I have no interest in becoming queen."

"Right. Merelani's shy, little sea worm. Or should I say 'bookworm,' since you'd rather read all day?"

"You are a menace!"

"What is it again—novels of girls falling in love? '*Riveting romance that'll shock your heart into feeling.*' That's on the back of one of your books, right?"

"Aalto, I love you. But you are the absolute worst—"

"Ah, ah . . . I'm not done yet." His grin turns wicked and his eyes brighten in amusement as they descend closer to the dome. "That L.H. Sirene gets awfully steamy. Should I tell father that you'd rather stay up reading those salacious land-dweller books instead of our tasteful nonfiction?" Aalto throws his head back in laughter, which makes Avarie narrow her eyes. "For Goddess's sake Avarie," he continues, "I think the Royal Garden's dying. Please pick up a plant book."

Her voice jumps to the highest of octaves. "They're far from salacious! They're—they're beautifully composed love tales. Plus—she doesn't *only* write romance. You can't ignore the fantastical elements sprinkled in, the *amazing* figurative language. She handles loss and grief with so much care. It's almost as if she's pulling from her own experiences. L.H. Sirene is far from crude." Avarie crosses arms around her chest with exasperation.

"How would you know? You've never met the girl; she could be as torrid as they come, and it frightens me that this unknown author could lead my sister down a trail of debauchery. I better tell father this instant!"

"Do *not* tell father! I'll never receive another human book again."

For a second, Avarie wonders how ridiculous they must look—two members of royalty hovering above Merelani's border and extensively discussing her *slightly* unwholesome reading preferences.

And maybe that's why she continues risking her safety. She just knows that L.H. Sirene understands her, maybe as much as her conniving brother. Maybe much more than her kingdom; they only see her as Aalto's meek twin. But the way Sirene composes her characters, gifting them layers upon layers of depth, she just knows that she'll see past the surface level of Avarie too.

Aalto grabs her by the hand again, the rings on both of their fingers clinking, hers a sun and his a metal moon, a secret to the nervous nature they once shared. He dips his head to the side, locs swaying in the same direction. "I wouldn't dare. At least one of us should have fun. But you have to promise me one thing." He squeezes their hands together.

Avarie notes the straightness of his lips, the lack of a sarcastic frown, and the weight of responsibility in his dead-set gaze.

"Our dome's surface grows ever more transparent and fragile. Father and I discovered that it deteriorates the most during the transition from midfrost to summertide, and it weakens even more every time it's breached. The dome can't expel nearby humans if it's fractured. Until the Enchantress crafts a spell to render it unbreakable and keep Merelani invisible to humans permanently, *please* stay within the barrier's limits. I want you to be happy. But more than that, I want you and *all* of Merelani to be safe." Aalto's stern expression softens. "You can breach the barrier all you want once it's secure—but I'm *still* not letting you out here without guards to ensure your safety."

Avarie squeezes his hand before pulling away. She wants to ask why he and Bruinen always leave her out of the loop. She had no idea that the barrier was on the brink of collapse, or that breaching makes it weaker—but it all makes sense now. Creatures are not confined to the border, they pass through the dome just as merfolk do. It doesn't help that the greatest migration of sea life happens when the seasons shift. Between Avarie's excursions and all the underwater creatures, the dome could truly break.

If she had known, she never would've come out here. But she speculates that Bruinen and Aalto had assumed she couldn't handle the news—because they find her as fragile as the barrier. Avarie opts for an easier question instead of asking why they didn't tell her: "Guards? Why multiple?"

"Whether you like it or not, you're next in line for the throne. We have to protect you at all costs. Oh, and the way mother would never let me hear the end of it if something happened to you!" He widens his eyes dramatically.

"I'm *hardly* as important as you are." Her sarcasm is loud, but Avarie knows Aalto can hear the faint whisper of inferiority in her tone.

Aalto drags Avarie into a hug. The embrace soothes her acutely somber mood. "You and Mairya are two of the most important beings in my world. When I become king, what matters to me will matter tenfold to all of Merelani. You are special, Ava. I know living in my shadow hasn't been pleasant, but I value your spirit, and your kind perspective on everything. I—I can't—I *won't* do this without you."

Somehow, her brother always knows what to say to silence her self-deprecation, and Avarie's more than grateful for it.

"Well, come on then. Stop stalling. We've got a coronation to prepare for," she says with a smile before swimming alongside her brother to their home—the royal palace of Merelani.

As they pass through the barrier, Avarie looks over her shoulder. The barrier shimmers before going still . . . But when the sun's rays touch Merelani's protective dome, Avarie swears that she can see an incandescent fracture. Her heart freezes. She blinks thrice.

When she looks at the barrier again, the fracture is gone.

Avarie decides to keep the strange occurrence to herself. Aalto doesn't need to worry about anything else today.

She shrugs. It's probably fine.

AVARIE FACES THE TILTED OVAL MIRROR RESTING IN the corner near her reading nook. The mirror's outer rim is embellished with a thick trim of gold; along it are traditional Merelani jewels, their hue a deep and mesmerizing dark green. These gems of varying sizes are embedded unsparingly around the mirror's circumference.

The mirror is around eighteen years, like Avarie. In her youth, it loomed over her like a paternal figure, watching her with the care and pride she wished her father would bestow upon her. Now, she's of a similar height to the mirror, with only the smallest of breaths between their individual statures.

Oh, but her favorite space in the room is the reading nook nestled underneath her translucent coral window. The window always gives a satisfying shimmer when the sunlight penetrates through it. Avarie likes to imagine that the near see-through coral mimics what the humans call 'stained glass.' Her reading nook, with its assortment of books stacked haphazardly around her chambers, is her safe place.

Avarie remembers the first time it clicked for her that letters became words, then sentences, and that sentences could be strung together into full-length books . . . Her fondness for reading has only grown with time. Avarie and her father were often at odds, her timid yet impulsive nature always clashing with his expectations of her. But one kindness he did for her was retrieving books from sunken ships, having the Enchantress waterproof them, and allowing Avarie to read for hours on end.

The waterproofing isn't perfect, but the Enchantress can restore the books with minimal page bleeding and tears. Avarie can't complain. After all, she's spent many nights with a book clutched firmly in her fingers until fatigue finally stole her consciousness. Avarie's bed may have the highest of thread counts and the softest pillows—but the nook is her first choice for relaxation.

Fond memories of consuming book after book bring a smile to her face. Avarie stares into the mirror, seeing the present and past duality of her 'Self' as she's being dressed.

Her maidservant, Mrs. Clara, who has been dressing Avarie since her youth, clasps Avarie's brassier behind her back. The gaudy garment is unmistakably regal, with its green and purple jewels that were heavy enough to sink her. Yet 'queenly' is something Avarie can never be—that's reserved for her mother, Cordelia. Avarie prefers a carefree lifestyle, sitting in her nook and devouring tales of love—of tragedy and comedy and horror, all of it—all day. But indulgence is not a realistic part of her world, it's incompatible with her royal duties. Avarie could never be queen. She doesn't *want* to be queen.

Thank the Sea Goddess, she wouldn't be, what with Aalto being the firstborn and all. But she'll have other duties—hosting community events, maintaining the Royal Garden, and whatever else her brother will delegate to her once he's too busy being king.

The light amethyst scales on her body darken with annoyance. Like color-changing cuttlefish, the scales of merpeople can alter pigment. Although for merfolk, it usually happens because of sudden or heightened emotions, not for camouflage. Avarie loves her brother wholeheartedly, but knowing from a young age that she'd end up serving his every whim left her feeling dejected. And she always wondered what it would feel like to abandon all her responsibilities.

Mrs. Clara slips a silk shawl up Avarie's arms and onto her shoulders. It was a luxurious fabric made from the rare secretions of a pen shell mollusk. She clasps a matching chain belt dotted with authentic pearls right where Avarie's stomach and scales meet. The layered belt has additional chains that drape down in half-moons on either side of her hips, a fancier version of the waist beads Avarie was wearing earlier.

The mermaiden begins applying ceremonial paint on Avarie's skin, a shimmery paste of crushed abalone and pearl. Intricate swirls, dots, lines across her neck, collarbone, and arms. Mrs. Clara avoids Avarie's midsection, as paste is only permitted there for expectant merpeople. In an aged voice, Mrs. Clara remarks, "How grown you have become, my dear. You look beautiful. I'm sure others have noticed too. Has anyone captured *your* heart recently?" The mermaiden waits for a response as she removes Avarie's crown from its glass encasement. The majestic headpiece gleams in the light filtering through Avarie's expansive window.

Avarie sighs. She knows that the merwoman means well, but everyone in the kingdom must be wondering the same thing too. "Not yet, Mrs. Clara. There's hardly any merwomen highly ranked enough to wed in this kingdom. Father doesn't take kindly to outsiders either." Avarie remembers the first time she kissed a mergirl. The king was furious. *How dare she press her lips to a commoner?* That was the first time she realized how different her life was compared to other merpeople.

Mrs. Clara laughs lightheartedly, her bob-length braids shaking along with the movement of her head. "Well, you never know, my dear. Love can ensnare you at the most unexpected, and sometimes inconvenient time." The mermaiden affixes the crown atop Avarie's head; her locs fall past her lower back, golden cuffs adorning some of its strands. The gold of her crown outshines the trim of the full-length mirror entirely. Mrs. Clara puts distance between the two of them and observes her handiwork. "Any woman would be lucky to have you. Now come. Let us make our way to the grand staircase for your announcement. The king would hate it if you were late, Princess Avarie."

Today, impulsiveness wins again.

Craving another moment to herself, especially after her thwarted venture ashore, Avarie makes a left out of her chamber's double doors and disappears down a side hallway and heads straight for the Royal Garden.

Despite Aalto's ribbing about the state of her plants, Avarie loves taking care of them. Nothing beats getting lost in a good novel, but she'll take tending to the garden as a close second.

Avarie swims faster at the sight of the first set of water-resistant arches leading into the garden, a feeling of contentment propelling her tail as she passes through them. The three arches were adorned with sea roses, their black vines intertwining through each of the archways' grooves. They are a sight to behold, and Avarie's favorite out of all the plants.

She loves the roses for their resilience, for the way they endure every season, and their beautiful mint hue and their mesmerizing scent that, somehow, could melt the stress from Avarie's shoulders with one sniff. She touches every arch past the entrance, and with each passing second, disappears into her own world.

The rest of Merelani can wait. Her plants need her.

Avarie hums to the centuries-old coral that exist in a vast array of hues, sizes, and textures. She read somewhere that communicating with plants helps them grow stronger. Her mouth waters, daydreaming about the savory crunch of coral chips. She hopes some will be served after the coronation.

The next garden patch is reserved for the intensely dark-purple kelp. A little too slimy for her tastes, but with a thickening sauce and a sprinkling of salmon, the stringy plant is tolerable. Avarie continues her light humming as she passes the wild stalks of seagrass. She wishes to sing, but that's impossible. Merfolk cannot sing as they please—that's the stark difference between them and sirens. There are only two reasons that merpeople sing: after birth, akin to a human baby's first cry, and . . .

Avarie refuses to think of the latter.

On her fourth circle around the garden, she hears her name being called.

"Avarie. I knew I'd find you here."

Avarie freezes in place, feeling like a merchild again. Her shoulders instinctively lift to her ears. She grasps onto an arch, dropping her nose into the nearest sea rose. Her shoulders relax.

"Momma Cordelia, I didn't notice your presence."

Her mother laughs with authentic amusement. "I know

you, daughter. If you aren't in your nook, you're with the plants."

Sheepishly, Avarie turns around, an embarrassed smile pinching at the corners of her mouth. She flicks the sun ring on her finger.

"I just needed a moment. A few seconds to myself."

Cordelia envelopes her into a hug and Avarie returns it without hesitation.

"Ah. Just like when you attempted to breach the shore earlier today?" Queen Cordelia raises a knowing eyebrow.

How does she know that?

Damn it, Aalto.

Avarie shakes away her chronic annoyance for her brother.

"Momma, you know everything, don't you?"

"When it comes to my twins, yes. Even if Aalto—" Cordelia pauses to laugh again, "Even if your brother had not shared it with me, it's intuition. Maybe one day you will experience that for yourself."

Avarie chews her lip. She's yet to manage a thorough thought about children. At first glance, the idea seems appealing. But the reality is that she couldn't, and *wouldn't* raise a merchild without a partner. Sure, it's possible, but it's not a choice Avarie wishes to make. Right now, these plants and her books are Avarie's progeny. "Maybe, Momma Cordelia. Maybe. Perhaps a discussion for another time? I suppose right now it's time to support Aalto. It's the most significant day of his life, after all."

Cordelia extends her hand and Avarie clasps it. "Very well, I won't lecture you. I'm certain your brother already did. Let's make our way to the Grand Foyer. We can't start without you, precious daughter."

Hand in hand, Cordelia and Avarie leave the garden. Unable to resist a final glance at her plants, Avarie peers over her shoulder and catches something that looks like a flicker of lightning. If she had blinked then, she would've missed it entirely.

Avarie tells herself that this irregularity from the usually serene sky and the barrier's temporary fracture earlier mean nothing.

It's probably fine.

Right?

Chapter Three

"Her Royal Highness, Princess Avarie of Merelani!"

The herald's voice booms through the Grand Foyer, carrying upward to her and below to the crowded ground floor. Avarie's sick of being announced first because she's the lowest-ranking member of the royal family. She prays that the announcer and the citizens of Merelani watching her cannot decipher the fear in her eyes. Avarie wants to appear calm, composed—but she probably resembles a panicked, out-of-water fish in desperate need of rescue. She digs her nails into the railing, grasping for purchase on her reality as she guides herself to the foyer's balcony where the thrones reside.

Avarie nods in acknowledgment. She barely manages to prevent her crown from slipping off, her shaky hands darting up to reposition it atop her head. She sits. The ornate, golden chair sends a chill up her spine. Since her shawl only covers her jeweled brassiere, the rest of her back remains exposed. Her long, crescent shaped nails tap the armrests. She hopes the coronation passes with haste.

The palace is massive. It has three cavernous floors and

numerous rooms. But a real testament to its size is the ground floor where the kingdom's citizens are gathering. Overhead, there's a rectangular sunroof casting a glittering light upon excited attendees. The waiting crowd is vast and densely packed, a kaleidoscope of diversity in terms of ages, skin tones, and genders. Avarie swallows a lump in her throat and flicks her ring as an anxiety-riddled afterthought.

It would be Aalto waiting in her golden seat had things been different . . . But instead, the pearl encapsulating her twin twinkled with life first. They were born from the same oyster, but Avarie took a little more time. Eighteen minutes to be exact. And so, she sits here, waiting for her family to arrive and for Aalto to be crowned king. She's okay with that; the anxiety of ruling a kingdom might just crush her. But that doesn't stop her from wishing the stigma of being secondborn would cease following her like a shark stalking its injured prey.

The herald continues, voice laced with pride: "Queen Cordelia of Merelani!"

Avarie's mother floats through the entrance, chin held high, her black box braids pulled smartly into a bun atop her head, with an ornate crown as the centerpiece. It would be the ultimate blessing from the Goddess if Avarie could exude even an ounce of the confidence her mother possesses.

"Now then, please rise if you have yet to do so." Merpeople in the crowd below straighten their posture and tighten their attention on the balcony. Avarie rises from her seat and adjusts her crown once more. Her father expects perfection. But she'll just have to give him her best.

"Presenting: His Royal Majesty, King Bruinen of Merelani!"

Avarie's father breezes past her, his crown the most decorated of them all, encrusted with small sparkling white diamonds, and the largest Merelani jewel Avarie's ever seen at its center. Momma Cordelia looks to Bruinen with tired, yet loving eyes. Over thirty-five years of ruling together, and now they may finally rest. It's Merelani's custom that the ruling monarchs pass the crown to their eldest offspring after they turn eighteen years—for it would not serve their kingdom to allow rulers to make decisions for a future they may not live to see.

With his arms splayed wide, her father takes over the introductions. His voice, deep and commanding, booms through the packed foyer. "It is with ultimate joy that I announce my eldest, my son, Prince Aalto of Merelani! May he serve all of you well. From the members of the royal court to our villagers that do the hard and necessary work to keep Merelani thriving. May he keep us safe from the land dwellers encroaching upon our territory, who steal our beloved fish and scales for their personal gain. The weight of the crown is harrowing, but I don't know anyone better suited to wear it."

Avarie looks down, disheartened by her father's candor. She knows he doesn't think she has what it takes to rule, but it's even worse to hear him announce it to the entire kingdom. Her father continues, "I present to you all my beloved son, Aalto. The new reigning King of Merelani."

Claps erupt from the crowd and little merchildren let out gleeful screams. Aalto emerges from the opposite balcony, looking every bit the king he's meant to be. His locs, though shorter than Avarie's, are contorted into an intricate twist down his back. Aalto's dark skin flashes against the gold paint on his bare arms and chest, and the golden clasp wrapped around the bulging muscles of his right arm. His straight white teeth gleam with outright pride. This is his moment, and Avarie couldn't dream of souring it despite her complicated relationship with their father.

Even the sun is managing to shine brightly, sending rays of hope and glee through the massive sunroof of the foyer. Aalto gives a regal bow to the crowd before swimming over to hug

Avarie and Momma Cordelia, and to clasp Bruinen's huge hands. When he leans in for the embrace, his hair smells just like hers, like freshly plucked sea roses.

The herald appears, holding a crown atop a royal-purple tassel pillow. Aalto bends down, accepting his new crown. He then gestures to someone and out comes Mairya, his bride-to-be, passing through the mollusk satin curtains. The tawny merwoman with straight black hair and almond eyes is beaming with joy. She leans in to kiss Aalto.

Sometimes Avarie wishes to be Aalto, to have what he has—affection from another, as well as her father's pride.

A longing begins nesting within Avarie's stomach as her eyes linger on Mai—then shame overcomes her. She looks down and isn't at all surprised that her purple scales have changed hue. Avarie only hopes that no one else has noticed. The amassed crowd didn't make her break composure, but somehow a stupid childhood crush that won't wash itself away, does. In more ways than one, Avarie remains second to her brother.

Aalto and Mairya come together to lift their conjoined fingers up to the sky. What a joyous, picturesque moment. Avarie swallows down her jealousy because, more than anything, she loves her brother. It's not his fault Avarie's spent too many years being secretly lovesick over Mai. It isn't his fault that Bruinen's an unfair, distant father to her either.

The crowd erupts into cheers again, many are waving at the couple and some are hugging each other. Servants at the banisters hoist up the Merelani flag, each enchanted cloth swaying with ease. Avarie loves to look at the flag. It encompasses so much gorgeous mystery and symbolism. From the starry night sky and the waves that meet at the dark horizon, to a slender brown hand reaching upward from the sea to cradle a single star. It's unquestionably the Sea Goddess's fingers reaching from the beautiful void below, signaling harmony between the sea and the world above. If only this were actualized in real life.

Avarie places a hand to her quickly beating heart. A new era begins today. An even better one, though their parents were fair rulers. Momma Cordelia often dealt out grace when Bruinen desired punishment—though Bruinen's stringent reign never resulted in fear or anarchy. But all that is now past.

Avarie's shoulders relax. She will work through her fear of public speaking and compromise with Aalto on whatever he asks her to do. This will be easy, painless, and Mairya will be there too, the future queen; the three of them grew up together, and despite Avarie's complicated feelings, they remain close. She hopes their closeness will inspire the kingdom further.

This day is truly shaping up to be perfect.

Then the world above Merelani shifts.

The sky darkens and a menacing, thunder-like boom deadens the chorus of cheers. Avarie falls back onto her throne, stunned by the lightning pulsing overhead, illuminating the dreary sky to reveal not one, but *hundreds* of glowing cracks in their barrier. High up and near the surface, a hulking ship appears right above Avarie's head, suddenly visible through the foyer's coral sunroof.

The one-way barrier should be concealing the kingdom from anything that does not live under the sea, if she can see the human's boat, then surely they can see Merelani as well. Then the ship births some sort of vessel. It plops into the sea and down, down, down it chugs slowly toward their dome.

Avarie squeezes her ring so hard, the pointy rays around the sun jewel's circumference prick her skin, drawing drops of purple ichor to the surface. She wipes the blood on her shawl and flinches at every additional flash of lightning.

Aalto shoots her a look of knowing apprehension. She

can't bear the intensity of his gaze, so she stares at her hands before shutting her eyes altogether.

The screaming starts after multiple flares, unleashed by the diving vessel, crash into the palace's sunroof and burst like perilous fireworks. Coronation attendees disperse like octopi scattering after they've released ink.

But all Avarie can register in her mind is that the land dwellers are *here*.

Everyone in Merelani is in danger.

And it's all her fault.

The coral roof cracks and jagged shards rain down on the merfolk who had been too frozen to vacate the foyer.

A drumming noise pulsates from somewhere far above them, reverberating in eerie waves that dance strikingly across the seafloor. It is followed by an even worse tune, that of a scratchy whistle building up, mimicking the screech of a creature screaming in abject terror. Others follow, joining the mighty instrument, crafting a symphony of high-pitched shrieks.

The disturbing music slices through Avarie's thoughts—it's deep, evocative. A haunting cacophony Avarie's only ever heard stories of. However, tales of the Poacher's Song do not do it justice; not the way it makes her spine tingle and her pierced ears prickle, or the way it evokes a chill deep in her bones that she can't shake.

Avarie's hand clenches into a fist around the fabric of her shawl, her nails piercing through the material and into the skin underneath. She watches as tension manifests all over her father's body. The dome had come into existence long before

Bruinen became king, and now it's in peril. His mouth contorts into a gruesome snarl and his hand, which was still wielding the royal staff tightens. His broad shoulders pull back, entire body taut like the war bows in Avarie's books. Bruinen's tail darkens to a murderous red hue. Avarie knows he's upset for two reasons:

Land dwellers have threatened the people of Merelani.

And Bruinen can't intervene because he's no longer king.

Aalto eyes the surface, gritting his teeth at the massive ship that's likely chock-full of poachers. His thick brows, identical to Avarie's, crinkle with distaste and apprehension. Her mother's face never falters, ever playing the role of a stoic queen. Avarie gathers next to her mother, burrowing into her welcoming arms, and whispers, "What is to be done?"

Land dwellers have never interrupted such a monumental moment—Avarie doubts the humans even know that—but worse still, in all the Merelani literature she's devoured, Avarie's yet to read about an interaction between their people that ends peacefully. And humans have never gotten this close before; poachers usually attacked lone merfolk who strayed near the surface. That's why breaching the barrier was discouraged—if you dared to go beyond the border, you could be lost forever.

Avarie peeks out from under her mother's embrace. They both shift their gazes to Aalto, who was caressing Mairya's hand. Avarie clutches her mother's forearm, and Cordelia places a hand over her frantic touch, their brown hands fitting together like otters grasping paws in the night.

There's a weighty silence before Cordelia speaks, "If we had time, I'd suggest your brother strategize with the Enchantress. There is nothing that powerful merwoman can't fix."

The Enchantress? Avarie's eyes widen. Of course, she can

solve their problem! She has to tell Aalto even if it goes against tradition.

Mairya squeezes their hands together, perhaps in a doting attempt to strangle Aalto's simmering rage. Yet by his eyes alone—the storm swirling inside of them—Avarie knows the merwoman's efforts are futile.

As Avarie starts toward Aalto, plan brewing on her lips, he speaks. "As your new king"—Aalto makes eye contact with every remaining commoner—"I will ascend to the surface. I won't allow measly land dwellers to poach from us or contaminate our waters. I will secure the barrier."

By yourself?

He can't be thinking that he'll stop them alone. The ship is large enough to catch thousands of crabs and large fish; they must have a sizable group with nets and weapons!

Avarie's grip tightens around her mother.

Mairya cries out and latches onto Aalto. She shakes her head with vigor as he, with tenderness, pries her slender fingers away. Aalto wraps Mairya into a hug and whispers something in her ear. Her shoulders shake, but she nods in agreement to whatever he says. Aalto removes the crown and returns it to their father. Bruinen claps a strong hand on Aalto's shoulder in acceptance.

"For safekeeping," her brother states.

Aalto dips his chin to Avarie and Cordelia before gesturing for three guards to follow him. The guards are already outfitted with sturdy breastplates, shields, spears, and helmets. But Aalto lacks the same protective gear.

"Come," he orders the guards, "to the armory! I will show these land dwellers that the new King of Merelani will take action, just as the former king had done." His speech earns him an immediate nod of approval from their father.

Aalto and the guards prepare to vacate the foyer for the armory nestled in the far back-left of the palace, just a few tails from the Enchantress's room. Avarie's stomach flops with nausea.

What does Aalto intend to do?

Body to body, limb to limb, all those remaining in the foyer huddle close. The storm above them continues to rage, and Avarie glimpses what must be a tangle of knots being thrown into the water. A net?

Avarie expects her brother to breeze past her and go straight for the armory, but instead Aalto stops right in front of her, grabbing onto her shoulders with both hands.

"Aalto, the Enchant—"

He shakes her and Avarie's voice falls away.

Like the gradual changes of a moon phase, Aalto's face transforms into the spitting image of their stern father. "Go to your chambers. We need you safe."

"Let me help you, please."

"Now, Ava. I don't have time to argue. I have to fix this."

I have to fix what you did, Avarie.

He doesn't say it, but the words hang heavily between them both.

And that's enough to make her flee the royal balcony, the sting of Aalto's unsaid words propelling her forward. Her breath comes in erratic spurts, the walls of the palace blurring as she retreats to her chambers.

She slams the door shut with shaky hands, recoiling as if the door handles burned her flesh.

It's your fault, Avarie.

You broke the barrier, Avarie.

"I-I didn't mean to," she laments in such a weak voice, she can scarcely hear it.

Avarie's body screams for her to collapse, but her mind compels her to swim with manic flair, from her bedpost to the window nook, back and forth like a tsunami of unbridled anxiety.

She imagines numerous boats brimming with hungry, human eyes waiting for the chance to attack. Heavy nets diving low into their waters, scooping away innocent merfolk. Each glance toward the curtain-covered window stokes her anxiousness to new peaks, and looking at her untouched ceiling only makes her visualize the Grand Foyer's demolished sunroof.

What is Aalto thinking? He *isn't* thinking. They both share the same touch of impulsiveness. But his proves far riskier since it hails from fury rather than curiosity. Lightning flashes against the window, jarring Avarie to a startled stop. She resigns to sitting on the bed and eyeing the glass separating her from the outside.

Suddenly, lightning and thunder rocks the palace and sends Avarie cowering beneath the covers, reminding her of the times Momma Cordelia soothed her when storms would shake her tiny world. Avarie longs for her presence now, but her mother must remain with Bruinen.

Soothing him.

Comforting him.

Attempting to make his darkened scarlet scales simmer down to their natural, bright red.

A bitterness swarms her heart for a second, awareness that she's alone with no one to comfort *her*. For now, Avarie can do nothing but shiver underneath the duvet, feeling every bit like the six-year-old that needed reassurance from her mother.

Until, eventually, she feels nothing at all.

Until her consciousness is a distant memory against the backdrop of thunder and human-made flares.

AVARIE WAKES UP IN HER CHAMBERS. BEFORE SHE can even begin to berate herself for fainting at such an uncertain time, the melody of a merperson's wail kills her every thought. The beautiful song brings tears to her eyes—and sickness. She hurtles to her reading nook and thrusts open the windows, dry heaving and hoping against hope that the enthralling yet frightening noise is only her imagination.

Merfolk only sing twice in their lifetime. When they are born . . . and as they are dying.

The unease from earlier mates with her current nausea, creating a new queasiness that Avarie has never experienced. Feeling trepidation, she clutches her finger, flicking the sun wheel on her ring. The jewelry was a gift from Aalto on their sixteenth birthday. Avarie had given him one with a rotating moon that same year. For a small moment, this is enough to still her troubled thoughts. Unfortunately, the self-soothing is usurped by a dread so powerful, Avarie wonders if it will destroy her nerves altogether.

Avarie slams the window shut and vacates the reading nook. She slaps her palms over her ears, hoping to drown out the noise. But it only creates a ringing in her ears. She floats over to her bed and covers her entire face with a pillow.

"No, no, no . . . this can't be," she whispers to herself. The now muffled singing dissipates, replaced by a familiar yet guttural scream; an eerie distortion of her mother's always calm, always collected tone.

"Mother of the Sea . . . please."

Avarie doesn't pray often, but she finds herself begging, pleading with the Goddess for everything to be alright. For that merperson's last song to be unsung. For her mother's wails to come to an end. Avarie can't imagine what Cordelia's face may look like right now. The anguish in her voice is nothing Avarie has ever heard. The knots in her stomach twist into something worse, pain that forces her to bend at the waist. She lets go of the pillows, wrapping her hands around the lower half of her tail in a fetal position she hasn't done in years. Avarie stays like this for a few seconds . . . but when the pain fails to dissipate, she gets up with a shaky sigh.

Avarie swims to the large, heavy entrance doors of her chambers and, with trembling arms, swings one open. She rounds the corner, flying down the stairs at a breakneck pace. Upon reaching the palace's foyer, she sees that the ship and its looming presence in the sky are now gone. The barrier shimmers, blemish-free, and disappears from view. But the day remains hideous. Her mother has collapsed at the center of the Grand Foyer's ground floor, a tiny, perfect dot over the Merelani crest engraved on the marble flooring. Cordelia's body is draped over something Avarie cannot see, rocking back and forth rapidly.

And her tail . . . it's so *green*.

A sickly, muted hue. Like vomit. Like infected sea roses. A stark contrast from its regal emerald.

The next thing Avarie notices is her crown. In her mother's franticness, her braids had fallen from their once precise bun, and her crown now lay upended on the floor. Royal crowns must *never* touch the ground, that signified weakness, defeat—

The sounds of her mother's sorrow increasing octave by painful octave washes away the rest of Avarie's thoughts.

As Cordelia screams, the guards surround her, preventing Avarie from seeing what her mother is cradling.

Or who.

As Avarie draws nearer, the solemn-faced guards allow her the smallest of space to swim through.

Avarie is unsure if she is ready to see what her mother is clinging to. A huge gulp slips down her throat before she kneels behind her mother, tail folding neatly underneath her. Avarie reaches up to place a shaky hand on Cordelia's right shoulder.

Her mother stiffens before looking at Avarie with hollow,

dark eyes. "Look at what they have done," she despairs. "My baby boy—my son—our king!" Cordelia collapses down again. "Monsters, monsters . . . monsters, the lot of them." Avarie doesn't think she can feel sicker, but her mother's muffled wails stir another wave of nausea inside her.

Avarie lifts herself up to gaze over her mother's shoulder, with the intention of a quick glance. But her eyes become glued to the desecration before her. A scream would not suffice. Her shoulders begin to shake with such violence that Avarie almost falls over. Straight away she's gasping for air, as if she, herself, has become a human that cannot breathe underwater.

There he is.

On display in such a horrid fashion. There's no way Avarie could conjure such a grotesque image on her own. But now, the sight of him is embedded in her brain. She will see this in her sleep, in those first few moments after waking—every day for the rest of her existence. Her twin brother's body, crumpled and lifeless.

Scaleless.

Each beautiful scale has been plucked cleanly off like flower petals, leaving the exposed flesh underneath a gaping, bloody mess. His immaculate, onyx fin is missing, severed. Carved into his bare chest is a symbol Avarie's never seen before; there, enclosed in a circle, a broken oyster and pearl missing from its center. It must belong to the poachers that took her brother. *This.* This is what she'll see in her sleep. This symbol of hate carved into his flesh. Avarie's scales darken to an unrecognizable color as remorse and desolation take over.

My fault.
My fault.
My fault.
I did this. It's my fault. I killed my brother.

Chapter Five

"How—how will the kingdom ever recover from this?"

How will I recover?

Her question is drowned out by the lamentation of the villagers who had remained in the Grand Foyer. They are huddled together, tails tucked beneath them, arms squeezing their loved ones. Looking at them, Avarie didn't think anyone would have an answer to her question.

The guards who accompanied Aalto to the surface are also nowhere to be found. Avarie's ears strain to hear what might be far-off singing . . . a distant chorus of voices. Or maybe she's losing it. Certainly, no one would fault her if she were.

Bruinen's howls shake the walls of the palace. But that's impossible, right? No voice is that strong. "Land dwellers will not sabotage our way of life. We will make them pay. Our king will be avenged!" His words carry through the once lively hall, reaching all those who had stayed awaiting Aalto's safe return.

With a shaky breath, Avarie nods in agreement, though not wholly comprehending her father's words.

Her twin is dead.

Her only sibling is gone.

Their king has perished.

Avarie attempts to rise, but she's forced back down to the ground. Her hands splay out behind her, softening her fall to the floor. Her limbs are unsteady, vibrating without her doing. Is she so distraught that she's lost command over her own body?

No.

The seafloor is shaking.

Villagers shriek. They begin flooding out of the palace with frantic eyes and jerky movements. Small chunks of stone and coral drop like rain from what remains of the Grand Foyer's ceiling. One hits Avarie on her temple, resulting in a hot flash of pain. Instinctively, she puts a hand to her head, and without both firmly planted beneath her, Avarie is thrown face down into the marble flooring.

"What's happening?" Avarie screams, but her voice is swallowed whole by the cries of merpeople escaping the palace.

Her mother doesn't move, still hyperfocused on Aalto. Bruinen stares upward, dodging the raining coral and stone. It's the first time Avarie's ever seen her father look worried.

Panicked shouts bounce around the near demolished foyer:

"She's angry!"

"They've disrespected the Goddess."

"We must flee before it's too late!"

Commoners rush to vacate the palace, but some get struck by falling stone. They are pinned to the ruined floor, their consciousness knocked swiftly from their bodies.

Avarie's ears start ringing again, she claps both hands over them. The room feels too warm, her line of sight too narrow, and her breathing is too shallow to even blow out an enchanted candle.

Damn it, she can't afford to black out right now.

Then—nothing—the quakes stop as quickly as they began. Avarie rolls onto her back, breath labored and temple aching. Villagers pause their anxious attempts to vacate the palace. All turn their eyes to Bruinen for an answer.

Bruinen clears his throat, wiping away all the unadulterated pain from his face. Avarie shuts her eyes, waiting for her vision to return to normal. "These seaquakes could mean many things. But I *know* they are not random. The royal family will confer with the Enchantress tomorrow. For now, disperse. Go home and be with your loved ones." Her father falls silent, allowing the slowly returning crowd to drink in his words. Slowly, like slinking eels, the villagers do as they're told.

Once everyone is gone, Bruinen addresses the remaining palace guards and servants. "Take our fallen king—" Bruinen's voice shakes as he issues the command. He squares his shoulders before continuing. "Prepare him for the burial ceremony, so that we may burn his body and return his ashes to the seafloor."

Servants float in. Their movements are brisk and efficient. They lift Aalto's corpse with care and take him away, leaving only drops of purple ichor behind.

Everything's happening entirely too fast.

Avarie's breath hitches. Aalto had carried her in his arms like that once. After one of their childish schemes—trying to see who could rush through the palace the fastest—led to a bruised fin and Avarie unable to move it properly for a week. How surreal to see her brother's body now being carried the same way.

Without her son's body in her arms, Cordelia's hands go limp. She curls into herself, placing her head to the marble floor that is now laced with cracks. Aalto disappears from sight so quickly that Avarie is bereft of the time to process his defiled body. Time slows as her father speaks again. His following words shake her to the core.

"And Avarie . . ." Her father's stern voice causes her to flinch. "You will do whatever it takes to heal this kingdom. *You are now the heir to the Merelani throne.*"

Her eyes widen, grappling with the command to accept the crown she is so ill-prepared for. Avarie wants to fling herself under the covers and weep for days to come. She has no idea how to heal herself, much less an entire kingdom.

Cordelia remains collapsed upon the Merelani crest where Aalto once lay, silent sobs rack her body. With a trembling hand, Avarie tries to console her mother. As she rubs Cordelia's back, she twists to face her father. Mouth agape, Avarie preps a response. But his face brooks no argument; the only answer is to seal her lips and obey. This is not a choice.

This is her fate.

Bruinen's eyes sear into Avarie's, squashing any rebuttal she might try to make. She nods, slowly, but she imagines it looks more like an erratic twitch. She accepts her assignment without another word, and her father finally drags his gaze away from her. He refrains from meeting her eyes again.

His dismissal stings, but she's cognizant of a far worse pain. Avarie sinks to the floor, staring at the spot where her brother once was. All that's left of him are purple splotches of blood; the hue of royalty. Something that should never be seen. Avarie averts her eyes. It's almost like it's her own blood, like her punctured heart is bleeding out. Avarie's lips tremble. She will bear this troublesome responsibility for her kingdom, for her lost twin.

Right now, she wants to mourn with all of Merelani.

Later, she will do right by Aalto.

She will. No matter what.

Midmorning the following day, villagers, servants, and the remaining royals gather just beyond the Grand Foyer's second set of doors, in the courtyard, the heart of the palace. Aalto's corpse, wrapped in the finest silk, is lowered into a smoking pyre made of seaweed. The enchanted fire flares as his body touches the algae, consuming Aalto's corpse almost all at once. Music begins playing in the background, a mere accompaniment to the crackling flames. The crowded courtyard—Avarie, especially—cannot appreciate the Royal Symphony's skill.

Eyes are rubbed, noses are sniffled, and hands are clenched together, forming numerous circles that surround the pyre. Avarie couldn't count how many individual circles there were. The kingdom of Merelani showed up in droves to send off their king. The circle nearest the pyre is what remains of the royal family—Bruinen, Cordelia, and Avarie.

Avarie's hands are being held by both of her parents. There's a similar intensity to their hold. Yet Avarie feels as though Momma Cordelia's touch is for comfort, while Bruinen's is derived from a deep, internal rage. Mairya merges into their chain of joined hands, replacing Bruinen's hand with her own. When their hands meet, Avarie's heart beats double time. She inhales deeply. There isn't time for this—for old feelings to resurface. She turns her mind to Mai's appearance. Mairya's scales are a pallid yellow, instead of its usual brilliant and sun-like hue. Instead of gold ceremonial paint, Mai's arms are swirled with a pitch-black pigment—the color used for mourning. Avarie and the rest of the royal family are wearing their own black swirls and swooshes on their arms.

Upon waking, Avarie took the time to draw the mourning tattoos on her arms, pushing away her mermaiden's pleas to do it for her. Some lines are jagged, slanted, thick. Others are wiggly, imitating the flare of fire. These are Avarie's favorites; they're catastrophic, unique, and illustrate her cyclical grief.

Her father breaks their circle, floating closer to the pyre and launching into a well-rehearsed speech.

Avarie strains to hear Bruinen's words, but the insistent knock of guilt and fatigue is the only thing she seems able to hold onto. There is pain, discomfort pulsing in her temples, coursing through her veins—it's all that she can seem to feel.

Her fault.

It's all because of her.

Because she wanted to breach the surface.

Because she was reckless and insisted on doing stupid things.

She called Aalto's impulsiveness worse than hers—but hers is what ultimately got him killed.

She can tell no one.

Avarie rubs her eyes, which are red from her tears and the absence of sleep.

She glances up at the spot. The dreadful spot in the barrier that started it all.

It looks perfectly unmarred.

And that visual somewhat angers Avarie. She tries to clench her hands into fists, but the pointed rays of her ring dig into her and Mai's flesh. A low hiss slithers from Mairya, and she stares at Avarie in displeased confusion.

Sorry, Avarie mouths to her.

Mai shifts her attention back to Bruinen.

Avarie's gaze returns upward, transitioning slowly into a glare.

Why couldn't the Enchantress just make a perfect barrier?

Her magic should be as vast as the Merelani Sea.

As her enmity for the faulty dome intensifies, Avarie swears that she glimpses something long and serpent-like in the distance, past the barrier.

Pearl-like scales with a sprinkling of black in between, a

fiery-red plume of hair along the length of its eerily long body, from head to tail.

Her mouth dries.

This is wrong.

This creature should not be here.

It's not yet their season for migration.

The appearance of a lone oarfish out of season is an omen of bad fortune, it spells unfathomable disaster.

Avarie's gaze grows frantic, flitting from the crowds of commoners gathered for the service, to her father passionately delivering a speech. But she cannot hear his words. All Avarie can do is stare.

Stare—as this herald of doom flirts with the fragile barrier of their kingdom.

Avarie opens her mouth, prepared to announce its presence, to get her father's attention. She waves to her father. He barely spares her a glance of acknowledgment, moving his hands in a shooing motion, pushing aside her concern before she can even utter a syllable.

She clamps her mouth shut, and peers upward once more. The oarfish is retreating, receding far away until it becomes nothing but an inconsequential dot in the distance. But Avarie doesn't miss its parting action—the way it flicks its tail against the dome. There's no sound, but the less-than-gentle tap still roars in her ears.

Avarie should say something.

She wants to say something.

But the look of almost resigned hatred from her father shocks her into a panic-stricken silence. Avarie stares at the seafloor, flicking her tail. Why was speaking up so hard for her?

Momma Cordelia squeezes Avarie's hand before addressing the crowd, her body still deliberately turned away from the pyre as she speaks. Avarie clears her throat, like a polyp made of sadness has taken up shop right next to her vocal cords.

Cordelia's composure manages to seep through her harrowing grief as she says, "Though King Aalto's reign was evanescent, we will cherish his memory for years to come." She shakes her head in disbelief before continuing. "But I believe that Avarie will lead us with a unique brilliance of her own. Though she is not her brother, she is her own being with a perspective I'm sure will push Merelani into a grand future we cannot wait to witness." Cordelia shifts backward, allowing for her last living child to speak next.

Avarie looks out at the hundreds of grieving merpeople, taking in the forlorn glances shared between mercouples and friends. Can she do this? Can she really lead the kingdom of Merelani as well as her brother might have? The courtyard fire dies down, almost encouraging her to speak.

As if Aalto is encouraging her.

Avarie had spent the last few hours repeating her speech over and over, like a mantra. She had paced the expanse of her chambers, not wanting any hiccups when directly addressing the people of Merelani—*her* people—for the first time.

"No one can replace Aalto—uh, King Aalto. My brother. What a heavy crown to wear, for he was raised knowing that kingship would be his sole purpose. If there is one thing I-I must strive to do, it will be to rule with the passion and fervor that I know he would have." Avarie looks to her father, searching his face for something, anything—approval for her speech, confidence that she can rule—but all she can see is a hardened, angry face. Avarie swallows, the nervous polyp finally traveling down her throat.

To her dismay, the remaining words in her speech escape her. With an awkward nod to the crowd, Avarie rejoins the royal circle, confidence tarnished by her foible.

The enchanted flames die out, leaving nothing but dust.

Cordelia scoops up some of the ashes into a small, shell-shaped necklace. She clasps the jewelry closed then turns to Avarie. "Here, daughter. May the ashes of your brother protect you. May the necklace's warmth guide you on your journey." She closes the necklace around Avarie's neck. It rests perfectly in the dip between her collarbones. Though the necklace is light-weight, the responsibility it symbolizes feels as though it were weighing her down.

May the necklace's warmth guide you on your journey.

Before she has a chance to thank her mother or inquire further, Bruinen interrupts by clearing his throat. "Today will be considered a day of mourning henceforth. Shops will be closed, schools will pause. After, Avarie will be coronated, and then the royal family shall meet privately with the Enchantress to plan our revenge."

Bruinen's last words send a twitch through Avarie's tail. She doesn't bother looking down to see her scales changing in tune to her chronic anxiety.

Revenge?

She never agreed to that.

Chapter Six

There's a comical absurdity to having a coronation less than twenty-four hours after a funeral. And Avarie can't help wanting to jest with her brother that she's going to be queen—but he's no longer here to laugh at her jokes.

A mourning period followed by faux celebration. She told the servants not to bother with festivities. She doesn't want to do anything besides tidying up the piles of books in her room that had been scattered by the seaquake. A distraction, yes. But one she hopes would keep her mind off this timeline that she never wanted to be on.

Avarie's coronation clothing rivals her own mother's intricate threads, but she can't appreciate the bejeweled shawl or yesterday's dark mourning paint still brushed upon her skin. The people of Merelani are watching her from the palace's devastated foyer. They are looking at her with sad eyes, angry eyes, eyes that are wide with uncertainty.

Avarie's grip tightens around the armrests of her throne. She can't look at those eyes. All of them want something from her, but she barely knows what she wants for herself. Instead, she focuses on the damage. The marble on the ground floor is riddled with cracks; the coral sunroof is completely gone, as if it never existed; the stone walls appear as though they were one light touch away from collapse.

The servants' chatter dies down as Bruinen moves in front of Avarie, head bare, with Aalto's crown in his hands. His grip is strong, as Avarie can see the veins bulging through the skin of Bruinen's hands. The crown will soon be hers, and it feels so wrong. But Avarie has no choice but to accept. Her chin dips low, ready to receive the crown, so low it just about grazes the silver shell necklace swaying at her throat. Anguish swells within her at the necklace's movement.

It's a fierce reminder that Aalto is gone.

Bruinen clears his throat and her head snaps upward. The sudden movement is jarring. She isn't used to the weight of the crown, which feels heavy upon her head and conscience.

Avarie whispers a 'thank you' to the Sea Goddess for concealing her tears with the surrounding water. But there is no time for pity. The sadness of an entire kingdom usurps her own. She must take care of her merfolk first.

Her father's voice carries through the Grand Foyer, though his eyes are locked on Avarie. "Merelani is one of the few kingdoms to have been resilient against land dwellers. We owe this to all the great leaders that have come before. Their strength has made our kingdom prosperous, and the merfolk we must protect numerous. Take this crown as a symbol of all the great Merelani leaders before you. And now, you are bound by that same duty. You are all that we have now. You will lead us into the next era. The Mother of the Sea smiles upon you. May you not disappoint her—or us."

Avarie's tail flicks; she feels nervous at the statement. Their entire life, Aalto had been molded for kingship, while Avarie merely trailed in his wake. How could the Sea Goddess be smiling upon her now? None of her land-dweller books prepared her for this twist of fate. Avarie nods as she's absent-mindedly tapping a scale to kill off her jitters. She refuses to avert her eyes from her father. Even if she lacks confidence, it's best not to display her weakness to Bruinen, or the entire kingdom.

"I vow to uphold the will of the Sea Goddess. I will bring honor to our people."

Bruinen cocks his head to the right, considering her words. Her hands tremble, in full view of the thinly crowded foyer. But again, shoulder to shoulder, she meets Bruinen's gaze. Though it isn't packed like Aalto's coronation, Avarie knows she is responsible for so many merpeople now. A lump forms in her throat, trapping her words within. She should say something else. Shouldn't she? Something queenly. But she can't form any words.

Her mother ventures forward to address the crowd, voice strong just like Bruinen. "I am sure Queen Avarie will bring honor to us all, just as her forebears have done. It is in her blood to succeed." Cordelia squeezes Avarie's shaking hand. The world goes still. For a moment, it's just her and her mother, and no one else.

Right now, that's exactly what Avarie craves. For her world to stop so she doesn't have to think of Aalto, or her father's mountainous expectations. Her mother has never made her feel like she wasn't enough—and Avarie feels content, even for this short moment, to know that she needn't do anything drastic to earn her love and affection.

Cordelia plants a kiss on her forehead. When her mother pulls away, Avarie notices how weary she looks, like the past few days have aged her. Avarie thinks Cordelia must be yearning for simpler times, when all she needed to worry about was missing her children in a game of hide and seek.

Typically, after a sovereign is crowned and the speeches have been made, the Royal Symphony will launch into Merelani's anthem. But there is no music now, no celebration. Only a severe silence. What little crowd that had gathered begins to file out until all that remains are servants returning to their duties.

Avarie knows this coronation is a mere formality. That it shouldn't be happening in the first place.

Avarie shouldn't be queen.

In a twist of irony, the enchanted light in their underwater kingdom begins to liven up, signaling that the setting sun will be replaced by the moon.

Yet it is Avarie who remains; the moon to her sun is gone.

Mairya taps Avarie on the shoulder.

"A word, Queen Avarie," she says.

SILENCE SWIMS BETWEEN THE TWO OF THEM AS THEY sit in Avarie's cozy reading nook. Words escape her thoughts. Avarie can't remember the last time she was alone with Mairya. Probably during a game when they squished into an armoire together to hide from Aalto. Now, Mai's attached to the hip with her brother. Well—she used to be. Avarie was attached to her twin too. Which must mean they both live in limbo now. When the silence begins to make Avarie's skin prickle, she speaks up.

"How are you, Mai? Truly. I imagine we're both not faring well."

"I still can't believe that Aalto's really . . . that he's—I'm sorry. I'm so lost without him. My path had been set so long ago. Aalto would be king, and I would rule beside him. This was what the Mother of the Sea intended, but now . . . Now what? Aalto is gone and, Goddess, I miss him, Ava. I loved him. I feel the absence of his warmth and care so deeply. The pain is like a million missing scales." Mairya's cheeks redden.

Avarie gives in to the sudden urge to hug her friend. She leans close to wind her arms around Mairya's thin midsection. Mai smells like a mix of waterlilies and freshly cut coconut. Her younger self would have given anything to enjoy this closeness, but Avarie is no longer a little girl who can indulge in whimsical crushes.

She can no longer think of Mai in this way.

She shouldn't. She can't—it's improper.

Avarie chooses to ignore the warmth spreading from her head to her tail fin as she hugs Mai tighter.

"It's going to be okay. I'll make it okay," Avarie promises. She blinks a few times, uncertain. *Can* she make it okay? What does *okay* even look like?

With a slowness rivaling a starfish, Mairya pulls away, staunching Avarie's rambling thoughts. But their faces remain close. "I must discuss something with you. It needs to be addressed with haste."

"What more needs to be addressed?"

Mairya clears her throat like she's preparing to deliver the most important speech of her life. "I was destined to be queen —it must be so, even if Aalto is gone."

Avarie's brow furrows.

"I could love you, just as I learned to love him. This is the best solution for our kingdom." Mairya leans in closely, too close, her full, pink lips poised to kiss Avarie.

Apprehension stabs at Avarie's heart. Everything is happening too fast for her to think. Mai draws nearer, and their lips meet with Avarie's eyes wide open. She hates herself for thinking it, but Mai's lips are surprisingly soft against her own. Avarie pulls away before the interaction can linger. She brushes a finger over her lips, confused.

"This is bad. We should not have done that." Avarie suddenly feels . . . strange, fatigued. Similar to the drowsiness one feels after ingesting dream angelfish—a natural remedy for insomnia. Has she fantasized about kissing Mai? Yes. But not in years. Not since Aalto and Mairya made their bond official. Guilt pools in Avarie's midsection.

She thought that she'd met her quota for the emotion, but it seems to have reached a new intensity now.

Avarie's eyelids adopt an unnatural heaviness.

Mairya cocks her head to the side, mere inches from Avarie's face. "Do you not find me beautiful anymore, Queen Ava?" Her eyes lock onto Avarie's, holding them hostage.

And Avarie hates herself for allowing her gaze to drift to Mai's flushed lips.

Before whatever feelings she still has can rise to the surface, Avarie stifles a yawn and responds as neutrally as she can: "Yes. Of course, I think you're beautiful. Who doesn't? But marriage . . . that would disrespect Aalto. His memory—all I have left of him." Befuddlement overcomes Avarie's mind. Regardless of her old feelings for Mai, courting her deceased brother's fiancée is out of the question.

Mairya grabs her hand as her almond-shaped eyes try reasoning with Avarie, "Consider it a bit longer . . . there are no other viable candidates for you." Which is true. While Merelani doesn't care about same-gendered relationships, *social standing* did matter. Avarie needed a respected merwoman to rule by her side. No exceptions. And they must produce an heir of noble blood. It wasn't unheard of for an heir to court a widowed merperson, provided they were of good enough standing. But courting Mai feels like the ultimate betrayal to Aalto.

Avarie's heart races. "I need more time to think, Mairya. I need solitude. I'll get back to you when I've made up my mind."

Mairya nods in agreement, then brushes a loc behind Avarie's ear. For a fleeting moment, she places a hand on Avarie's bare shoulder. And to Avarie's dismay, she isn't put off by the touch. "I await your decision, my queen." Mairya gives Avarie a soft smile before exiting. As she's turning away, Avarie notices Mai's bright yellow scales darkening for a brief moment.

Avarie floats back and forth from her reading nook to her chamber doors. But all the pacing in the world couldn't help her decide.

She can't marry Mai.

Not with the wound of her brother's death still so fresh. It hasn't even been a full two days since Aalto died. Avarie reaches up to clasp the shell at her neck. The grooves and carvings of the metallic shell are smooth under her fingers. She squeezes the charm with such force that she feels it might break in her grasp.

Avarie relinquishes hold of the necklace and sucks in a deep breath.

"Aalto, what should I do?"

Avarie collapses on her bed, no longer strong enough to fight off the peculiar lethargy that's been weighing on her since Mai kissed her.

Maybe it's just another one of her inconvenient fainting spells.

AVARIE AWAKENS IN THE DEAD OF NIGHT. SHE shakes away the images of her disfigured brother clawing into the forefront of her mind. Her ears prick up. Someone's outside her door.

Two voices.

Why are her parents up so late?

"I think we should reach out to a neighboring community. We can join forces and attack the humans. They won't expect it," her father says.

Cordelia's sigh seems heavier than Avarie's new crown. "You're no longer king—that's impossible. A *huge* overstep of Ava's authority. Plus, give our daughter some credit. Do you truly think she can't handle the next steps on her own?"

"I *know* she can't. Look at her—she locks herself away in her chambers and reads all day. Her reclusive nature rivals that of the Enchantress! How will she stop the seaquakes? How can we expect *her* to take decisive action when she balks at the idea of addressing the kingdom?"

Avarie flinches at his words.

Bruinen asks, "Where did you go wrong with her?"

Momma Cordelia's voice is a hushed whisper, but the sharpness of her tone makes Avarie sit up in bed. This is an anger she's never heard from her mother before. "I raised her as I did her brother. It's you who went 'wrong' with her—you gave her all those books, and now you criticize her for reading them! Have you even considered that, perhaps, she considers those books to be her only connection with you? And so, she reads and reads—in the hopes of gaining your approval, of impressing you with the knowledge she's gleaned?"

"Spare me, Cordelia. She's obsessed with fiction. Make-believe. What help will that be in stopping the seaquakes? For the first time in Merelani history, we may have to search outside our kingdom for new leadership."

Cordelia scoffs. "You wouldn't dare. Give her a chance."

"She may not give me a *choice*, Cordelia."

"I suggest you take the spare bedroom tonight—and the following nights until Avarie proves herself and rights the wrongs done to us." Her mother's tone is cold. And as wonderful as it is to hear her mother standing up for her in her absence, Bruinen's cruelty clouds her mind. Avarie grabs her blanket with a fierce intensity, no longer interested in hearing her parents whisper in the halls.

For anyone else, perhaps Bruinen's lack of faith would

spur a fire within them, encouraging them to prove him wrong.

But for Avarie, it just makes her sad.

And she's unsure if her mother's confidence in her will be enough. Avarie curls up into a tight ball, wishing she could just disappear.

Chapter Seven

Rays of light shine down into the water and through Avarie's grand chamber windows, prompting her to wakefulness. It was a frightful sleep. After overhearing her parent's argument, images of Aalto's mutilated body continued to haunt her for hours on end.

She lets her eyes wander around the big expanse of her room. Memories of Aalto and their childhood cross her mind when her gaze lands on the various things there. Avarie clings to them, desperate to think of something other than her parents. There, in the armoire, was where she often hid from Aalto during their games of hide and seek. Her gold encrusted dresser still has the smallest of cracks from their roughhousing. Even the enchanted driftwood of her canopy bed, with its lavish rose-gold linen sheets and mountains of pillows, are hiding etchings that they carved into the wood. Misspelled phrases of an old nursery rhyme decorate the wooden frame:

> Here the song of life and death
> Blessing or eturnal rest
> First or last breath, find out befor long
> If theyre alive oar forever gone

Avarie hadn't read into the words too much when she was young. But now, she comprehends how unsettling they are. *First or last breath . . . alive or forever gone.* Merfolk only sing twice in their lifetime; Avarie didn't know that's what the words meant when they were reciting it while chasing each other around the palace.

This wasn't to be confused with the equally concerning nursery rhyme a preteen Avarie—who possessed a stronger understanding of spelling—carved into the opposite side:

> Drown her, drown her. Watch her go.
> Down, down to the waters below.
> Impostor, impostor. Seek her out.
> Find her quick, ignore all doubt.
> Drown her, drown her. Return where sirens lie.
> If you don't, land dwellers may die.

Avarie's knowledge about this rhyme is limited; some tale about a merwoman walking on land and humans being frantic to return her back to the sea—because her existence in their world must *surely* equate to their deaths. Or whatever the humans believed. *A bunch of whale crap,* Avarie decided years ago upon her first reading of it. A well-established land-dweller rumor that made its way to Merelani via a human poetry collection from Bruinen.

But it sure was catchy.

With a sigh, Avarie shrugs on a shawl and exits her chambers, the memories of adolescence weighing on her chest like a sunken ship.

Even if Bruinen hadn't ordered the royal family to meet there after yesterday's coronation, it was obvious where she needed to go, and who she needed to see: the woman who makes Mairya a suitable partner for Avarie—the Enchantress.

THE ROOM OF ENCHANTMENT WAS A PLACE AVARIE hadn't seen since birth. It gave her the creeps. Plenty of good spells were made here, but Avarie has a forever sinking feeling that just as many bad ones were crafted here as well. Avarie's seen servants scuttle past the room, heads down and bodies hunched. She's heard their conspiratorial whispers. Of power unimaginable. Uncontrollable.

Avarie flicks her ring and scans the space. The Room of Enchantment is a strange place filled with trinkets, potions, and the wildest magic any merperson can think of. Reminiscent of a cave, the room is made of stone, with glittering Merelani jewels embedded throughout the entirety of the floor and disrupting its flat surface. Tables of black ore are littered with green or blue glass bottles filled with mystery contents. An eeriness overshadows Avarie's feeling of sadness. Her parents are already there, along with Mairya. Despite the minimal lighting, Avarie does not struggle to interpret their demeanor.

Momma Cordelia is feigning calmness, but Avarie knows this is a farce by glimpsing a lone box braid sticking out of her bun at an odd angle. It should be perfectly wrapped, instead it's tangled with Cordelia's crown. Bruinen does not mask his anger, he couldn't even if he tried. A dark aura of impatience is surrounding him. Mairya, though silent, is wearing a hopeful smile. Avarie hates how pretty she looks—hates that Mai is rushing her to make a decision she's not ready for.

The Enchantress, herself, is facing away from all of them, toiling away at something on a table, humming to herself. Tattoos speckle her arms, white dots of varying sizes that are luminescent in the dim lighting. Waves intertwine among the dots, swaying in real time as the well-respected magic weaver lifts an arm to pour a handful of powder into her free hand. Avarie watches with wonder, too entranced to say anything.

But Bruinen didn't bring his patience today. "Avarie you're late. Time to take guidance from the wise Enchantress. Her wisdom will cure our plight."

Avarie notices that her father has yet to refer to her as queen. But after last night's whispered conversation near her chambers, she isn't surprised.

Upon hearing her name, the woman turns around, her pearl white scales flashing against the light. She places the mystery object behind her back. "My dear Avarie," the woman's deep and smooth voice purrs, "it's been so long. I detest the circumstances in which we are meeting. Come, I'll show you how you'll bring the poacher that killed King Aalto to their knees."

Though trembling, Avarie nods. "Avenging Aalto is my sole purpose now, Enchantress, that is what I desire most." She dips her head in reverence.

But it's all a bald-faced lie.

Avarie wants nothing but to cower underneath her sheets, to fight off images of Aalto's death or that creepy oarfish from entering her dreams.

The merwoman floats forward, hovering a few inches from Avarie. "You will drink a potion. This will allow you to live as a land dweller for two weeks. Only two weeks, not a second more. In that time, you must infiltrate the town of Deniz and destroy the poacher's heart. The life debt will be paid and the seaquakes will cease. Harmony and safety will return to Merelani."

Confusion racks Avarie's thoughts. If potions exist to transform merpeople, why is surface dwelling uncommon? Maybe that old nursery rhyme holds some weight. Avarie expected revenge could get ugly . . . but murder? She's unsure about killing another.

The Enchantress offers an understanding smile. "The main ingredient used in the potion of transformation comes from the scales of the legendary and rare oarfish that only appears every ten years. And we're about nine years shy of seeing another one."

Avarie's brow furrows. "Then why did I see one yesterday?"

The Enchantress laughs. Avarie detests the mocking tone. "Impossible. The aura of an oarfish is difficult to miss. None are set to migrate to our waters anytime soon."

"Well, I saw one, I know I did. I've seen pictures of them in my books—"

"Avarie." Her father seethes. "Do not waste time with your foolish questions."

Avarie stiffens at his harsh tone.

"Though your quest for knowledge is commendable, your father is right. Our Goddess is displeased. See what she has already done? These seaquakes will not cease until justice has been served. Everything we know could be destroyed if the land dwellers go unpunished."

Avarie resists the urge to glower at the powerful merwoman. "Why has there been no talk of a truce? Humans. Merpeople. We don't have to hate each other. My books say—"

"I knew those damn books would do you no good. Kindness for the monsters that killed *my* perfect son?"

"He was my brother *too*!" Avarie hates that her voice cracks.

My fault. My fault. My fault.

Avarie feels herself swaying but quickly grasps onto a counter to steady herself.

"If it weren't for Aalto, you would have nothing Avarie. Not one human book to taint your mind."

"What—what do you mean, father?"

Bruinen's gaze hardens. "Aalto begged me to save a book that fell overboard from a ship. I would have let it succumb to the void had he not suggested that we enchant it for you."

"I thought you gave me all those books because you loved me?"

Avarie clutches her fingers to her chest.

"I gave you those books to appease the future king."

A stinging silence ensues.

The weight of a dozen anchors tug on Avarie's heart.

But she will not cry.

Only Aalto deserves her tears.

After a shaky breath, Avarie steers the conversation down the previous path. "Seems like this oarfish potion is invaluable. One that comes with a high cost."

The Enchantress nods, gaze darting between Avarie and Bruinen. "The potion does come with a debt of its own. But I know how you can pay it . . ."

She trails off, looking at Cordelia and Bruinen, addressing only them.

"Many years ago, the two of you came to me in need of an heir. Cordelia, your womb was barren, and it remains so to this day." Cordelia's eyes narrow with indignation. She clutches the jewels around her neck. "But I generously gifted you life. I took the love you and Bruinen have for each other and transformed it into an oyster shell that not only produced an heir two years later, but twins. An invaluable service. One many cannot afford." The Enchantress faces Avarie again. "The price for this miracle was to have the growing daughter in my own womb become queen."

Collective gasps echo from Avarie and Mairya, though Avarie can't help but notice that Mai's reaction seems a bit manufactured. Avarie never knew the gritty specifics of Mairya's betrothal to Aalto. It was just an established fact when they got older.

Cordelia's response is almost a whisper: "We would have paid you handsomely for the service. But money was not what you wanted." She blinks in quick succession then looks away from the merwoman.

The Enchantress continues as if the former queen said nothing at all. "I would like this bargain to be upheld. Upon Avarie's safe return, I would like her and Mairya to marry. The girl was born to be the heir's queen, after all."

"Greedy beast!" Bruinen thunders. "Don't you think you've held enough power over the royal family? I should have you banished."

As though to signal the Goddess's displeasure at Bruinen's outburst, the potion room begins trembling. Avarie grasps onto the nearest table to steady herself. She holds on tight, waiting for the ground to stop convulsing. Others in the room follow suit. After fifteen seconds, the seaquake quells to a few tremors before ceasing. Avarie doesn't want to think about the damage caused in the upper levels of the palace if so much had been destroyed here: from ripped open cabinets to shattered, dark vials spilling their contents everywhere.

"But you won't." The Enchantress cocks her head to the side, gesturing to the disheveled room to prove her point. "Did you forget that as Enchantress, the Mother of the Sea communicates her desires to me? The quakes will *not* cease until the

Sea Goddess is appeased. And no one else can create this potion for you, Queen Avarie. It is best that you keep me and my daughter happy."

Bruinen clenches his hands over and over, rage building in his eyes. Avarie must act fast before more vials in the room are broken.

"I—I'll do it." Avarie's voice sounds like a ghost of itself. "If that's the only way to pay for this potion, I'll marry Mai when I return to Merelani."

Even if every part of her being tells her to not do so.

Because that is what Merelani needs to survive.

A satisfied yet wicked smile takes over the Enchantress's face. Her pointed teeth and the jewels embedded in them gleam sinisterly. "Perfect. You have chosen well. A good ruler knows how to compromise . . . and it's best not to destroy the long-established bond between the crown and its line of enchantresses. When the time comes, I will create a shell just for your heir, like I did with your mother; free of charge."

Her smile makes Avarie's stomach churn. She looks over to Mairya, who is wide-eyed with disbelief as she stares at her own mother. Avarie glimpses something else on Mai's face too —Happiness? Triumph?—nothing that helps settle the apprehensive waves in her stomach.

Before Avarie or anyone else can get another word in, the Enchantress continues: "It's settled. Come nightfall, Avarie will swim to the surface and go to the pier where the sea is a hairline from meeting the shore; from there, she will drink the potion and her transformation shall begin."

Avarie only nods, frightened by the merwoman's words.

"Two weeks. You'll only have two weeks, young queen." The Enchantress smiles that awful grin again.

Chapter Eight

White stars dot the sky when Avarie's head pops above the sea, rivulets of water streaming down her face and into her eyes. She blinks thrice. It's quiet, the first calm moment in what seems like a long time. But she is not alone.

Guards wait below, watching for unanticipated danger. Mairya rises above the surface as well, close enough to bump elbows with Avarie. Her jet-black hair sticks close to her skull, and a weathered, dark-brown satchel is hanging from one of her shoulders. "Are you ready?"

Avarie nods, which is a gargantuan lie. She was not afforded much time to prepare. After leaving the potion room, she retired to her chambers, wishing to brush up on everything she'd learned about humans through her books. The rest of her free time went to cleaning up the mess caused by the seaquake. Avarie hates that her deepest wish of venturing ashore has come true for the worst reason. For revenge.

For her brother.

For Aalto.

He didn't deserve such a gruesome death. He didn't

deserve to die at all. He would have been the perfect king. Stern like Bruinen. But noble like their mother. An amazing merman and brother. Avarie, herself, can barely tell which of her parents she best resembles. Perhaps this journey will reveal that in due time.

Will she be like her father, guided by anger and dead set on revenge?

Or will she favor her mother's cool composure and find a gentler path?

Avarie shifts to face Mairya. "I'm surprised your mother sent you. Thought she'd want to administer the potion herself."

Mai shrugs. "She trusts me. I've been apprenticing under her watch for years now. I am meant to be the next Enchantress, after all." Mairya uncovers an intricate bottle. It's a deep blue that's so dark Avarie can't see its contents, with gold markings decorating the surface. Mai uncorks the container and a fetid stench floats around them.

Avarie wrinkles her nose in disgust. "I had no idea oarfish smelled like that. Mother of the Sea, that's bad."

A small laugh filters out of Mairya's mouth. "If you hate this, don't even think about sniffing moray eel. Its mucus is great as a salve, but it'll fry your gills clean off." Avarie can't help but laugh at her humor, though Mai sobers up soon after. "I didn't know, by the way."

"Know what?" Avarie asks, even as she senses what Mairya is alluding to.

"I had no knowledge of the deal my mother made with your parents. We are meant to use our enchantments for good. To help. I'm sorry that was not the case. To hold a rare potion just out of reach from the royal family . . . it's—it's bold, I'll tell you that."

"I believe you." But Avarie can't shake the image in her head of Mai looking pleased during the unveiling of the shady deal. Could Mai be lying? And why? "I guess I'll be coming home to an elaborate wedding then."

"I suppose so." A shy smile spreads across Mairya's mouth. "Um, let me finish your . . . briefing. Perhaps those are the best words for this situation. Once you drink the potion, you'll transform into a surface dweller. I have clothes for you in this satchel. It's enchanted to be water resistant, so it and its contents won't get damp. Put them on once ashore."

"Any advice for me—Mai the Enchantress's daughter?" Unease knocks at the door of Avarie's mind. She can't believe she's really doing this.

"Be back before the moon cycle's last crescent. We're in the Last Quarter now. Let the moon and the Mother of the Sea guide you. Sometime during the Waning Crescent, you'll transform back, whether or not you've made it safely back to the water. Be sure to always close your eyes when you transform, the bright light has potential to blind you."

Avarie's tail twitches, her scales glow bright with unease. "Mai, I'm scared."

Mairya grabs onto Avarie's right hand. The motion of kindness helps still the tremors a little. "You've got this, my queen. But I can help you." Mai relinquishes hold of Avarie's hand and places a featherlike touch beneath her chin. "Tilt your head back," she encourages.

Avarie makes no attempt to disobey, though this moment mirrors the mysterious sleep-inducing kiss they had shared days ago. She tilts her head backward, locs falling from their natural place in front of her shoulders. The bottle comes to her lips and Avarie parts them with slow caution.

The potion slithers coolly down her tongue, leaving a vile aftertaste that has Avarie coughing and gasping in shock. She steels herself and swallows. Mairya wipes Avarie's bottom lip, pocketing a small, lingering drop back into the bottle. If

Avarie had blinked, she would have missed the swift movement.

"For safekeeping," Mairya whispers.

Avarie isn't sure how much liquid is still in the opaque glass bottle. Nor does she have time to even process Mairya's words, or the lingering meaning behind them. Without warning, her tail begins tingling. Unlike the unwanted spasms she feels when she's nervous, this one *burns*. The fiery sensation runs from her hip to tail fin—back and forth, to and from, the pain doubling with each lap. She squeezes her eyes shut then cries out as a blinding light emits from her lower half. It feels as though her tail is being severed in two. When the light vanishes, Avarie opens her eyes, staring down at her midsection in utter disbelief.

Legs.

Long. Thick. Dark-brown legs.

She cries out again. This time in awe. The excruciating pain is fleeting, but her new legs don't work as she assumed. Avarie sinks below water; her arms are useless, rising above her head like when Aalto dragged her back to the palace.

Salty water rushes into her mouth, and to her shock, it burns down her throat. She's coughing like a novice swimmer underwater. Her entire frame sinks below, her eyes smarting from the salt. Avarie squeezes them shut just as hands grab her waist and push her toward land.

Avarie scrambles forward inexpertly on her hands and knees, her bare ass out for any land dwellers to see if there had been any around.

Mai remains a safe distance away, careful not to breach the boundary between shore and sea. She tosses the satchel to Avarie then glances over her shoulder.

"Leave us now. I can take it from here."

Dark shadows—guards—recede farther into the waters until Avarie can no longer see them.

"No need for them to see you in this vulnerable position, my queen."

"Th-thank you, Mairya." Avarie hadn't bothered to catch the satchel. Though her arms felt normal, massive fatigue took hold of the rest of her body. Breath labored, she rolls over to unzip the satchel.

"Anytime. I will allow you some privacy as well." Mai averts her brown eyes and stares down into the sea. She drifts farther away, placing distance between them until only her neck and head remain above water. "I'm still here for you, Ava. For anything. Every night I will come here for you. To relay news of the palace. To receive updates from you that I can share with your parents. All you must do is return to this exact spot on the shore and call my name." With that, Mairya descends below the surface, leaving Avarie naked and afraid—a mermaid with human legs.

AVARIE CLUTCHES THE CLOTHING WITH A DEATH grip, staring down at her new . . . legs. She wiggles her toes, bends her knees. She's not ready to explore anything else down there. Her patch of missing scale now resembles a jagged scar, puckered and discolored from the rest of her bare, brown skin. Aftershocks of tingles reverberate through her legs. Avarie braces for the visceral pain, but it doesn't come. The odd sensation passes the more she moves her legs. A relieved gust of breath flows from her mouth.

She rolls onto her side—in true fashion, like a fish out of water—and wiggles on an undergarment that is tight around her frame. She frowns. *How constricting. How do humans live like this?* she wonders.

Suddenly, Mairya's head pops above the surface, earning a mild shout from Avarie. "Apologies, my queen. I forgot to give this pouch of coins to you." Mai tosses a rose-gold pouch ashore. Like the bag, Avarie doesn't bother to catch it. The pouch settles into the sand with a light plop. "How are your legs, Ava?"

"Strange."

A small nod of understanding. "It will take time, but you will adjust. I believe it. But be careful. You cannot breathe water like us. You can drown."

Avarie recalls the old nursery rhyme about a mermaid drowning at the hands of land dwellers. It never made sense until the seawater burned her throat. "Got it. Don't drown. Find the poacher. Avenge Aalto."

Mai smiles. "I must go now. But don't forget, I am here; your lifeline back to the sea." Without warning, Mai reaches out to caress Avarie's ankle, wonder and awe sparkling in her dark eyes. "You are beautiful in all forms, Avarie. Goodbye for now." Mai sinks below the surface again with a sense of finality.

ALONE ON THE SHORE, AVARIE PERCEIVES HER NEW surroundings. The deep-purple sky grants passage for the sun to transition to other parts of the world. And with the sun gone, so is her vision. At least that's a constant, mermaids aren't known for seeing well in the dark either. Something barks in the distance, sending prickles of panic crawling over her skin. With her vision a useless blur, she listens to the animal until the noise fades away. Chirping insects add to the cacophony of Deniz. It's all so loud, yet somehow it's in the most minuscule of ways.

Funny, she realizes, the book that was stuck in the sand is nowhere in sight. It seems like a decade ago since she spotted it. It all seems so silly now.

The weighty, hydrophobic pouch jingles when Avarie shakes it. Money. She'll need that. Avarie starts investigating some of the satchel's items. She grins. Mai thinks of everything. Simple wire frame glasses are the first thing Avarie scoops up. She puts them on, and the view around her reaches a new clarity.

Next, she pulls a shirt over her brassiere. In all the stories she's read, Avarie can't recall one where people walked about in their undergarments. But the way it blankets her skin feels constricting, heavy and foreign on her body.

Her stomach rumbles at the sight of her favorite treats: seaweed and thinly sliced coral chips. But she'll save them for later. Who knows when her next meal will be. The cozy blanket is a nice touch, she can't help Aalto if she freezes to death.

The final item puts an end to her investigation. A jagged knife with a pearlescent hilt. Its intricate carvings are so small that Avarie can scarcely recognize them in the night. This must be the tool she's meant to use on Aalto's murderer. It seems too early in her quest to nurture the festering doubt on whether she can kill someone. Instead, she sets her mind on what needs to be done tonight.

"Think. Think. What do I do next?"

A gust of wind rolls over the shore, sending chills over her skin.

"Shelter. Shelter first."

Every adventure book she's read touts shelter as the most important step.

Not ready to trust her legs yet, Avarie rolls onto her stomach and shifts her gaze from the shore. Just faintly visible in the distance, past the sandy beach, is a dilapidated house. Even from a hundred feet away, and with her weak eyesight, Avarie is certain of its battered state. But it will have to do for tonight. With darkness beginning to press down on her, and her legs still wobbling like a human infant, this is her safest option. In fact, her heart tells her that's where she needs to go.

With nothing but a feeling and her intuition, Avarie pushes herself up to her knees then makes her way to a standing position. Her toes scrunch in the sand. There's no way she's putting on those foot contraptions. The boots must wait until tomorrow, until the mere sensation of sand between her toes no longer bewilders her. It will take some time for her to get to the cottage.

Time.

She tries not to think of the metaphorical hourglass that are her legs. How fleeting the enchantment is. Avarie has less than two weeks now to formulate a solid plan to avenge her brother.

To kill his murderer and stop the dangerous seaquakes.

The responsibility seems so daunting that it makes her want to bury herself in the sand and hide from her duty.

By time she reaches the rundown cottage, the sun has completely withdrawn. A near pitch-black sky stretches overhead with scattered sprinklings of stars. Her glasses are rendered useless without proper lighting. Her locs drip water onto her itchy clothing, but the drops bounce off with ease from the garments. How does the Enchantress do it? She'll have to ask Mai's mother one day.

Avarie can't help but think back to Mairya's slight smile as her mother asserted her claim to the throne. It wasn't sinister, but Mai's expression didn't rub her the *right* way. Avarie would much rather be able to *choose* someone to rule with her, and on her own accord. But that option seems too grandiose for Merelani's circumstances right now. Avarie sighs and pushes all thoughts of the arrangement away. She's got more pressing matters to focus on.

It may be dark, but at least her hearing is not an issue. She presses a pierced ear to the chipped door. The house sounds empty, except for the soft scuttle of bugs. She pushes on the door with minimal effort, and it swings open with a soft creak. She closes herself inside though the door doesn't lock.

It's dusty inside, tepid smelling, and the floorboards are near rotten—truly a place fit for a queen. Avarie has a feeling that she'll be humbling herself a lot during these two weeks. Thankfully, her favorite author has somewhat prepared her to live among the land dwellers.

The floorboards moan in protest as Avarie crosses the cluttered threshold, the near empty corner in the back of the room is her target. Books litter the floor, though she cannot read the titles without ample light. Dust enters her new set of nostrils, resulting in a high-pitched expulsion of air from her mouth. Her eyes widen in surprise. So that's what a sneeze feels like. Underwater, she'd expel a trail of small bubbles from her lips.

Her chosen corner is the perfect spot; there's a broken window just above her head. She'll be awakened by sunlight passing through it. It will be like when Mrs. Clara draws open her curtains every morning.

Legs aching and thighs quivering, Avarie slides down to the floor. Wishing for her new legs to be free, Avarie rips off the uncomfortable leggings. A satisfied *ahhh* erupts from her mouth. Pants are pointless.

Her stomach growls, gurgling for some sort of sustenance. She frowns. Avarie wanted to save her snacks for at least until the morning. Until she can find stable shelter and a steady food supply. But the coral chips call to her, and she gives in, ripping the thin, cloth-like packaging open.

She layers two coral chips at a time on her tongue, relishing in the taste. A wonderful, crunchy reminder of the sea. Her happiness wanes. Avarie didn't anticipate missing the palace so fast. Her mom, the people of Merelani. Even her stern father. Water pricks at her eyes. She wipes the developing tears away before they have the opportunity to race down her face.

Determined, Avarie grips the necklace at her throat and forces herself to take a few, deep breaths. She can do this.

Maybe.

She *must* do this.

For Aalto.

Avarie nods to herself. "It's my fault all this is happening. I have to fix this." She fishes around the tattered satchel—it and its contents were likely salvaged from a shipwreck—for the blanket her hands had grazed earlier.

Avarie drapes the warm fabric over her chest and exposed, thick thighs. She drifts off to sleep, memories of her brother weighing on her mind and heart.

Chapter Nine

Shuffling feet jolt Avarie to an upright position on the floor. The sun hadn't awakened her like she'd hoped. Recurring grief and the laborious journey to the cottage must have left her exhausted. Through the broken window, clouds drift by, hiding most of the sun's rays. She rubs her sore back while looking about, remembering where she is and the task at hand.

Delirious fatigue planted strange memories of Aalto in her sleep. On more than one occasion, she woke up gasping for breath, muttering her dead twin's name over and over. Underneath the sadness is a sliver of anger. Why did he act so rashly? Aalto left an entire community in mourning, and Avarie is beginning to believe that their grief is eternal.

But as her disdain for Aalto's recklessness begins simmering again, a swell of self-hatred surpasses it. Avarie rubs a tear from her face and immediately feels embarrassment, as if her father is witnessing her vulnerability. She shakes her head, casting Bruinen out of her mind, if only for a moment.

The books that were too dark to read last night are recognizable now. Once upon a time, these texts were beautiful . . .

but now they smell acrid and their leather bindings are damaged almost beyond recognition. Avarie investigates further, wrinkling her nose at the combined feel and scent of the discarded books.

How odd.

Most of them belong to her favorite author, L.H. Sirene. Despite the wear and tear of most of the novels, the author's name remains resilient. If Avarie could meet Sirene, she'd know what to do. Anytime her main character was at a loss for what to do next, the author created the most intricate plot to progress the story forward. In one novel, the main character was trapped in an underwater cave and couldn't hold her breath anymore. Her last conscious act was to pull out a single scale from her satchel and rub it like a genie lamp. Sure, scales didn't work like that in real life, but the creativity was unmatched. As the girl lost consciousness, her mermaiden rescued her, taking her to a rocky shore and willing her human to live through the power of the love she felt for her. Excessively sentimental? Yes. But Avarie's curiosity for land dwellers grew tenfold after reading it. Why? Because it was staggering to her mind to read about a mermaid loving a human. Caring for them with zero animosity.

Because that damn rhyme and their shared history asserts that humans and merfolk can never safely coexist.

Avarie crawls on her hands and knees to grasp the nearest book. Black soot sticks to her fingers. She rubs the grime back and forth then deposits the remaining mess on her shirt. To her dismay, the contents of the book appear as disastrous as the cover. It's obvious that chunks of pages have been ripped out. Why would someone destroy such a wonderful story of young love and triumph?

And why do so many of the books belong to Sirene?

While preparing to investigate another novel, voices stop Avarie in her tracks.

"Let's check Cast-out Cottage."

"What do you think we'll find? That's where junk goes to die."

The voices have a lightness, a carefree flair to them that suggests the boys may be a few years younger than Avarie. This doesn't relax her tense shoulders though. What if they're the sons of poachers?

"Hide," she whispers to herself. "I must get out of here."

She'd read enough books to know that a lost girl shouldn't trust the first people they run into. Especially men.

But what do they mean by 'Cast-out Cottage'? Is this truly a place where people dispose of things they never wish to see again?

Looking every bit foolish and lowly, Avarie crawls backward to the corner, trying her best to remain quiet. She redresses, rolling her eyes at the pants contraption ensnaring her legs, before slipping the satchel on. Wind blows through the broken window, biting into her skin like an angler on a fishing hook. She'll need a shawl soon.

And food.

Her stomach rumbles at the thought. What Avarie wouldn't give for her favorite Merelani dish right now—scallops garnished with pink water lilies. By the Goddess, there must be a market nearby. She decides that finding one will be her next task.

Too afraid to reopen the front door, Avarie crouches low, heading for the cottage's backdoor. Her thighs wobble from the small exertion. Looking over her shoulder, she sees three boys walking past the broken window toward the front of the cottage. They're all pale-skinned, and the boy in the middle towers over the other two. She can't determine what they look like without a full view of their faces. Avarie tugs on the backdoor with haste, her hands melding to the knob as if the sweat on them is glue.

It doesn't budge.

Could it be boarded up from the outside?

Avarie's heart hammers against her ribcage. She places a shaky hand on her chest. She mustn't get caught; she's barely spent a full day on land.

Her eyes trail back to the window she slept under, taking in the remnants of jagged glass that she couldn't see last night. Her mouth goes dry.

She'll have to jump through.

Her exit isn't too high up, just a little above her hips, so the jump may be more of a hurdle.

Avarie throws a leg out the window, her pelvis narrowly avoiding the glass shards. Awkward, she hops, a bare foot landing on the rocks outside. She holds onto the frame as she lifts her left leg over. When her graceless legs meet again, Avarie tries her first attempt at sprinting.

Rippppppppppp!

Her satchel snags on a stalagmite-shaped glass shard. Avarie's breath quickens even more as she jerks the bag free.

"What was that?"

The sounds of feet trampling grass flood into her ears. Before the trio can get a chance to see her, she hobbles into the woods, farther away from the safety of Merelani and into the unknown.

AVARIE RECOGNIZES HOW LUDICROUS THE situation is—her, a mermaid *queen*, scurrying away from human boys. How pitiful. But the truth is, she has no idea what could have happened if they had seen her. Better to avoid potential danger as best as she can since there's no one she can call for help now.

No one here to help her but herself.

The realization takes a toll on her confidence. These legs are still so strange, so new. They weren't stick thin like the boys she ran from, but plump, solid limbs. She admires their thickness though, the strength in each stride. Avarie takes a moment to marvel at her new body, though her quick escape had resulted in some minor chafing. She pats the insides of her thighs but that doesn't do much to help.

Avarie tucks behind a tree. Her oval toes dig into the dirt. Her back presses into the stocky trunk. She stays this way until her heartbeat settles and the voices fade. Something gold catches the light.

Coins.

Avarie digs into the satchel and her pointer finger sticks straight through the bottom. She groans. She'd forgotten that the bag tore in her scramble to escape. Avarie chucked the supplies into her satchel; the coin bag must not have been pulled shut. She should be more careful. She scoops up the currency, using one hand to sift the dirt away. Shiny dots decorate the forest floor. How many coins did she lose? She'll need to mend the bag soon.

Avarie takes a deep breath, brushing off the mistake. No need to get herself worked up over something that can be fixed. There might be plenty else that can't be remedied during this journey. She tucks the coin bag into her brassiere then tugs on the boots after having avoided them for so long.

They aren't terrible. But if her sensitive feet could continue barefoot the whole time, she'd choose that option without question. Avarie tests her feet in the shoes, stomping them on the forest floor. They pinch her toes a bit. The minimal cushion was fine for now, but she had a feeling the thin padding would become cumbersome in the future. She needs to get moving and find better shelter.

It would also be best if she gets her story straight. What's the story behind this human character she is masquerading as?

Who *is* Avarie the human?

What does she do?

Where is she from?

Why is she visiting Deniz?

Time stretches forward as Avarie crafts exactly who she wants to be.

"I am confident. And no one can intimidate me. My father is proud of me. I know how to talk to people. I'm—I'm a shoe maker. No—that's stupid, I barely like the things on my feet now. I'm an artist. A painter. I'm here to capture the Denizian landscape while on vacation. I'm on vacation because—"

Her ramblings peter out as the forest transitions from tree after enormous tree and opens up to a boisterous market.

At the market's center is a huge stone fountain with a mermaid statue. The mermaid is leaning forward, her hand reaching up for what seems like the stars. Seashells are embedded on the outer circumference of the fountain. There are wooden booths surrounding the fountain, topped with red, orange, or blue canvases to shield hagglers and sellers alike from the sun. The booths venture farther than Avarie's eyesight allows.

The disorienting voices stop Avarie in her tracks for a moment. Just minutes ago, she'd grown accustomed to the calm sounds of the desolate forest. Now there are feet pounding against the gray cobblestone, ratty picket signs announcing the vendors' wares, and screaming children weaving their way through the crowd as parents scold and chase after them.

It's utter chaos.

She'd been to the Merelani market a few times. Calm instrumentals floated through the air. Merkids, in low voices, played in a designated safe area. Sellers had no problem adjusting their prices, there was no need to yell at all.

What a complete one-eighty.

Avarie clutches her bag and turns in a circle, absorbing her surroundings with a slack jaw and widened eyes. Then she stops herself, dropping the astonished look like a hot dish. Maybe she shouldn't look so lost. Maybe she should act as if this were a normal day in the market.

She nods in confirmation.

Good idea. Act normal. *Completely* normal.

She takes a few steps backward to recalibrate, to orient herself to the new environment. While backing up, a strong force knocks her off balance. Well, not much force was needed. Her legs aren't at optimal use yet. Avarie teeters on her feet for a few seconds before collapsing to the ground. Pain explodes from her knees as she hits the cobblestone.

Avarie looks up, her glasses slipping down her nose, and finds the sun glaring right back at her. She drapes a hand over her eyes just as a tall and skinny brown girl fills her vision, blotting out the sun with her massive curls. She smells of sweetness and sea sorrel, and she's looking at Avarie with a sheepish expression. The girl gives her a floundering smile and reaches out to help her up.

Avarie fixes her mouth to admonish the girl, but before she can even get a word in, a wooden cart rolls by and splashes them both in muddy rainwater. The water seeps into Avarie's hair, latches onto her skin, chilling her bones in ways water has never done before. Her enchanted clothing is no match for the mixture of mud and water. She's drenched. The human world sure has a rude way of welcoming her.

Chapter Ten

"Oh God, I'm so sorry," the nameless girl says, her voice softer than the velvet curtains in Avarie's reading nook. "Some people"—she shoots a glare at the still moving wagon—"can be so careless. Take my hand."

Avarie frowns. First the cottage boys, then she gets muddy water thrown on her, and now, this—wait, what is *this*? She studies the stranger for a moment longer, really drinking in the girl's features. She has breathtaking, speckled skin. An enriching score of light and dark-brown, and the palest of melanin decorate her arms, face, and neck, with trails of more likely lurking beneath her clothes. Mermaids don't have such wonderful, pigmented skin where she comes from.

Her deep-auburn curls are beautiful. Avarie wishes she had the patience to take care of such wonderful hair; that's why locs work best for her. The girl's comely, dark-brown eyes meet Avarie's.

Wow. She's *so* pretty.

Avarie has never had the pleasure of meeting someone so unique until now.

She then remembers she's meant to grasp the girl's hand.

Avarie reaches out, extending her hand. As the two connect, the girl sucks in a sharp breath, just as a strange, calming warmth floats up Avarie's arm. But it's not just her body, the necklace at her throat heats up as well.

May the necklace's warmth guide you on your journey.

Avarie can imagine it now. Aalto teasing her about this girl, about how she's so tongue-tied. He'd probably prod Avarie into asking her out. A smile grows on her face. But it's brief. Aalto's gone. There will be no teasing, no joking threats about snitching to their father. This necklace is meant to guide her to his killer, not the love of her life.

With minimal effort, the stranger pulls Avarie to a standing position, then goes further as to dust dirt from her shoulders.

"Thanks. Maybe I should have been paying more attention too," Avarie responds. Their hands stay entwined until Avarie realizes she should pull away. The energy generated from the initial touch felt genial, comforting. But she wasn't here for that, whatever *that* was.

"My place isn't far from here. You can wash up—if you want. Do you, er, want to wash up? I assume you would. You're too pretty to—"

Avarie cuts her off, an embarrassed heat warming her cheeks. "Sounds like an offer I shouldn't resist." This is an opportunity to learn more about Deniz from a local. And a queen should never remain so dirty. Plus, this seems like a step in the right direction. Her necklace says so . . . at least, that's what she tells herself.

Avarie's certain there's a novel or two about following a stranger into the woods and never returning home. And yet Avarie can't help but insist, something about this human feels as though she can be trusted.

Only time will tell.

"I'm Avarie, by the way."

"Lahna. Greetings, Avarie." Lahna smiles, innocent charm spewing from her oval face and strong cheekbones. The smile almost stuns Avarie into a dazzled stupor, a spell that rivals any the Enchantress could concoct. Avarie shakes her head. *Focus.* She needs to focus. She's not in Deniz for cute girls. How maddening it would be to explain to Bruinen that she failed her mission on the first day—thwarted by a pretty stranger— she would never hear the end of it!

Avarie takes a steadying breath then tries her best not to wobble as she follows Lahna back into the forest, somewhere between the abandoned cottage and market. Her legs are growing on her. Though Avarie admits she misses the feeling of treading water with her tail. She'll get back to that sensation soon enough.

Avarie cradles her satchel in front of her like a newborn and Lahna takes notice.

"Something happen to your bag?"

"Uh, yeah. I poked a hole in it . . . clumsy me." Embarrassment from her rudimentary lie makes Avarie drop her gaze to the forest floor.

"Ahh, okay, seems like you've got a knack for accidents."

"I just might with the way today's been going," Avarie admits.

"Well, maybe I can change that." Lahna shoots her a hopeful look. And Avarie thinks she might just melt. She doesn't trust her brain to say anything useful as a response, so they walk in silence for a bit. Avarie tries to memorize their surroundings, but it all seems like an endless forest. It's a wonder how she didn't get lost on her own earlier. Then there's cottage after cottage after cottage. All of them similar in build. She needs time to learn Deniz. Maybe Lahna can be her guide.

Not just because the girl is cute and Aalto probably would have approved of her. Having a local at her disposal will help her get home faster—and the necklace's warm response to her can't be forgotten either.

After minutes of silence, Lahna revives the conversation. "So, where are you from Avarie? Any Denizian resident would know not to stand in the center of the market. Chaos is bound to happen." Lahna chuckles.

Avarie stiffens for a moment, but Lahna doesn't notice as they walk side by side. Everything she was rehearsing earlier is seemingly dumped from her mind. She never anticipated needing a backstory because visiting Deniz, much less meeting a nice human, was never something she thought could happen. This is why they should have let her prepare more before sending her off to shore, but the raging seaquakes insisted that she leave as soon as possible.

"Uh, I'm from the north. North of Deniz," she eventually tells the girl.

Lahna raises an eyebrow. "Oh really? Which village? Think I have a third cousin in Alameda."

"No . . . not from that one." Avarie purses her lips. She's so unprepared, she *must* be blowing her cover right now. No human can know she's from the sea. Not even a nice, cute girl who offered to help her clean up . . . Not with everything at stake.

"Okay," Lahna's grin widens, showcasing a dimple in her right cheek. "Let me guess! I'm pretty good with geography."

"Sure, take a gander." Avarie's stomach sinks, heavy with unease.

"Tallis?"

"No."

"Wonne?"

"Nope."

"Adahy?"

"Yeah, that's the one." Avarie's voice squeaks a little, resulting in an uncontrollable wince.

"Knew I'd guess it!" Lahna triumphantly thrusts a balled fist into the air.

Avarie can't help but join in on the excitement. "I believed in your sound knowledge of geography."

Lahna nods, eager. "How's it way up there in Adahy? Have you visited the castle? That's the northernmost village I can think of. Never been though."

"Haven't gotten a chance to see the castle, to be honest. Adahy is . . . chilly." Lahna shoots her a confused look as she says 'chilly.' Avarie wishes for the ground to split open and swallow her whole. How can she be this bad at making conversation with a human girl?

It's because she's attractive.

Avarie shakes her head.

Stay on task.

As she's attempting to redeem herself, a resplendent cabin comes into view. The cottage from last night is paltry in comparison.

An aged but well-cared-for stone fence lines the perimeter of the home, adorned with vines and lush green plants that Avarie can't name, and which contributes to the cottage's overall feeling of seclusion. A white-painted wooden door rests in between the stone fencing. Lahna nonchalantly slides the metal rod keeping the door closed then walks through the gate.

An intricately embedded stone walkway leads to the front door. Robust grass with a variety of wildflowers fill the blank space on either side of it. Beige brick rock encompasses the exterior of the cottage while a roof as dark as night decorates the top with neatly positioned bricks and a chimney.

Granted, Avarie spent her life in an underwater palace, but if she were human, a cottage such as this would be the ultimate goal to own.

"Goddess . . ." Avarie exhales under her breath. She can only imagine what the inside looks like.

"Hmm?" Lahna eyes her.

"Goodness. Your home, Lahna. It's astounding."

"Thank you, I'm flattered." Lahna looks down bashfully. "My father possesses a lot of wealth. It's a gift from him, or, well, a punishment, actually."

"Punishment?"

"Yes. I'm his only child, and I refused to go into business with him. So he gifted the outlandish chalet he planned for me to his third wife—which is fine—I prefer this one much more. It has"—Lahna pauses for a moment—"a calm beauty to it. It's not gaudy like that thing my ex-stepmother resides in."

"Seems like you lucked up."

"I did. I truly did."

AVARIE STANDS AWKWARDLY IN THE MAIN ROOM OF the cottage, absorbing her surroundings, just as she'd done outdoors. Lahna disappears down the hall and Avarie is unsure if she's meant to follow or stay put. Her right foot moves forward. Then she stops in place. She clasps her hands together, rubbing her sun ring. Avarie can't help but wonder if she bears resemblance to a crab digging in the sand, one that sporadically pauses to make sure the coast is clear. She opts to stay in place and look around instead.

The main room is immeasurably cozy. From the brick fireplace to the sparse wooden furniture. Simplistic. The more Avarie observes, the more she believes she has an even better idea of who this human girl is.

Lahna returns with wooden buckets filled with water, that same relaxed, calming smile adorning her face. A smile that intrigues Avarie, one urging her to get to know Lahna just a little bit more.

To gather information on Deniz, of course.

Because Aalto's murderer is here. And I've got to stop the seaquakes. Plus, I'm sort of betrothed? Should I tell her I'm getting married soon? Does it matter? No—she doesn't need to know. That's probably weird to announce to someone cute—someone I just met. Ugh, she is cute though—I have more important things to focus on!

"I'll save you the trouble of cleaning up in my small washroom. You can get clean here." Lahna sets two buckets down next to a stool, along with a change of clothes that was folded underneath her arm. She shuts the flowy light-blue curtains, granting Avarie more privacy before returning down the hall she came from.

"Th-thank you!" Avarie calls out, but Lahna is already gone. As if she needed *more* time and solitude to overthink . . . She plops down onto the stool, her thighs flattening out. Avarie removes the dirty garments from her body, plunging them into the bucket, over and over. Quickly, the sudsy water transitions from clear to brown. A bubble floats into the air and pops in front of Avarie's nose. She sighs. As merkids, she and Aalto would compete to see who could blow the biggest bubbles from their noses. He always won. Which Avarie never considered a true victory, because who wants to win at being the grossest?

I miss you, Aalto.

She wrings out the newly washed clothes before setting them on the floor, unsure of exactly where to put them. Avarie takes a rag and wipes it across her arms, legs, and all the in-betweens. She shivers as the warm water cools her exposed skin. She quickly towels off then slips into the provided garment. It was a tight fit, but she'll make it work. The knee-length dark-blue dress felt snug around her chest and thighs. Her legs stick to each other in ways the leggings had prevented. Avarie doesn't know how long she'll survive in this. Hopefully, her original clothes will dry soon.

Lahna returns, wearing a yellow tunic and fitted cream pants, looking almost ethereal with her hair pulled back into a huge bun; free coils line her face near her ears. Avarie jumps at the chance to thank her before Lahna can disappear elsewhere.

"I wanted to express gratitude for—"

"It's the least I could do." Lahna shrugs, picking up the buckets and heading in the direction of what Avarie assumes must be her washroom. Over her shoulder, Lahna throws out the words, "Gotta give our tourists the five-star treatment."

Avarie wanted to ask what other perks tourists received, but when Lahna returns, her eyes bright and alluring, Avarie swallows down those bold words with a nervous gulp.

"I'm-I'm just saying . . . I came here on somewhat of a—a whim, and I wasn't expecting such kindness. So, thank you. I owe you," Avarie stammers, rubbing the back of her neck. She notices that her hand is hot, clammy. Suddenly, she's hyper-aware of her body in contrast to Lahna's.

How her breathing has become irregular.

The way her mouth is stretched in what's probably a stupid grin.

And how she's counting how many paces it would take to walk to Lahna.

"Oh, an undetermined favor where I can ask for anything at any time?" Lahna smiles as she leans on a wall a few feet from Avarie. "I need to bump into strangers more often."

"Something leads me to believe you may have ulterior motives." Avarie purses her lips in faux concern. "Do you bump into every girl you see that's lost in the market?"

"Only the beautiful ones."

While there was a playfulness to her words, Avarie can't help but note the earnest look in Lahna's eyes. She bites her lip, there's a sprightly innocence to it, but the action makes Avarie's stomach flip nonetheless.

Oh, Goddess.

She knows this feeling. This stupid, stupid feeling she reserves for individuals she can never have—infatuation.

She should run away right now.

" . . . you must bump into beautiful women quite often, no?" Avarie continues, surprising herself.

Lahna's head tilts to the side, her curls springing along with the subtle motion. "Can't say that I do. But there's a first time for everything, *no?*" She imitates the drop in volume Avarie used just seconds ago. But it didn't seem like she was mocking her. It was more like Lahna was somehow attuned to the slightest inflection in Avarie's voice. And something about that makes her feel heard.

"I truly have no witty response to that," Avarie admits.

Lahna pushes herself off the wall, laughing. The sound of it rivals the beauty of Merelani's Royal Symphony, twisting strings in Avarie's heart she didn't know existed.

"That's okay. I'm a bit of a wordsmith."

As Avarie grasps for a clever response, her growling stomach blessedly interrupts the conversation.

"Sounds like someone's hungry. How about I hang your clothes outside to dry, sew your bag, then we head to the market?"

At this point, Avarie's stunned into silence by the girl's unyielding kindness. How did she get so lucky on her first day? If everyone in Deniz were kind like Lahna, then her mission could be done in a breeze.

Then she remembers everyone can't be as nice. Humans *murder* merfolk. Someone butchered Aalto. No matter how nice Lahna seems, she could be just as evil as the one who killed her brother. She might only be kind since she believes

Avarie is human. This reminder wipes out the sprouting joy in her heart.

"So, THE MARKET IS SPLIT UP INTO THREE sections," Lahna explains. "Food is closest to the front, near the mermaid fountain. You know, where the *incident* happened." Lahna wiggles her eyebrows for dramatic effect. They're back at the market now, except Avarie feels less overwhelmed than her first visit.

Avarie chuckles. Having a speeding wagon throw mud on her was beyond frustrating at first. But now, it's probably the best thing that's happened to her. Lahna's been so amicable since their initial meeting. Avarie's wet garments are drying on a clothesline at Lahna's home, and her bag has been patched together, almost like new.

"Oh, the *incident*, however could I forget? The travesty is still vivid in my mind."

"It's hard to forget." That calm smile returns to Lahna's face as she continues showing the way. "About halfway through the market, you'll find vendors selling the usual household tools. Firewood, cleaning supplies, you name it. The very back . . . specifically the far-right corner, are all the 'unspeakables.' My advice—avoid that section. No good can come over there."

Avarie's pierced ears perk up at the word. *Unspeakables.* She tugs at the small hoop earring in her right ear. Sounds exactly where she needs to go. "Unspeakables? What's that about? We don't have that in . . . *Add-uh-he.*" Her tongue stumbles over the pronunciation Lahna unknowingly provided to her hours before.

Lahna frowns, her reassuring smile twisting into something unfortunate. "The vendors and hunters sell awful things there. They call it the 'Unspeakable Corridor.' I don't travel down that far into the market."

Lahna doesn't offer anything more after that, making a point to stop at the invisible line drawn between the regular and the shadier vendors. *Hunters?* Avarie makes a note to visit the darker side of the market on her own time.

The sky above is already transitioning to a vibrant purple sunset. Watching the sun's retreat from the surface almost matches the beauty of seeing it set from her chambers. But it also signals that it will be dark soon. She should find a place to stay before her vision worsens. These human eyes cannot brave the dark like her true ones. Avarie clutches her bag, now full with a newly purchased outfit and some food, before asking Lahna one final question: "I'm in need of a place to stay for the night, any suggestions?"

"I'd go with the Siren's Rock. One of our better overnight lodgings. Good prices. Tell the inn owner that Lahna Hart sent you. He might give you a discount. You can cut through the market, actually. Make a right at the fountain and keep walking straight until you see it."

"Wow, you're overflowing with generosity tonight. Thank you." Avarie beams.

"Anytime, Avarie." The captivating smile returns. "Stop by my cottage when you get a chance. I'd like to see you again before you leave—how long are you here for?"

"A little under two weeks," Avarie can't help but smile back. This human girl was growing on her in unexpected ways.

"Ahh, so a short visit then. We should make the most of it."

We?

A fuzzy feeling blossoms in Avarie's chest. And then it fizzles out.

I'm not human. And I won't be here long. What's the point in 'making the most of it?'

"Oh, and your clothes," Lahna continues, "you should pick those up too. I work from home. So, feel free to pop in whenever."

Avarie can only muster a few words. "Absolutely. Will do."

"Great! It was nice running into you today, Avarie. Until we meet again." Lahna gingerly grabs Avarie's hand—the one that isn't attached to her satchel—and caresses it. Her thumb and pointer fingers massage both sides of Avarie's hand.

Avarie's knees almost buckle from the interaction. A knowing simper appears on Lahna's face before she squeezes the affected hand once more and retreats from the market, leaving Avarie standing alone in a giddy stupor.

No mergirl ever made her feel this whimsical, not even Mairya. What was it about this human that makes Avarie almost forget her purpose on land? She flexes the hand that was briefly warmed by Lahna's long, slender fingers. And that fleeting warmth reminds Avarie of the heat the necklace produced when she met Lahna.

This girl feels like trouble, but it's trouble Avarie wants to crash headfirst into.

Chapter Eleven

Avarie finds the Siren's Rock with no trouble, what with Lahna's simple directions playing on repeat in her mind. She doesn't know if she's replaying the words to remember them . . . or just to remember the smoothness of Lahna's voice. Signs point to the latter.

The inn doesn't measure up to the subtle magnificence of Lahna's cottage, but it will suffice for her short time on land. And short it will be. She doesn't want to think about failing Aalto, but she can barely bring herself to touch the blade in her satchel.

What will Avarie do when she finally discovers the killer?

And what of her parents? Bruinen has shown over and over that he finds her incapable. Proving him wrong means casting aside her morals. Failing means disappointing her mother.

It's not just about her anymore. If the seaquakes never stop, what about Merelani's future? There won't be one.

Failure is not an option.

Despite all this pressure building up like a tidal wave . . . there's something she's ashamed to admit.

Never seeing Lahna again stirs the hugest feeling of unease in her stomach. It's childish. Not at all the personification of a queen striving to save her kingdom. But Avarie can't help but feel like this anyway.

Avarie brushes away *all* those feelings as she walks up the inn's slanted stairs. After reaching the landing, she wraps a hand around a wine-colored doorknob and tugs the door open. A gust of warm air hits her face, a welcome sensation in contrast to the steadily cooling outdoors.

The bell attached to the door chimes loudly, signaling the arrival of a newcomer. Just then, Avarie's necklace grows hotter. She looks down and places a curious hand over it. When she looks up again, she finds the men inside had turned to gaze at her like sharks smelling blood in the water, distracted from whatever card game they were playing.

They were seated around a large table at the center of the room; underneath their feet is a circular maroon rug that spans the entirety of the chairs and table placed atop it. A fireplace off to one side is casting the room with orange and yellow hues.

The men, older and a little grimy, are leering at her from head to toe. Avarie's unsure if it's because she's a new face here in Deniz, or simply because she's a woman. Either way, a blanket of discomfort settles on her skin, making her look frantically for a way to abandon the undesired attention.

Avarie's eyes lock onto the innkeeper at the front desk. She speedwalks to him like her life depends on it. The man, older and just as grimy, stares at her. But not in a way that makes her skin crawl. His cerulean eyes only betray curiosity with a hint of fatigue.

"Welcome to the Siren's Rock. Unfortunately, we're full for the night, young lady. Why don't you come back tomorrow?"

Avarie frowns. This isn't going how she wanted. Not at all.

She has nowhere else to go. A few hours in that dreadful cottage was alright for the first night, but she didn't know how long she'd survive for several *days*. She could ask to stay the night with Lahna. Avarie peers out the iron-barred windows. Utter darkness. The fatigue she'd been trying to suppress hits her. She needs rest right now. Avarie looks over to the hungry-eyed men at the table whose gazes seemed to desire something other than food. She needs a room at the inn tonight. One with a lock. There must be a way to make it happen.

"I'll be in Deniz for a few weeks. I need a room, please. It's dark out."

The man purses his lips yet looks set in his decision. "There are no clean rooms, ma'am. Nothing I can do. I wish you safe travels." But the kindness seems empty, like he would rather Avarie got out of his face.

"I'm a—" Avarie pauses for a moment, trying to find the proper words. "I'm a friend of Lahna Hart. She said I should mention that," Avarie continues, feeling a little sheepish yet giddy that she referred to Lahna as her friend.

The man's tired eyes widen. With what—is that a trace of fear? "Oh! Any friend of the Hart family is welcome here. My apologies, miss. Let me . . ." The man trails off, frantically searching the desk for something. Then he lifts up a tarnished metal key. "This room isn't our best. The fireplace is tricky. And it could use some tidying. If you give me a moment, I'll clean it for you. Our maid is out for the night."

"Yes, thank you," Avarie mutters with barely contained astonishment. Who is Lahna Hart? Why did her name cause a grown man to panic? The men playing cards have gone quiet too. Only the sound of the crackling of wood in the fireplace can be heard. When Avarie turns around, the men at the table hastily avoid eye contact. She returns her gaze to the front desk. Avarie plans to milk this for as long as she can. She leans forward, placing both hands on the counter. "I'd like the fireplace lit as well. And an appropriate discount on the room and board."

"Ab-absolutely! What name should I use for the logbook?"

"Avarie. Just Avarie."

The man nods quickly, suddenly awake. "Of course, Miss Avarie, give me a moment and your room will be ready. Why don't you take a seat in one of our comfortable lounge chairs? Then I'll escort you to your room."

Avarie settles into the red velvet lounge chair near the fireplace. The heat feels every bit wonderful against her bare legs. She thinks her father would be proud of her for asserting herself and refusing to take 'no' as an answer. But there's a feeling of concern lingering over her too. What about the women who get turned away that don't have connections? The frown returns to Avarie's face. What about *their* safety? She crosses her arms and legs and waits, overthinking the different ways this night could have gone had she not met Lahna Hart today.

AVARIE'S LODGING ISN'T ANYTHING SPECIAL. SHE collapses backward onto the bed, her arms spread wide like the limbs of a starfish. The bedding doesn't feel the best against her skin, but it's better than Cast-out Cottage.

Curiosity swims laps in her mind at the memory—how could anyone destroy L.H. Sirene's books? What's not to like? Other human literature that she's read uses the terms 'mermaid' and 'siren' interchangeably. But Sirene writes with such a great respect for both species, that Avarie is wondering if the author were masquerading as a human like she's doing now.

Fatigue cements itself into Avarie's bones. Today has been quite eventful, and she's glad to be off her feet for the rest of the night. Avarie closes her eyes.

She's tempted to stumble her way back to shore and rehash everything with Mai.

Oh, Mairya.

Avarie feels embarrassed that she's almost forgotten about her. However, not only does she want to gossip with Mai now . . . but she *has* to. She promised. What about their nightly recaps?

What about their eventual engagement once Avarie returns home? Avarie *should* be relieved that she needn't worry about finding someone to rule Merelani with.

But she's not.

Avarie refuses to entertain the crazy, reckless thoughts about Lahna lingering at the back of her mind. It's pointless.

Lahna belongs on land.

Avarie belongs to the sea.

She shakes her head. *Such, foolishness.* She can't allow a stranger to lead her astray from her duties. That won't bring honor to her family. That won't save her people from the wrath of the Sea Goddess. Bruinen would be most displeased . . . and she risks disappointing her mother too.

She thinks of Cordelia's wails, how broken she had looked as she cradled Aalto in her arms. How could Avarie return home and say she failed to avenge her brother—their slaughtered king—because she got waylaid by a crush? But then, Avarie thinks about the way her necklace had reacted to Lahna; the warmth that felt keenly like her brother's approval.

The necklace also seemed to signal trouble, like when the men from the inn were leering at her. But the warmth she felt when she met Lahna had been different, hadn't it? It must be a sign—but Avarie can't like her.

A sigh of frustration leaves Avarie's mouth.

Focus, Avarie.

She'll visit the Unspeakable Corridor tomorrow.

She won't miss another meeting with Mairya.

She won't like Lahna . . .

Avarie slips beneath the scratchy linen and hides beneath the covers.

Nevertheless, she can't help but smile at the thought of getting to know Lahna more.

"This little infatuation just might come back to bite me in the tail—ass?"

Avarie shakes her head, embarrassed even though no one can see her beneath the covers. She squeezes her eyes shut and lets the fireplace's warmth lure her into a dreamless sleep.

Chapter Twelve

Avarie shields her eyes against the sunlight peeking into her room. She jiggles her legs, attempting to banish their stiffness. As time passes, her new limbs no longer seem as foreign to her. Avarie removes the covers then goes to stand in front of the full-length mirror, truly viewing her human form for the first time. Heat from the furnace lingers, but it's less intense now.

Lifting the dress, she takes in her bare legs, twisting and turning them side to side. She's comically short. Her mermaid tail must have lent most of her height. Either way, she's significantly shorter than Lahna.

Why is that human suddenly at the forefront of Avarie's mind?

She shakes her head, banishing all the 'Lahna Thoughts' away.

Avarie's hips remain the same, curving out at an arch. Now she just has thighs to match. Avarie examines her missing 'scale,' the scarred over patch of skin on her thigh. She wishes she had known then that there were other ways to reach the surface. With a sigh, she releases the fabric of the dress, it falls to its natural place at her knobby knees.

Avarie rifles through her bag, grabbing the jerky Lahna bought for her last evening. It differed from the taste of crustaceans, but it wasn't gross. Just something new. She rubs the underside of her bag, feeling the mended threads and thinking of Lahna's overflowing well of kindness. She'll need to think of a nice way to repay her.

Here she goes again with the 'Lahna Thoughts.'

Avarie opens the bathroom door, her focus turning to the clawfoot tub. She twists a golden handle, and warm water comes rushing out. She dares not touch it; steam billows out to caress the skin on her face.

This is a land-dweller custom, it's only right for Avarie to try it out. She should try to enjoy some of her time in Deniz. It doesn't escape her that she's only experiencing something she's longed for—the human experience—because of her twin's death.

Avarie frowns.

She twists the handle again, turning the water off and slams the bathroom door shut.

THE MIDMORNING TRANQUILITY OF AVARIE'S SHORT walk to the market fades as she reaches the outdoor shopping area. Like yesterday, various noises compete for dominance. Children scream with glee, hagglers haggle, vendors argue. It was overwhelming at first, but now it's full of familiarity that quiets the anxiousness in Avarie's chest. Sweet and savory smells find their way into her nose, reminding her that food is a priority. She follows the savory scent to a single booth with a sign that reads 'Sarahi's Eatables.'

An older woman with gentle dark eyes and brown skin greets her. "Hi, dear, what can I get for you today?"

Avarie assesses three rectangular metal pans that are heated underneath by a small fire. Two out of three dishes look unfamiliar. The farthest pan to the right holds braised shrimp with some sort of grain intermixed. The first pan is filled with grilled meat paired with a bulbous green vegetable. The middle pan has another unrecognizable meat with what Avarie can identify as carrots. This meat's a little red in the middle, with a bone sticking out.

At a loss, Avarie inquires further. "What would you recommend? I'm . . . new here." New to land. But Sarahi needn't know that.

The vendor stares at her for a moment, trying to see if she's serious or not. But when Avarie leans forward with interest, awaiting the woman's answer, she finally speaks. "This first dish is grilled chicken drumsticks and peppered brussels sprouts. The second is lamb quarter with carrots. Lastly, this is shrimp and brown rice. All are good. They're fairly common items you can get from any market."

Not the Merelani market. But Avarie can't say that. She flashes two copper coins. "How much of the shrimp and rice can I get for this?"

Sarahi quickly grabs the coins and tucks them in a pouch on her waist. "A heaping spoonful. Eat it before it goes cold." She takes a wooden spoon and plops a portion into a metal bowl. "When you're done, return the bowl to a nearby waste bin. There's a place to set them on top, I'll grab it later. Here you go." The woman pushes the bowl and a utensil toward Avarie, dismissing her as soon as she'd come.

Avarie takes the bowl and finds a secluded spot underneath a tree to eat. She watches the bustling market as she takes her first bite. The shrimp wasn't fresh. None could be as lively as the underwater shrimp brought to her just moments after they were caught. But the rice was tasty, if a little plain. The food will fill her stomach. That's what matters. The way Sarahi took her coins is worrisome, however. Maybe she shouldn't tell merchants she's new. They could take advantage of her naivety. She should ask Lahna market prices when she sees her next.

And oh, how she couldn't wait to see her again. A blush warms Avarie's cheeks. Despite the minor hiccups, being a land dweller has been treating her well so far. Now, if only Avarie could find the poacher who hurt her dear brother.

AVARIE REACHES THE FURTHEST END OF THE MARKET at the sun's highest peak. Sweat lines her brassiere and brow. It wasn't a long walk, but it was certainly hilly. She wipes the wetness from her face on the hem of her tunic. The sun is unrelenting, so Avarie is grateful for the tarred canvases pulled taut above the walkway. The shadows they cast are welcome, even though the darkness seemed to signify that she's reached the most daunting part of the lively market. Avarie slips on her glasses for good measure. She doesn't want to miss a thing.

Vendors aren't as loud here; they speak in caliginous whispers and murmurs. As though to signal what is to come, the sun hides behind the clouds and darkness breeds itself further. As Avarie walks along the cobblestone, nearly avoiding a tumble from the uneven ground, she spies the 'corridor' Lahna spoke of. The concrete walls are ashen and the soot covering it contributes to its overall sense of foreboding. As Avarie braces herself to venture into the unknown, she's dismayed by the appearance of a cloaked figure blocking her passage.

"You don't belong here," the cloaked face growls.

And they're right. Avarie has no idea what possessed her to

visit the sketchiest part of the market alone. She doesn't believe dropping Lahna's name will help her out this time. She'll have to do this on her own.

"I'm looking for something." Vague, but true. Avarie doesn't know exactly what she needs to find. But the sudden warming of her necklace tells her answers lurk just beyond this stranger.

"You must be lost, little girl," the voice spits out. "If you don't have the code, you are not welcome here. Be gone. Now."

A code?

That's the next step in her quest then. *Find the code. Get into the dark market. Discover who the murderer is. Make them pay.*

Avarie must have hesitated for too long because the man rises to his full height and shoves her. She staggers backward and falls on her ass. Her brows furrow with indignation as pain explodes through her body. Avarie scrambles backward on all fours.

Like a cornered animal.

Not like a queen.

"You—you don't know who I am," she stammers, holding the man's gaze despite wanting to tuck tail and run. Avarie stands on shaky legs and dusts herself off.

"And who are *you* exactly?" the voice mocks.

Royalty.

Someone on a mission to save her kingdom.

But Avarie knows she can say neither of those things. Gaze collapsing to the floor, her confidence crumbles.

Avarie retreats with a few murmurs of apology under her breath. She bumps into other people while fleeing from the Corridor. She needs to regroup. With discouragement floating freely in her heart, she decides to pay a visit to Lahna. Maybe learning more about Deniz from her will make her look less of a tourist. Maybe Lahna knows this elusive code.

That's her excuse to visit. It isn't because Avarie desires Lahna's presence. Or that she suspects the human will uplift her spirits.

Plus, she needs to retrieve her clothes.

That's what Avarie tells herself while leaving the market.

BEFORE HEADING TOWARDS A CERTAIN COTTAGE IN the woods, Avarie washes away the dirt and humiliation clinging to her after being shoved to the ground. Even if she's only submerged in a tub, it feels invigorating to be surrounded by so much water again without the fear of drowning. She redresses in a rush. Time to visit Lahna.

With a hopeful feeling blooming in her heart, Avarie raises a hand, poised to knock on Lahna's front door when—

"You're being ridiculous! It's time for you to grow up!" A male voice booms from within the confines of the home. Avarie almost mistakes it for her father, the wrath and disappointment it carries is similar in tone. The voice grows louder as it nears the front door. Quickly, Avarie dashes to the right, out of sight around the corner of the house. When the front door bursts open, she timidly peeks around the edge. A burly, masculine figure emerges through the door. Waves of agitation seem to roll off his shoulders. Avarie shrinks away, hand at her naked throat. *Huh.* She must have forgotten to put her necklace back on. She watches as the man grumbles incoherently to himself while flicking a pocketknife in his left hand open and closed.

At the sight of the weapon, a near intelligible gasp escapes from Avarie's lips and she winces. The man stiffens, hearing her slip up. Avarie recedes farther behind the cottage, going so far as to assimilate with the small shrubs lining its side. In an instant, she feels silly. But maybe it's just enough to hide her should he round the corner. Avarie tucks her head and tries to become one with the shrubbery.

Please, Goddess. Please don't let him round this corner.

The idea of the man discovering her cowering alongside the foliage, sends tremors through her limbs.

After a moment that feels like an entire sunrise and sunset, the man stomps away, demolishing innocent wildflowers in his wake. Avarie releases an anxiety-riddled breath as his heavy steps fade away. She waits a few minutes for her breathing to slow before returning to the front door and knocking.

Who was that man? And how could anyone be so angry with someone as bright and kind as Lahna?

Chapter Thirteen

Avarie cautiously knocks on the door, the recent outburst from the unknown man fresh on her mind. Lahna snatches the door open with a huff, displeasure written all over her features. No calm smile in sight.

"Oh. It's you." Her face softens upon recognizing Avarie. The disgruntled crease etched between her brows starts to vanish. "What can I do for you?"

"Are you okay? You look . . . upset." Avarie doesn't dare mention what she saw. She can't imagine a scenario where it would ever be appropriate.

Hey Lahna, you seem so calm and collected. Care to tell me why a scary man turned your smile upside down?

Absolutely not.

Avarie continues: "I came by to chat. And to retrieve my clothes."

Lahna pauses, pursing her full lips for a moment. "Had an unwanted visitor. Hope you missed them?" Her eyes stare curiously into Avarie's, waiting for a response.

The foundation of their new . . . friendship is already

based on a lie. She has no idea where *Add-uh-he* is. More importantly, she's masquerading as a human girl . . . Avarie doesn't wish to tell another lie.

But she has to.

"I just came from the market; didn't run into anyone on the way over. Is everything alright?" Hopefully, her last few words don't come off as suspicious.

"Sure, sure." Lahna nods her head, relaxing a bit. But stress still clings to her frame like a succubus to her prey. "If you don't mind, I'd like to get out for a bit. Decompress. You're more than welcome to come with me, Avarie."

"I'd like that, lead the way, Lahna."

With a fishing rod clutched in one hand, Lahna steps through the cottage gate. Avarie expects to catch its handle but to her delight, Lahna holds it open for her. She breezes through, accidentally brushing up against Lahna's chest, and as they lock eyes in that brief moment, Avarie's resolve melts under her dark-brown gaze.

All of a sudden, she's mousey. Shy. Though timidity seems a regular thing for Avarie, something about this human pushes things into overdrive.

They follow a winding, stoney trail behind the house, which eventually peters out to dirt. Maybe it's a good thing Avarie didn't try to visit Mai last night. She's sure she would have lost her way. But now this pathway looks familiar.

Avarie sees Cast-out Cottage growing closer as they continue walking. This seems like a safe subject for her to inquire into. "What's the story with that cottage? Do you know?" Avarie does her best to keep pace with Lahna, but it's a huge feat given their differences in stature.

Noticing that Avarie's falling behind, Lahna makes her steps slower. Her wistful eyes lock onto the cottage as she responds. "Do you want the fairytale? Or do you want the truth?"

"I absolutely need the fairytale." Avarie's lips curve into a smile.

"As you wish." Lahna stops a couple paces from the cottage and meets Avarie's gaze. "Once upon a time, there was a beautiful maiden who visited this cottage every ten years. Not necessarily the same maiden, but *a* maiden. She fixes up the cottage, tends to the garden. Then disappears for a decade. Typical ethereal maiden stuff.

"One day, a visiting prince hears the tale of the Ten-Year Maiden. And because this is a fairytale, the timing of the prince's arrival coincides perfectly with the maiden's ten-year cycle. On the maiden's last night in Deniz, the prince follows her. He watches her wade into the water where she changes into a mermaid and disappears. Amazed by her transformation, he begins to call for her every night at the shore. And on the fifth night, she finally appears. They fall in love—you know how that goes."

But Avarie doesn't know. Fraternal love, parental love, even love shared between friends differ. She knows that. A seahorse-sized jealousy builds in her stomach. For her lack of experience or Lahna's alleged experience, she can't tell.

"Yeah—yeah I get it," Avarie says.

"People from his kingdom wonder why the prince never returned home. There are treaties to be signed, territories to be claimed. An adviser is sent to Deniz to retrieve the missing prince. But what the adviser finds frightens him. The prince is waist-deep in the water and entwined with a mermaid. Different variants of the story mention the severity of their entanglement. For your sake, let's stick to the child-friendly version—"

"You don't think I can handle the adult version? I'm eighteen years of age, you know." Avarie crosses her arms in false indignation.

"I'm twenty-two, but even the adult version makes *me* call for some sort of decorum."

"I want to hear it! Don't skip on the details," Avarie insists.

"Okay, okay . . . well the prince was in a state of . . ." Lahna trails off, searching for the proper word. "A state of undress. As was the mermaid, well as much as a mermaid can be, I suppose. Anatomically speaking, I have seen some sketches of mermaid anatomy, so the sex is possible—"

"Wait, why do you need to know mermaid anatomy?" Avarie asks. But the true burning question that she wouldn't dare to voice is 'in what ways is *it* possible?' Avarie's cheeks warm at the less-than-innocent inquiry.

"For research . . . that's beside the point," Lahna laughs. "Do you want the full story or not?"

"By all means, continue," Avarie's smile turns into an amused smirk.

"The adviser catches the prince and the mermaid intimately involved, and he sounds the alarm. Metaphorically. He really just gathers a mob of Denizian townsfolk in an attempt to capture the mermaid. Now do you want the happily ever after, or the grim conclusion?"

Avarie deliberates, but it doesn't take her long to reach a decision. Her life right now aligns much closer with tragedy. Even though she's currently living a lie, Avarie doesn't want the truth softened for her.

"Grim. I'll take the grim ending please."

"The adviser and the mob mistake the mermaid for a siren. A *succubus of the sea*—the story's words, not mine. So, they kill her then throw her back into the sea. The prince returns home, only to die of heartbreak. And the cottage is burned down, never to be inhabited by a Ten-Year Maiden again." Lahna almost looks apologetic as she finishes the story.

"Well that royally sucks." The intrigue on Avarie's face dims.

"You're not wrong," Lahna shrugs her shoulders. "And to this day, we still mistake mermaids for sirens."

We?

Avarie almost rejects the word before she remembers that she's human right now. "Ri-right. I hope one day that's no longer true."

"You and me both. And sorry, that was a little somber. Why don't we keep going so we can lighten up the mood?"

"I think that's a grand idea," Avarie says.

"Great, we're not too far from the pier now," Lahna extends her hand and Avarie's breath catches. She stares at the appendage for a beat.

Grab the hand, you fool.

Avarie springs forward, perhaps a bit too eagerly, and intertwines her fingers with Lahna's. She wishes nothing more than to burst into giggles like an excited merschoolgirl. For now, she'll indulge this feeling. Because it's so much better than dwelling on her true purpose here. Offering only a shy smile, she allows the girl to pull her forward.

AVARIE CAN SMELL THE SEA BEFORE SHE SEES IT. Scents of sandalwood, a fruity-vanilla musk, and saltwater welcome her. She can't believe two days have passed since she's been near the sea. Her heart yearns to caress the flowy waves, to snatch up fresh seaweed for a snack. But neither of those actions seems appropriate in Lahna's company. Instead, she lets her hands sway nonchalantly at her sides.

The spot they pick is a couple of paces away from where Avarie first gained her legs. Lahna's curls play in the breeze, flitting through the air, carefree. A calm, wistful smile appears on her face. And Avarie can't help but wonder if the Ten-Year Maiden looked as ethereal as Lahna does right now.

Somehow, and a little to her annoyance, Avarie's thoughts drift to the Enchantress's bargain with her parents and how, almost two decades later, Avarie's made a deal of her own. One she can't back out of. The Enchantress will probably curse her if she tries. Plus, Merelani requires two leaders. Mai serves as an ever-constant reminder of Aalto. A reminder of her silly, unrequited crush. The guilt of having wanted someone her brother genuinely loved stabs at her conscience. Now she's getting what her younger self longed for. It feels hollow. Because a marriage to Mai isn't true love, it's a commitment to duty. Obligation. A barren victory . . . just like Avarie's wish to walk among humans.

Lahna confidently stabs a fishing pole into a weathered crack in the pier they're standing on. Her knee-length tunic dress sways in time with the light breeze, leaving most of her long legs bare. Like her face and arms, there's a beautiful mix of brown tones on her legs, which leave Avarie speechless, enthralled. In an instant, Avarie is lost in the beauty of the sea and Lahna's—

"Hey, you paying attention over there?" Lahna raises a playful eyebrow.

She'd been caught; no lie will save her this time. "Sorry, no. What did you say?" Heat glows beneath Avarie's cheeks.

"Do you fish often in Adahy? I hear there's great rivers up in the northern settlements."

Avarie stalls for a moment. She could fabricate the truth again, but if Lahna asks her to fish, there's no way she can do that without making a fool of herself. Sure, Avarie loved eating fish. But fishing underwater differs vastly from fishing on land or from a boat.

Avarie prefers tending to a garden over catching fish, but she'd do almost anything if it meant more time with Lahna.

For research of course.

This *is* for research, she reminds herself.

"Don't laugh, but I've never actually gone fishing before," Avarie says.

"Oh, so I've got a princess on my hands."

Avarie stiffens. Lahna smirks.

She can't mean that.

Besides, Avarie's *technically* a queen.

Avarie responds coolly, "Princess? I'm far from royalty. I prefer my fish from the market, that's all." She shrugs a shoulder for good measure.

"I'm just teasing, Princess Avarie. Come here," Lahna motions with her left hand. "Let me show you how it's done."

Avarie walks to her, legs wobbly as ever. But this time, it's not because she's new to walking. Lahna's soft hand wraps around Avarie's, the warmth so inviting, she wonders what a hug from the land dweller would feel like.

Lahna places the fishing rod in Avarie's hands, encouraging her to wrap her fingers around the pole. From there, she goes to stand directly behind Avarie, leaving no space between them. Their closeness wears away at Avarie's resolve not to like this human. Lahna winds her arms around Avarie to clasp the pole atop Avarie's hands.

Avarie's breath catches in surprise while her heart pounds strangely.

"Let's pretend we have bait already on the hook," Lahna says smoothly. "You're going to bring your hands behind your right shoulder then thrust them forward. Enough to land the hook in the water. See?" Lahna gives an example, pulling the fishing rod backward while simultaneously bringing her and Avarie closer. After a few more motions—long enough that Avarie is certain she's memorized the outline of Lahna's body through their close contact—the girl inquires, "Got it? Or do we need to do it a few more times?"

Truthfully, Avarie could do this for an eternity. But she didn't have that much time. She tilts her eyes to the bright sky above. The slowly moving clouds annoy her, a reminder that time is moving too and she's yet to find answers for Aalto. She can't spend all her time welded to a cute girl, no matter how much she wants to.

"You know what? I think I've got it. Thanks."

Lahna gives Avarie a reassuring squeeze before letting go of their joined hands. It takes everything in Avarie not to pout. She'd never been held so closely before. And the feeling is something she knows she'll long for later. How is it that the first person she meets on land can spark so much joy . . . during the most expansive sadness Avarie's ever experienced?

She's able to do it on her own now, thrusting the baited fishing pole into the sea. But it doesn't compare to her touchy, too-short lesson with Lahna.

Avarie takes a break, allowing Lahna to use the wooden pole as she rests on the pier's edge, legs dangling and jovial. "So, Lahna, I take it you like to fish regularly?"

She smiles in response. "Yeah. This rickety old pier holds a host of memories for me. Back then, I didn't know what the world was—if that makes sense. Does that make sense?"

"I get it. When you're young, it's not your responsibility to know the evils and misfortunes of the world."

"Exactly," Lahna says with a sigh. "A lot of fathers took their sons fishing, but it was my mom who took me. This reminds me of her too."

Just as Avarie motions to ask about Lahna's mom, the overwhelming sadness on her face stuns her into silence. So, Avarie grasps for a new subject, anything to wipe the melancholy from her face. "Sure wish you were around in Adahy to lend your fishing skills."

"I'm alright. It's still a huge shock to me that you've never gone fishing there. My cousin, my mom's niece, tells me about all the stuff she's caught during her summer visits. Mom used to call Keeya her favorite niece. The joke is, she was my mom's *only* niece.

"I miss her. She's a busy, married woman now. She skipped out on me last year, but maybe she and her wife will visit this summer." Lahna locks eyes with Avarie, blushing. "Sorry for all the word garbage. Feels like you're a good listener. Like I can talk to you about anything. Is that strange because we've just met?"

Avarie beams. "I don't think it's strange. I find it refreshing. I'm enjoying getting to know you, Lahna."

"Same here. I'm a bit of a hermit if you haven't noticed. Keeya's my best friend, and you know we only see each other once a summer if I'm lucky." Lahna laughs awkwardly.

"Hermit crabs are well traveled," Avarie confirms with a head nod. "They have everything they need with them. And if you're lucky, they'll share their space with you. Not a bad attribute, if you ask me."

Lahna puts down the fishing pole and sits beside Avarie, trying her best not to laugh. Her closeness sends a giddy jolt through her. "I wasn't thinking of that kind of hermit, but you make a good point. I have everything I'll ever need with me. Moving is no issue."

Her cheeks redden. "Apologies, I have a love for sea creatures."

"I don't blame you. Sea creatures are cool." Lahna playfully bumps her shoulder.

"You . . . you can call me Ava, if you'd like. My friends do."

"Ava it is." Lahna smiles.

The cogs in Avarie's brain turn faster, her imagination suddenly ready to write a script too elaborate for real life. After she stops the seaquakes, she'll likely never see Lahna again. There's no way Lahna can come home with her. To

Merelani. What would the kingdom think? Her parents? Mairya?

Not to mention, there's the whole *breathing underwater* thing that humans struggle with. Divine intervention is what it will take for Avarie to keep Lahna in her life after this.

A splash of cool water licks at Avarie's bare feet, sobering her thoughts. "So . . . Lahna, I get the sense that you're pretty well known around here, can you tell me a bit more about that Corridor you hate? Specifically . . . what's the code to get in?"

"For starters, my family name is known around here, not me. And I don't know the code. Sorry, I can't be of more help." Lahna's sudden cold tone bristles against Avarie's warm, inquisitive one. She continues: "Those card players at the inn, those are the people you need to talk with. I'd start with them. But they don't trust outsiders. Maybe if you can beat them in the card game they're always playing, they'll have no choice but to give you the code."

Avarie hides a frown. Did she ruin the moment? Lahna seems almost angry about that Corridor. As much as she wants to keep the peace, Avarie knows she *should* want retaliation for her twin much more.

Lahna stands up again, ready to resume fishing. Unsurprisingly, between the two of them, she performs better, catching three fish during their session. Avarie almost caught one, but it was a little trickster, stealing the bait and escaping below.

They talk more about Deniz. The best vendors, proper market prices, everything Avarie wasn't briefed on prior to coming ashore. But what hangs over Avarie the most is that she must beat the shady men at a card game—a traditional Denizian game, no less, that Avarie has no idea how to play.

"It concerns me, you know," Lahna says. She shoots Avarie a brief look before staring out at the sea.

"What concerns you?"

"Why does that Corridor intrigue you so much? I can't stress enough that it's empty of honor. Integrity."

Avarie purses her lips. She should inch closer to the truth in order to make this lie work.

"I'm just looking for something for my family, is all."

"Hm."

"Hm?"

Lahna catches her gaze. Her eyes are almost haunted. Like they hold a secret. One Avarie lacks the confidence to ask about.

"I don't know why you want to get into that Corridor, and I don't want to know. But I can teach you the card game." Lahna's tone denotes displeasure, but her body language is somehow welcoming. "Come over tomorrow evening. After I'm done working, we can practice. If you'd like to, of course."

There's no place Avarie would rather be. Arguably, she's going exactly where she needs to go. Learning the card game from Lahna could get her into the Unspeakable Corridor. Avarie ignores the tell-tale twist of guilt in her heart. She's doing this for Merelani.

For Aalto.

She isn't letting her feelings usurp her plans.

Nope. Not one bit.

Chapter Fourteen

Instead of laying around like one of the lovesick characters from her books, Avarie decides to explore more of Deniz while waiting to meet up with Lahna. Her purpose on land is clear—avenge Aalto, save the kingdom—but this is also a once-in-a-lifetime chance to experience the human world.

Avarie wishes she could show him everything. Tell him everything.

Would he like the loud market?

Would he like the human food?

Would he like Lahna?

Avarie smiles. Aalto would have definitely liked Lahna. Her smile alone can win anyone over, just like his had done.

Her eyes well with hot and angry tears. Avarie just used past tense when thinking of her brother. She sits on the bed a moment longer, ignoring the fact that she's a little off schedule. Avarie curls her hands like strong vises, her bones and tendons protesting.

Why did he say he wanted her to be happy only to rush to his death?

Why didn't he bring more guards?

Why did he refuse to stop and think things through?

Her shoulders shake, and the movement reminds her of the necklace at her throat.

Aalto's ashes.

He's still here with her. Not in the way she prefers. But all the same, her brother lives on, still protecting Avarie and wanting her to be safe.

Avarie squeezes her eyes shut and just tries to breathe.

Aalto the King. Aalto the son of Bruinen. He had so many roles. But my favorite of his was . . . brother. Aalto the sibling . . . But I guess that role never ends. Even if he can't be with me physically, he's alive in other ways.

Avarie stands, clutching the necklace at her throat, a silent vow to never remove it again.

She grabs her mended satchel, bolting down the hall and out the inn's doors.

Ten minutes later, Avarie makes a right at the mermaid fountain, trying her best to block out the noisy market, and then strolls right past the Unspeakable Corridor. She makes sure to avoid eye contact with the man that denied her entrance yesterday. Though she avoids looking, she can still sense his eyes boring into her back as she passes by.

The cobblestone turns into a wide expanse of grass, by far the greenest Avarie has seen while on land. It's a little overgrown; the tips of the foliage tickle her bare legs. Avarie squints through her glasses, farther up ahead is a collection of . . . cottages? Some buildings. Businesses, maybe.

Coming closer, it seems as though Avarie's assumptions were correct. The cottages are all built similarly but serve different purposes. First in the neat row of buildings is a bookstore, then some sort of eatery—this building is the largest—and at the end is a building with the weathered words 'library' sun-stained on the wood.

Avarie's heart swells. Books! It feels like a lifetime since she's laid eyes on the pages of a story. Avarie breezes past the other buildings, eyes trained on the library. Merelani's library was minimally stocked and didn't get any visitors. It was located in the palace, and the visitation hours weren't considerate of the schedules of working merpeople.

That will be her first act as queen when she returns home: expand the library, make it accessible to all merfolk. Avarie tugs on the door with glee and to her surprise, it doesn't budge. *Hm.* They must be closed. She'll have to visit another time. What a letdown. Hopefully, the bookstore won't disappoint.

ABOVE THE FRONT DOOR'S CHARMING BOX PLANTER, which is full of wildflowers, is a timeworn sign saying 'Deniz Books: Local Authors and More.' Avarie pulls open the store's entrance, the hanging bell on the door rings a cheerful greeting. Inside she's met with the scent of roses, not as fragrant as her sea rose, but amazing all the same.

No one greets her. At least the business is open.

The inside is cramped but homely. Wooden shelves are stocked with books, everything from romance to nonfiction. It's a little dim, being that the only lighting stems from the door's window. But the available light is enough to show Avarie the full selection. Fiction and nonfiction are split, with novels organized by the author's last name. Avarie knows exactly where she wants to go.

She winds through the shelves, kicking up a bit of dust as she explores. Avarie drags her hands along the way to the authors with surnames starting with 'S.' In truth, she'd read nearly every book by L.H. Sirene. But perhaps there was one she'd missed. They were relatively new, having only been published within the last few years. But she was prolific as well.

Five books in three years? Avarie couldn't imagine the dedication that takes. Sitting at a desk for hours on end, feathered quill in hand pouring an infinite amount of thought onto paper. Sure, Avarie had considered writing . . . but so far, she only has scribbled journal entries. With so many gaps in between the dates, she might as well not chronicle her life at all. Maybe one day she'll try her hand at fiction. For now, she'll stick to reading.

Avarie, with an eager smile, reaches the shelf where L.H. Sirene's books should be. Her lips flatten. Where are her books? They should be right here. She looks to the shelves on either side. Nothing. The sign outside said they support local writers. The backs of L.H. Sirene's novels were vague when it came to describing the author. Avarie could only discern her gender. But wording existed about the writer being a Denizian native. How strange. She'll take a look around all the shelves. Maybe they're misplaced or on display elsewhere.

After five minutes of aimlessly wandering the shop, Avarie circles back to the same place where her favorite author's books should be. She sighs. This is beginning to be a bit of a disappointment. Resigned, Avarie decides to give up and leave the shop, taking heavy steps in the direction of the front door.

Just as the bell rings a second time, a whoosh erupts from the back of the store. Avarie turns around to see a woman pushing past a dusty curtain.

"So sorry! Please don't leave yet," the woman exclaims. "I was doing inventory in the back. Didn't hear the bell ring when you came in. What can I do for you, dear?" The woman has a kind face, with crow's feet decorating the corner of her eyes. Her pale skin is sunburned, with a particularly red and itchy looking splotch on her nose. She wrings her hands on her checkered apron then adjusts the bandanna tied across her auburn hair.

"I'm visiting from Adahy and happened upon your shop. Do you have any L.H. Sirene novels here?" Avarie inquires.

The kindness on the store owner's face dissipates. She haughtily places her hands her hips. "No. We don't sell that author in Deniz. They're banned."

"Banned? What do you mean by that?" Avarie's confused. Stealing is banned in Merelani; so is selling imitation jewelry meant to resemble the Merelani Crown Jewel. But books? Avarie has never heard of such a thing.

"The content, miss." The owner scratches her nose with exasperation, skin flakes raining down like water droplets. "I'm not selling books that humanize sirens. No, not in this shop, I won't. And that interspecies love? Disgusting. I won't allow our youth to read such filth. Theorizing that sirens and humans can fall in love?" The woman rolls her eyes. "Straight nonsense. They need to ban that author everywhere. You go on back to Adahy if you're looking for filth like that." She makes a shooing motion.

Avarie doesn't hesitate. Befuddled, she exits through the front door without a backward glance. This was all so new to her. Bruinen let her read whatever she wanted, even at a young age. Granted, Bruinen placing a book in her hands feels a little less special now that she knows her brother requested it on her behalf. But Avarie was able to read freely, and she feels as though it was to her betterment. She's certain of it. She understands more about the human world than any other merperson does.

How strange it is to outlaw books that might help someone understand more about themselves or others.

Racing thoughts burn through Avarie's mind:

Were all the books gifted to her despised on land?

Bruinen couldn't have traveled ashore for them, and Avarie had always thought they came from wrecks. But what if they'd been thrown overboard, cast into the sea for what they contained?

Does her library collection only contain banned books?

The questions plague Avarie as she retreats to the inn. She walks through the front door, barely hearing the bell as she makes her way upstairs.

Tucked inside the confines of her temporary home, Avarie tries to distract her antsy mind by moving. She rises to the tips of her toes and waltzes across the space. Then she marches around on her heels. Avarie rises to her toes again then stomps about with her heels, admiring the different pressures each one allows. She spins in a quick circle and nearly falls. Avarie steadies herself and stares into the mirror. She imagines the traditional music of Merelani and sways to the imaginary beat. Right to left, she shifts her hips then tentatively steps with her feet. Avarie twirls in a circle, her tunic catching in the breeze, her thighs caressing each other.

There's a stark difference to dancing with legs on land versus a tail underwater. Avarie can't help but cringe a little at her lack of poise. She's floundering like a fish out of water. Then a thought occurs to her: does Lahna enjoy dancing?

What would it be like to join hands with her, and spin in endless circles to music from her home? The music in her head suddenly vanishes, cut off like an instrument's string being severed. Lahna will never hear Merelani music.

Avarie collapses onto the bed in a huff, her desire to dance vanishing into thin air. Lahna would probably cut her scale to scale if she knew the truth. Avarie's bottom lip quivers. Mermaid and human love stories are just that—stories. It's best to leave the romantic daydreams on the pages of L.H. Sirene's books. She's probably the only human who will give a mermaid a chance.

Still, Avarie tries to imagine herself swimming to a desolate shore every evening just to meet Lahna, just close enough not to lose a scale. When it became available, she would take oarfish potion to be on land for two weeks. She would be like the Ten-Year Maiden. It all works out in her head.

But *this* is the real world. A place where merfolk are hunted viciously for their scales, and where humans will drown them for even attempting to step an enchanted foot on land. Where Enchantress's potions come with too hefty a price.

A tear rolls down Avarie's face. Life just isn't fair.

EVENING CHASES THE AFTERNOON AWAY IN WHAT feels like a matter of seconds. Avarie throws the satchel over her right shoulder, her infatuation with Lahna and her duty to Merelani compete for dominance in her mind. She wants both to win.

Avarie eyes the men playing cards in the lobby. Loud guffaws and howls surround the oval table. They pay her no attention, the game holding their focus. One man slaps down a card with a triumphant shout while the others groan in disappointment. The winner beams with a bright smile. But the light is in his eyes, not his discolored teeth.

The timid sounds of chairs brushing against the carpet fill Avarie's ears as she exits the Siren's Rock. Soon enough, she'll be seated at the table, meeting the men's objectifying gazes with confidence.

Well . . . at least she hopes so.

LAHNA OPENS THE DOOR, HER SMILE WELCOMING Avarie even before her lips part with a greeting. Avarie spies black ink speckling her hands and some of her forearm. A quill with an extraordinary feather is tucked into her curls.

"Good evening, Ava. I trust you had a pleasant day?"

Avarie can't help but grin, she truly enjoys seeing this woman. "It was a day full of insight; I'm thankful. Now, what's that decorating your arm?" With an unexpected burst of confidence, Avarie runs a hand down Lahna's left hand and forearm. A tingle shoots through Avarie's body from the action. Lahna leans into the touch, warmth flowing easily between the two.

Lahna's gaze trails to the ground. She rubs the arm without ink. Is she nervous? "I'm . . . a writer. I write things."

Avarie's heart nearly jumps out of her chest, like a dolphin popping out the water. "A writer! You should have told me this sooner! I love reading—I went to the library today and was disappointed to find it closed. The bookstore woman was a letdown too.

"Oh, but I *love* L.H. Sirene. She's my absolute favorite." Avarie's gushing trails off as a sheepish smirk transforms Lahna's face.

"L.H. Sirene, you say? I should probably show you something then." Lahna grabs her hand and whisks her into the cottage. They wind their way through her home, stopping at a closed door that Lahna opens in a flurry.

Inside the room, there is a huge and prestigious-looking desk placed underneath a window. The glossy wood shines under the light of the setting sun. Three drawers with ornate, golden knobs are lined up along the desk's left side. Paper scrolls are rolled up and displayed across the desk's surface. A rectangular holder with "L.H." carved into the wood houses tons of quill pens. Their colors vary from a vibrant, artificial sea green to the muted brown of a speckled owl's feathers.

Avarie's jaw drops as she canvases the room. Her feet sink into the fluffy rug, its hue matching that of the owl feather quill. A glass cabinet adjacent to the desk is filled to the brim with books, literature that has yet to reach the mermaid community. She blinks a few times, in utter disbelief and questioning her vision. Lahna truly is a writer.

"This is my writing room. I don't allow anyone else in here, but I feel like I can make an exception for you." Lahna tugs her deeper into the room and points to the squishy, weathered couch on the wall farthest from them. "Why don't you sit there? I'd like to share something with you, but I fear you'll pass out."

"Do I look that bad?" Avarie wonders aloud, fingertips touching her face.

"You look gorgeous. But also, like, you should sit," Lahna replies with a timid grin.

Avarie wades to the furniture, Lahna's words melting away today's stress. She plops onto the couch; it engulfs her with instant comfort. What more does Lahna have to share?

Lahna walks to the cluttered cabinet and plucks a familiar brown book with an elaborate gold leaf trim. She returns to the couch, skipping like a joyous child in the market. With care, she places the bound book in Avarie's hands before joining her on the couch.

Avarie and Lahna read the title aloud: *"Siren's Last Song."*

"My favorite book," Avarie says just as Lahna declares, "My favorite book I've ever written."

"You're kidding!" Avarie exclaims. *"You're* L.H. Sirene? What? How?" She claps a hand over her mouth preventing any more words from escaping.

Lahna chuckles. "That's my pen name. L.H. Sirene. Lahna Hart Sirene. The 'Sirene' part is for dramatic effect. A suggestion from my dad, actually, since I write mostly about monsters of the sea."

Avarie would take offense to the *'monster'* part if she hadn't read all of Lahna's novels. All her books display a kindness and love for sea creatures not often told by land dwellers. She still can't believe Lahna is L.H. Sirene! Avarie clutches the warm necklace at her neck with excitement. Aalto was so, so wrong! Her favorite author is far from debaucherous. She's kind and confident and gorgeous and smells like sea sorrel. Lahna's damn near perfect.

"A pen name? But your work is amazing. Why keep it a secret?"

Lahna's eyes darken for a moment. "Some people find my books too . . . free. Hiding my identity is also for my safety. And my father doesn't think writing is a viable profession. Yet he paid for all my writing classes . . . the irony. He'd prefer Denizians to not know about my writing—that, and he's disappointed I'm not going into the much more profitable family business. So, I spend most mornings and afternoons here, writing in secret."

Lahna's father paid for her writing classes . . . just like Bruinen supplied me with books. Parents are sometimes strange in their support. And what's the family business?

Before Avarie gets a chance to ask, Lahna brushes away the subject. "But enough about my father. He already takes up enough space in my head. It means a lot to me to finally meet someone that appreciates my work. You have no idea, Ava. I never knew my books reached the northern settlements," Lahna gushes, her brown eyes brighter than before.

Guilt brews in Avarie's stomach. She has no idea if Lahna's books sell in Adahy. She's never been, couldn't describe the landscape even if she tried. Her lies are crawling into places Avarie couldn't imagine they'd ever reach.

"L.H. Sirene is all the rage back home." Which isn't a complete lie. *Siren's Last Song* seeped into many a conversation Avarie has had with her mermaiden and her brother. It's just not the place Lahna envisions.

"Ah!" In a fit of happiness, Lahna puts her hands over

Avarie's, sandwiching the book between them. "That's encouraging to hear. I've been thinking of giving up lately. Especially with all the book bans . . . but now I can't. Doesn't feel right knowing people actually care. Thank you, Ava. This is honestly the best news I've heard all week."

The guilt progresses into something monstrous in Avarie's midsection. Her stomach turns in on itself. She sends a half smile to Lahna, unsure if it looks more like a grimace than a smile. "Seems like a once-in-a-lifetime chance to be ran over by your favorite author," Avarie teases. "So, if you don't mind, could you tell me your writing process? Everything that helps you get words on paper? I'd love to hear about that."

Lahna pops up from the couch, eyes wide with delight. She's so cute when she's excited. Beyond cute. Lahna's adorable. The way she paces excitedly from wall to wall is reminiscent of a flying fish darting above and below the sea line. Avarie shakes the thought away, but she knows it will linger at the outpost of her mind.

"Absolutely! I'll put on a pot of tea! Do you like tea? I love tea. Chamomile relaxes me. I drink a cup often before bed."

It seems like Avarie isn't the only one full to the brim with words today. A genuine smile blooms on her face as she stares at Lahna pacing the room, a buzzing bee full of energy. "Tea sounds great. Let me help you."

THEY GUSH ABOUT THE ELEMENTS OF WRITING AND Lahna's characters for hours on end. Before long, nightfall lands in their world like a fleeting caress. Lahna shuts the curtains on the growing darkness outside. The cerulean teapot is empty and cold to the touch. A groggy Avarie fails at keeping her yawn a secret. She covers her mouth, but it's much too late.

"Why don't you stay in my guestroom tonight? No need to walk back in the dark to your room. It could be dangerous."

Avarie stretches out her tired limbs. They had been on the couch for ages, sometimes leaning against each other while chattering excitedly. Time passed at an astonishing rate. It seemed like she had just left the bookstore and settled into the writing room with Lahna. How could she have let time slip away so carelessly? It's true that she's only been on land for three days. But what have those three days looked like for Merelani?

Avarie's certain that Mairya's most displeased. This is the second time Avarie's blown off their nightly meeting.

A little glum from this realization, Avarie only nods to accept Lahna's offer.

"Okayyyyy," the words are drawn out as Lahna yawns. "Follow me. We can tackle the card game in the morning."

Avarie yawns again. "Sounds great, Miss Sirene."

Chapter Fifteen

Avarie wakes up underneath the comfort of the heavy sheets in Lahna's guest room, blanketed by a gentle warmth. Sunlight peeks through the two square windows in the room, and there's a happy trill coming from a family of birds just outside.

Avarie gazes upward, her eyes observing the unmoving, canopy sheets. They're white and fluffy like sea bunnies, reminding her a little of home. With a homesick sigh, she heaves the downy comforter off her body. It's already the fourth day, and she has yet to find a clue pointing her to the poacher. The remaining days might pass by in the blink of an eye; she must learn that card game now.

The game doesn't guarantee that she'll find the answers she needs. But every clue, every stone must not go unturned.

The kingdom depends on her. These life-threatening seaquakes and what they are currently doing to Merelani churn her stomach. What other parts of the kingdom have been destroyed since she left? What disaster will Avarie come home to?

She saunters over to the wooden door and pulls it open, searching for Lahna.

Well—*L.H. Sirene*. Avarie feels giddy, recalling the night before, when they were squished together on the couch in Lahna's writing room and talking for hours into the night. When neither of them could keep their eyes fully open, and they lamented their need for sleep. If only Avarie had her copy of *Siren's Last Song* with her, she might have asked Lahna to sign it.

Avarie rounds a corner, momentarily lost, but then she follows a cluster of noises: clinking pots and pans, water flowing, an eager kettle screaming 'I'm ready.'

The kitchen comes into view. Lahna is standing in front of the stove, hand wrapped around the handle of a skillet, moving it back and forth with precision. She's wearing a long nightgown, her hair pulled up into a disorganized bun. Tendrils of curls hang freely at the nape of Lahna's neck, and Avarie wants to brush her fingers over them.

At the sound of Avarie's footsteps—she's still learning how to walk silently—Lahna turns around with her characteristic smile. "Good morning, Ava. Did you sleep well?" She sets down the skillet and crosses the room. She wraps Avarie in a hug, extinguishing any remaining sleepiness from the mergirl's mind.

Her arms are strong, purposeful, like there's nothing else they could be doing at this moment. And what warmth! Avarie could linger in her arms for an eternity. Her short stature somehow works with Lahna's height, with the top of her head landing right at the human's shoulder.

"I slept better than I have in a while," Avarie finally says. "The inn does its best to make travelers comfortable, but nothing can replace a soft bed in a cozy home."

"That's great to hear." Lahna leans back to flick a curl from her face. Avarie cannot help but stare, stunned by

Lahna's effortless beauty. "How long did you say you'll be in Deniz?"

The reminder of her limited time on land makes Avarie's heart stutter. Nevertheless, she offers a prayer of thanks to the Sea Goddess for this time with Lahna.

"Less than two weeks now."

"How tragic! I hope you come back and visit. I'd love to see Adahy as well. Maybe I could visit you and we can catch fish there sometime." Lahna's hopeful tone feels like a gut punch.

"Of course, I'd love to come back and visit. I'm enjoying my time here so far." Avarie swallows the lump in her throat, unable to say anything more. She cannot invite Lahna to a home she's never been to. Her lies are stacking taller than Avarie can reach.

And at some point they'll come crashing down and hurt someone in the process.

Lahna turns away from Avarie and faces the stove, returning to the task she'd abandoned. Avarie doesn't miss the look of disappointment on Lahna's face. She knows the taller girl picked up on the way she neglected to invite her to Adahy.

"How—how about we start on that card game? I'm sure you have much to teach me." Unable to look at Lahna's face any longer, Avarie shifts her focus to the stove, fidgeting with her sun ring.

"There's plenty of time for that."

No, there isn't.

Avarie wants to argue. She wants to scream that there isn't enough time in the world for her to kill her brother's murderer. She doesn't want to do it, but her Goddess *demands* blood. She has no one to talk to about this either. Mai will judge her uneasiness. And Avarie just might alienate herself from the one girl she's ever liked that probably likes her back. Murder? Lahna would be so damn disappointed in her.

"We can't do anything well on an empty stomach." Lahna throws the words over her shoulder, focus still on the stove, turning the pan of fluffy yellow clouds and rectangular, maple-scented crisps over onto a large glass plate. "Grab some. Let's eat."

Avarie clenches her eyelids closed. She takes a shallow, shaky inhale, as if she can smell disappointment reeking from her pores, then picks up a plate.

"The goal of Drowner is simple. The player holding the Mermaid card must avoid detection until the game ends—in which case, that player wins because the Mermaid gets to 'return safely back to the sea.' Or the rest of the players—the 'townsfolk,' if you will—must figure out the Mermaid's identity and drown them."

Lahna explains everything in a matter-of-fact tone, laying cards down on the kitchen table as she explains. She doesn't notice—or at least, Avarie hopes Lahna doesn't notice the nervousness filling her because Deniz's most popular card game is aligning too closely with her real life.

"Drown a mermaid. How exactly would one drown a mermaid?" Avarie hopes her voice doesn't shake, and if it does, that Lahna mistakes it for incredulity. Of course she knows the answer to that question, but Lahna doesn't know that.

"Supposedly, a mermaid might masquerade as a human, and in that form, they are as vulnerable as any land dweller." Lahna is still seemingly unaware of Avarie's discomfort as she explains. "The game has some . . . history to it."

"Like the Ten-Year Maiden."

"Yes."

"That's a bit morbid," Avarie comments, trying to keep her voice level.

With a repetitive *fhwip fhwip*, Lahna throws five cards face up on the table. Her hands are spread wide, and Avarie very much wishes to cradle them in her own.

Lahna shrugs. "I agree. Unfortunately, some Denizians are very set in their ways, usually older gentlemen, like the players at the inn. Now, listen here as I explain the five roles.

"There's the Mermaid, of course, and then the four townsfolk: the Blacksmith, the Vagabond, the Milk Maiden, and the Baker. Each role has a specific strength. For example, the Milk Maiden can automatically use a salvation card against an attack on their life, while the others need to roll an eight or higher to do so."

"Okay, so how does the game start?"

"The game begins after each player has chosen a role at random. No one can reveal what their assigned role is, they can only 'play their role,' and do so at the start of each round by putting down an action card.

"There are two types of cards that you can put down. An 'action card' or a 'salvation card.' Each player's hand will be a random mix of both, totaling to five cards. But salvation cards are infrequently dealt since there's only one per role.

"Now, the Mermaid's goal is to trick the rest of the townsfolk into thinking they're one of them. But if they put down an action card that aligns with something another player might use, then it could draw attention to the Mermaid—"

"Sorry to interrupt," Avarie says. "But hold on . . . if all the cards are dealt from the same deck, everyone has a chance of getting role cards that don't align with their character. How does that work out?"

Lahna smiles. "Good question. Say you're a Milk Maiden, but you pull a 'harvesting crops' card. Playing that might come off as suspicious. So, you can put that card in the discard pile and pull a fresh one. Do that as many times as you'd like. But you can hold no more than five cards at a time."

"Hmm okay. Makes sense," Avarie muses.

"Ah, where was I? Action cards should align with your character. Mermaids have it hard since any card they use can raise the hackles of other players. The alternative is for them to play it safe by putting down generic action cards—like 'picking flowers' or 'cleaning the family wagon'—something a Milk Maiden or Baker might do—but using too many in succession could make the other players suspicious.

"There's a total of five rounds per game. At the start of each round, players will place down one card a time in a clockwise fashion. After the cards are revealed, there will be a debate to decide who the Mermaid is.

"For the first two rounds, this decision making is done silently. The players will keep their thoughts to themselves. However, for the last three rounds the accusations are done aloud. Each player will make a case for who they think the Mermaid is, votes will be tallied, and if the majority votes correctly, the Mermaid is drowned—"

"Wait, it seems like the odds are stacked against the mermaid." Avarie frowns.

"Yes, it is, unfortunately. However, if the Mermaid can pull a salvation card and roll an eight or higher with the ten-sided dice, the player can call upon the Sea Goddess to save the Mermaid and have her safely return to the sea."

"But the odds of that seem near impossible!" Lahna's eyebrows lift up as Avarie's voice rises. Avarie reminds herself that it's only a game, even if the humans made it at the expense of her people. "I mean, what about the other roles? What do they do if they're wrongly accused?"

"Actually, you'd be surprised what persuasive players can do during the accusation rounds. There's not much you can do about the role you're dealt, it's all about how you play it, how you 'sway the mob,' as it were."

Avarie nods. "Okay, I think I get it. You know, the Mermaid doesn't feel like a role you'd want to play."

Lahna grins, warming Avarie all over. "Not exactly. The Mermaid is the most unique character, if you ask me. You have to be extremely clever to survive in the role. I admire the skill. There's no other character I'd rather play. That is, if I still played this game."

"Why don't you play anymore?" Avarie leans forward, casting a curious gaze at Lahna. The woman truly is gorgeous. And her smile? It melts Avarie like the butter spread upon their breakfast toast. Her eyes take in the uniqueness of Lahna's skin. There's an oval patch on her left cheek, not exactly an oval, it's a little bit misshapen, yet beautiful, paler than the rest of Lahna's brown face. There's a trail of lighter brown on her neck. To put it simply, Avarie is nothing short of enamored. Lahna was what the land dwellers would describe as 'a catch.' From her outward beauty, to the creativity swimming and flowing freely from her mind. Avarie longs to spend as much time with her as possible.

If only she could.

"I know it's just a card game, but it seems so tasteless and cruel. Some people"—Lahna grimaces—"still hunt mermaids today like they're some kind of monsters, but they're not. The hunters are the ones that are monstrous. I've never had the privilege of meeting a mermaid, but my first instinct certainly wouldn't be to *kill* them."

Imagine all the bloodshed that could've been avoided, all the loss that could've been prevented if more people thought like Lahna. Avarie thinks of Aalto and the guards who were with him. She shakes the thought out of her mind as quickly as it arrives, thinking about them now will result in tears she cannot explain away. "Is that why you write tales of the sea then?"

Lahna beams. "Absolutely. I'm hoping my books will

change the hearts and minds of the people who will read them. If they could only learn . . . see that merfolk are just like us, perhaps they may be persuaded. After all, it's a grotesque fear of the unknown that drives some people to commit acts of violence."

"Wow, I couldn't agree more, Lahna. I swear you're the smartest land—er, *girl* I know." Avarie clenches her hands together under the table, the action concealed by the decorative, droopy fabric. Where was this carelessness coming from? Just because Lahna says she wouldn't hurt her kind, that doesn't mean she won't. Ideals are nice, but they're not facts, just blanket statements.

Be more careful. Remember Merelani. Remember Aalto.

"Thank you. Well, that's the outline of Drowner. Think you can handle some actual gameplay?" Lahna smirks, unphased by Avarie's unsubtle slip of the tongue.

"I think someone's given me some useful knowledge. Think you can handle losing?" she playfully retorts. She's only flirting to further distract Lahna from her slip up and . . . flirting never hurt anyone.

Right?

THEY PLAY A HYBRID VERSION OF DROWNER. WITH only two players, each of them assumes two roles. It's a little more complicated, but it allows Avarie to learn more about the roles and how best to play them.

After two games—Avarie *accidentally* brushing hands with Lahna each time she returned the cards for shuffling—the human retreats to her writing room to work for the day. She shuts the door with a soft thud, allowing Avarie to explore the cottage alone. Avarie hunkers down for the moment though, studying the cards, trying to remember their individual purposes, and memorizing the rules.

She flips through the cards while pacing back and forth in the living room, speaking their descriptions aloud like a mantra: "The Baker can use 'the Roller' without throwing a dice to defend themselves if they have their salvation card. A Vagabond can do the same with 'the Shooting Star' card."

Avarie rubs the gold-outlined cards in her hands. They're thin yet sturdy. And so colorful. The Mermaid card is the most beautiful of all. The creature's scales are a rainbow of radiant colors practically leaping from the paper. Avarie thinks this must be what true happiness looks like; her tail only ever darkens with anxiety. She imagines her scales would be darkening now with displeasure. Despite how beautiful the colors are, the way the mermaid is drawn rubs Avarie the wrong way. The mermaid is resting on a rock with her chest sticking out and her fin curled underneath her. Is this what land dwellers think? That mermaids are just sexual creatures?

She frowns, what a misjudgment on their part. For example, Avarie's as inexperienced as they come. But she was beginning to feel a strange yearning for a certain land dweller. She could tell by the way this new hunger manifests in her belly and spreads throughout her body every time Lahna looks at her.

Lahna's books are mostly tame when it comes to intimacy. Often, romance isn't even a focal point of the plot. But when it is, the characters always disappear behind a door and wake up the next day with blankets shielding them. Now, Avarie finds herself longing to know what transpires after the door closes. Maybe even experience it for herself too.

Avarie runs a hand through her locs, eager to disrupt these ideas. An irrational fear that her loud thoughts can be heard by Lahna takes root. She places the cards down on the living room table, now ready to explore. It doesn't seem right to invade Lahna's room, so she just keeps to the one she's in, observing the decorations and trinkets spread throughout.

The living room couch is cozy, though it's as comfortable as a brick when compared to the one in the writing room.

An exceptional fireplace neighbors the front entrance, its grandeur commanding Avarie's attention. The brick-patterned headboard of the fireplace is intricately designed with a mix of light and dark blocks. They interchange diagonally before ending at the cleanly swept mantle. The dark-brown mantle hosts an array of pictures—four to be exact—the ages of the people captured behind the framed glasses vary in ages. At the end of the mantle, there's a peculiar-looking whistle.

Avarie lifts one frame, bringing it closer to her face. The black and white photograph features a smiling woman with dark skin holding a swaddled baby close to her chest. A fraction of the infant's face is visible. A young Lahna, maybe?

Avarie plucks the next frame up excitedly. She could recognize that smile anywhere.

An adult Lahna is smiling at the camera, holding a book with the same care the woman held the baby. Waves of delight fill Avarie's heart, fed by the mirth on Lahna's face. Like yesterday, Lahna's forearms and hands are riddled with ink stains as she clutches a copy of *Siren's Last Song*.

The third photograph seems more recent. Like the second, it lacks the antiquated appearance of the first. It's simply a grinning Lahna looking up from her writing desk with a quill clutched tightly in her hand. Papers haphazardly decorate the desk and, as expected, ink adorns her skin, appearing darker or brighter in some places depending on where it hits her vitiligo.

Who took these pictures? Did Lahna have a special someone behind the camera? Someone that lights up her life the way Lahna is beginning to for Avarie?

Avarie and Lahna are from two different worlds, so it doesn't matter.

The cold reminder stings.

And anyway, a marriage to Mairya is awaiting her back in Merelani. Yet Avarie remains uncertain. If Aalto were alive, they would never be together. Mairya doesn't truly want Avarie. She only desires the crown promised to her.

The only reason Avarie is in Deniz is for Aalto. Her sole purpose here is to avenge him—not to fall in love. And yet, to her own embarrassment, taking the life of the one who murdered her brother feels wrong.

She reaches the final photo frame. It's face down, next to the whistle, and it looks to have gathered a considerable amount of dust. Whose picture could it be?

Avarie reaches forward to turn it over. Then she pauses. This is an invasion of Lahna's privacy. She shouldn't do that. She retracts her hand and returns to the couch, sinking deep into its cushions. On the table a short distance away from her is what looks like an advanced reader's copy of *Siren's Last Song*. Avarie's read the finalized version so much, she knows she can spot any differences.

It's tempting to flip through its pages.

But she should really study Drowner more.

She tucks her feet underneath her on the couch and resumes her studying.

All the while, she steals glances at the face-down photo. She can't possibly focus until she knows what it hides. She puts the cards down and creeps back, feeling compelled to sneak since a part of her knows this is wrong. But with how warmly her necklace becomes with Lahna around, maybe turning over this frame could be useful?

It's probably not. She's just one nosey mermaid. At least she waited a bit before indulging her impulsiveness.

Avarie reaches the fireplace, right hand poised to grab the

dusty frame when she hears Lahna pull open the door to her writer's room. She jumps back and flattens both hands at her sides. Her heart pumps furiously in her chest. But not only because she was almost caught snooping. One look at Lahna and a budding longing for her slumps like sludge in Avarie's heart. It's too thick, too heavy, too inconceivable to ignore.

"I'm famished!" Lahna exclaims, not immediately sensing Avarie's moody mix of unrequited longing and melancholy. "Care to make a date of it and attend the market with me?" Avarie can't help but reciprocate Lahna's smile, though hers is meager in comparison.

A date? A first date . . . with Lahna?

Of course, she wants to say yes. This must mean that Lahna is single, that she likes Avarie, *and* enjoys her company. It would be ridiculous to decline such an exhilarating opportunity. *But . . .*

Lahna stares at Avarie, eyes wide and hopeful. When Avarie does not immediately respond, she casts her eyes down to her inky arms, tracing the stained skin as a distraction.

Even though Avarie didn't want to disappoint Lahna again, she must.

"I—I should go, actually. I wish to study these cards more. Could I borrow them, if only for a few days?"

Lahna's upturned lips turn into a straight line of disappointment. Her eyes darken for a moment. "You may have them, Ava. Let me escort you to the door then." The muscles in her face twitch in protest as Lahna fakes a smile.

Scooping up the cards with a quick flourish, Avarie walks to the door clumsily, her legs the equivalent of an infant's first steps. Why did she say that? Why say no? What would it hurt to go on *one* innocent date?

But she already knows the answers to her questions. It didn't feel right to have fun when her brother was murdered just days ago and she hasn't made significant progress finding his killer. When she has neglected to meet Mai.

A small part wants her to reconsider.

No.

She'll have a bit of fun after she gets into the Corridor and not one second before. Avarie likes to think this discipline would make her father proud. But why does she care so much anyway?

"I'm . . . sorry." Avarie offers, but nothing could make this moment feel less solemn.

"I must admit, I got ahead of myself. I didn't imagine a possibility where you'd say no. Maybe I read too much into things. We had such a good time with . . . everything. I'm sorry." Lahna cocks her head to the side, tumultuous embarrassment on her face.

Avarie should correct her, absolve her cute, puzzled face. She certainly doesn't want Lahna apologizing like this when she's done nothing wrong. If anything, Avarie should be the one to do so a million times over if it could take away Lahna's frown. But maybe things are better like this? This way, neither of them gets hurt when Avarie returns to Merelani, never to be seen again. Lahna is just a stepping stone to get what she wants —just a way inside the Unspeakable Corridor.

Nothing more.

Chapter Sixteen

Vulnerability and nightfall greet Avarie simultaneously. The lack of light and Lahna's absence weigh on her. She discards her shoes for the moment, her toes squishing the sand of the Denizian shore. She relishes in the ephemeral distraction, her mind easily returning to earlier that morning, when Lahna's face wasn't so crestfallen.

Overhead, Avarie can just barely make out the blurry stars. When she puts on her glasses, the stars appear a bit clearer. She takes a deep breath, knowing that she can only stall for so long.

Here she goes.

"Mairya of Merelani, I desire your presence." She speaks to the lackadaisical waves, feeling immediately silly. Mairya wouldn't come. She's probably in her chambers preparing to sleep. She's probably mad at Avarie for not showing up the previous nights.

The water stills, like the waves are ready to slumber too. Then a disruption happens, the sea sloshing more energetically upon the shore and on Avarie's legs and toes.

Mairya's head pops above water, her expression weary, serious. "My Queen, you've called." She looks beautiful in the moonlight. So much so that Avarie crawls on her hands and knees to get a little closer. Almond-shaped eyes with wispy, long lashes stare unwaveringly at Avarie.

Avarie doesn't *want* to bombard her with questions, but it's been so long since she's talked to another merperson. "Mai. How are you? How are my parents? How's the kingdom—"

Mai holds up a hand, cutting Avarie off. Her nails are sharp, pointed. Blood red.

"Where have you been? We were worried sick about you —*I* was worried sick about you. My mind jumped to terrible places, all the horrible things that could keep you from me. What will happen if Merelani loses its other heir? What will happen to me if you were to perish? We're all restless, waiting with bated breath to hear from you.

"Cordelia refuses to leave her room. The palace is falling apart, and your beloved room full of books has caved in, along with the rest of the southern wing. Did I mention that the seaquakes have not ceased? The seafloor vibrates with malice, we're living on very shaky, uncertain ground. At the very least Avarie, have you located the heart?" There's an air of fatigue in her voice, intermixed with the anger. Mai conceals a yawn behind her manicured hand.

Avarie's throat grows dry. She knew it was foolish, but Avarie had hoped the seaquakes might have abated for at least a bit. From what she's seen above water, the waves had been peaceful, and she had hoped that might have meant that it was peaceful in Merelani too.

Here comes the guilt, rolling in like the misleading waves she's watching right now. She's beginning to think she'll always be swamped with it. The small steps she's taking are not yet enough to surpass the huge hurdle of duty she must jump over. Maybe her father was right. Maybe it's time to break tradition and seek help outside Merelani. If the only help that Merelani has right now is a nervous, grieving, barely-a-queen mergirl . . . is that truly any help at all?

Avarie's reply is as parched as the sand: "I haven't found the heart, but I've discovered a secret Corridor that markets illegal goods. Whoever's responsible is likely to be lurking there. If not, I'm certain I'll find someone who will lead me to them."

"That's great! Are you going to the Corridor tomorrow? The sooner you get to the Corridor, the sooner you can come home. We miss you, Ava. All of Merelani does." Mai swings her hips side to side with excitement, an attempt to stay afloat amid her sudden buzz of energy.

" . . . No, I can't go tomorrow. I must master a card game first." Avarie's cheeks burn, aware of how frivolous this sounds aloud.

"A card game?" Mairya quirks an eyebrow, incredulous.

"Yes. I need a passcode to gain access to the Corridor. Something only Denizian card players know. Apparently. I know it sounds silly." Avarie crosses her arms over her chest, wishing to ricochet Mairya's judgmental gaze elsewhere.

"Well, if you feel that's what you must do, I trust your judgment. Whatever gets you home the soonest. How are you liking the surface?" Mairya mirrors Avarie, arms crossing, revealing nothing.

"I've made the acquaintance of a kind land dweller. She's very knowledgeable. A Denizian native. I'm glad to have run into her." Avarie doesn't feel right freely offering up Lahna's name to Mairya. Especially since her and the land dweller's relationship seems as tattered as her satchel on her first day. Something's telling her to hold her cards close to her chest for as long as possible—because Mai, like all of Merelani, are not fond of humans. Especially right now.

Mai frowns. "I see. Is there anything else I can do for you, Avarie?" Her tone is biting, like the chilly sea breeze.

"Just give my love to my mother; tell her I hope to be home soon, to help rebuild all we've lost. And Mai? I apologize for missing our check-ins. I won't do it again, I promise."

Mairya stiffly nods, then disappears below water.

She doesn't return.

Confusion racks Avarie's brain as she stumbles back to the inn—even with the glasses, her vision isn't perfect in the dark. Was Mairya jealous? Or just displeased by her slow progress? Mai couldn't know that Avarie likes Lahna.

Avarie pauses, her hand squeezing the inn's doorknob.

She can't know that I like her.

Oh.

Somehow, the realization banishes the rising tide of guilt and anxiety in Avarie's chest, if only for a moment. She smiles to herself.

Yeah. She likes Lahna.

On Avarie's fifth morning in Deniz, she returns to the library. And this time, it's blessedly open.

Time to do some research.

The smell of old and worn books greets Avarie as she strolls through the library's double doors. She always wondered what older books smell like. The enchanted books in her chambers are near perfect, but not quite. They had no scent. Probably a symptom of the enchantment. These library books smell musty, earthy. They make her nose wrinkle, but in a good way.

As the doors shut without a sound behind her, Avarie scans the moderately sized room. There are at least fifteen shelves, each one with a placard labeling its contents. There's a man with thick glasses seated behind the single desk in the room, aggressively stamping a pile of books.

He must be the librarian.

Avarie beelines for him, not that she needs to. The only other beings present is a reader seated well across the room with a sleeping animal, perhaps a cat, nestled at their feet.

"Hi, I'm Avarie. Are you a librarian? I've never met a librarian before. How do you get your books? How long have you worked here? What sort of tasks do you do?" The questions flow freely from her mouth, leaving her with a need to gasp for air.

The man's brown face phases into an amused smile. "Ah, a first-time visitor. I'm Florence. Do you not have libraries back home?"

"No, not like this." Avarie's eyes wander around the room again in wonder.

"Well, welcome to the Deniz Public Library! I am a librarian—the *only* librarian," he mutters the last words to himself. "Been here a couple years. The pay isn't much, but the reward is keeping literature in the hands of Denizian townsfolk . . . for all ages. I wear many hats," he taps the nonexistent hat atop his head of black curls. "Right now, I'm withdrawing books from circulation."

Avarie frowns, confused. "Why would you take away library books?"

A tired crease appears between the man's bushy eyebrows. He tugs at his collar. "The nice answer is that we're making room for new books. The less pleasant answer is that some of our once popular books are no longer being checked out. Some are not very well liked, others are damaged beyond repair, so it's best to remove them."

Avarie picks up one of the books that the librarian has already stamped with a large, red X on the cover. She was not familiar with the author, but the cover is gorgeous. It has ornate, golden borders with a rich, forest-green backdrop. Avarie flips the book in her hands and finds that there are stars decorated sparingly all over the cover.

"Why was this book withdrawn?" Avarie lets her right hand brush through each page. She remembers the book she saw embedded at the shore so many days ago.

"To make space for others. Nothing tragic about this book's demise," Florence jokes.

"And what do you do with them?" Avarie wishes to pull up a chair and sit right next to Florence, she could talk to him all day.

"When I had the time and the staff to do so, I used to deliver them to neighboring settlements, to give them a second life. But now, I often take them home to stock my husband's library. That way they don't end up kindling at Cast-out Cottage."

Avarie stares at the book hungrily but doesn't dare say what her mind is screaming for her to ask.

As if reading her mind, Florence says, "Would you like to take this one? We already have a copy at home." Avarie nods eagerly.

"Yes! I'd love to keep it."

"Very well, consider this your official welcome to Deniz. I hope you enjoy your visit, Avarie." Florence pushes away from the desk and stands. "I need to pull more books from the shelves. Is there anything I can help you with before I go?"

Avarie tells him what she needs, and Florence directs her to the history books for her to browse. Even with the librarian's expertise, she finds nothing of particular value. She does discover an incredibly accurate book on mermaid anatomy that has her blushing—perhaps the same resource Lahna uses for her stories. Avarie's cheeks heat, her mind dwelling on the notion that the human's well-versed in the private intricacies of Avarie's true form. Avarie shakes her head, perilously close to succumbing to her inclination for romantic daydreaming.

BACK IN HER ROOM, AVARIE FINALLY MEMORIZES every card for Drowner. She feels as though her eyes might disintegrate. Even back in Merelani, she never had to study this hard. Remaining cooped up for three hours has left her limbs feeling antsy, but she does not dare to stretch her legs around the market and risk running into Lahna.

What would she even say?

In a fit of angst, Avarie flops onto her bed like a struggling fish. "Ugh! I should've said yes! Now she probably thinks I'm just using her, but—"

Isn't that what Avarie is doing? Using her until she leaves Deniz and Lahna's life forever. A heaviness lodges in her throat. She's a fraud. One taking advantage of Lahna's kindness. Avarie rolls over to her right side, purposelessly staring at the door.

Avarie wishes she can just let Lahna know that she cares for her. But she can't.

Her duty comes first. If Lahna knew what Avarie's true intentions were, she'd never forgive her. She thinks of the misfortune that has befallen her kingdom, the blood seemingly already on her hands. And before she leaves Deniz . . . there will be more blood spilled.

With a quick huff from her lips, Avarie decides she will talk to Lahna about something she *can* share. She has questions about Drowner . . . but mostly, she wishes to apologize. Again. The sadness on Lahna's face yesterday is something Avarie cannot erase from her mind. It pains her to think that Lahna might believe that all their interactions were objectively transactional. Avarie doesn't have the courage to tell

Lahna she likes her, but the least she can do is reiterate her remorse.

AVARIE CHICKENS OUT LIKE A SQUID EJECTING murky, black ink to escape its opponent. She doesn't go to see Lahna. Instead, she goes to the shore. It's beautiful even alone. Well, she's mostly alone. Farther down to her right, small children are playing a game, running to sea then retreating once the tide arrives. Some are building sand structures with their parents, their gleeful exclamations like a loud, searing alarm in Avarie's head—as though she can hear them calling her a coward.

She feels like one, sitting cross-legged here, as close as she can be to Merelani without getting wet. Sunrays warm Avarie's dark skin, giving it an ethereal luminescence she's never seen before. She marvels at the display of melanin, and she notices that others along the shore are staring as well, albeit harmlessly. The beautiful weather was unexpected, It had stormed last night, considerably enough it seemed to shake the foundations of the Siren's Rock. Thunder had woken Avarie while flashes of lightning sent her farther underneath the covers. She had feared that the Goddess's wrath had finally reached Deniz. Except when the dome had fractured, Merelani rarely experiences similar storms.

Avarie digs her bare feet deep into the sand. It's exactly how she remembers it—gritty, warm. In another world, this sensation might have brought her genuine happiness. Instead, it's serving as a reminder that she's only ashore to kill someone.

She has tried not to think about it, but she must face reality sooner or later.

Get the code.

Find Aalto's murderer.

Kill them.

That last one sends a chill through her body. Stealing someone's life—even the life of the cruel human who ripped Aalto away from the world, the human who changed Avarie's life forever—is nothing to take lightly. Avarie's hands claw into the sand.

She shouldn't be queen.

She shouldn't be betrothed to her brother's widow.

Not even his widow. They never got a chance to wed.

It's Avarie's fault—as much as it is the poachers'.

If she hadn't weakened the barrier . . .

Aalto would be the king and Mairya would be ruling by his side.

But Avarie cannot bring her brother back.

Nothing she does will ever bring Aalto back.

Her eyes burn. She pats away the sand on her fingers so she can wipe her tears. Being at the shore *could* have been a peaceful time. Instead, it's only a retelling of her shortcomings. Avarie pulls her knees to her chest, cradling them as she wraps her arms on either side of her body, feeling exactly as helpless as she did when she heard Aalto's final song.

How can she ever move on?

Why won't time stop? Rewind?

This is all wrong.

Avarie's head rises to the sky. Overhead, the grayness of the day dissipates, leaving only a rainbow weaving through the clouds and ending at the tree line in the woods, close to where Lahna's cottage must be. She touches her necklace. If this isn't a sign for Avarie to harness her courage and go speak to the girl, she doesn't know what is.

Avarie dusts the sand from her bag and body, and she dabs away the tears on her cheeks. She trudges to Lahna's place, no matter how much her legs shake as she grows nearer.

AT FIRST, AVARIE KNOCKS LIGHTLY ON LAHNA'S door. But with no answer, she decides to knock with more urgency.

Still no answer.

Avarie frowns. It's midday. Surely Lahna can still hear the front door from her writing room. Of course she can, she'd come straight from that room the last time Avarie knocked on her door.

Maybe she's not home.

But where could she be?

With her plan thwarted, Avarie returns to the Siren's Rock, not in the least relieved that Lahna didn't answer. She needs to see her, regardless of the awkwardness that is bound to ensue. Avarie misses her in the same way she craves her home under the sea.

The door bursts open from the inside just as Avarie is reaching for the curved handle. She lands flat on her behind. But before she gets a chance to rebuke the person who knocked her down, her angry words die in her throat.

Ever the elusive woman, Lahna is there, peering down at Avarie. Her curly hair is pulled back into two intricate braids with small seashells woven throughout. It's as if she belongs to the sea more than Avarie does at this moment. An image of the two of them swimming under the sea, hands intertwined, flashes briefly in Avarie's romance-starved imagination. If only it weren't a mere daydream.

"Ava. I've been searching for you. To apologize." Lahna holds her hand out and Avarie shakily grasps onto it, allowing herself to be pulled up.

"Apologize? If anything, I need to be saying sorry to you." Avarie dusts herself off then straightens her glasses.

"No, no, I—" Lahna quickly steps to the side, away from

the door's perimeter. She tugs Avarie with her before continuing: "I may have read into things. Things I imagined. It was never my intention to cause you discomfort. I thought things were going well, and I enjoy your company. But my imagination likes to run wild, I suppose. And not just in my stories. You know . . . my father always told me my imagination would lead me to nowhere but disappointment. And maybe he's right. I wish to remain friends—I'm okay with us only remaining as friends—if you are?" Lahna absentmindedly rubs Avarie's hand as she speaks, but when she realizes what she's doing, she reluctantly lets go.

Avarie is taken aback by Lahna's candidness. She's wrong about it all. She didn't imagine things. Their bond—Avarie doesn't even know what to name it—is the only good thing in her life right now. And Avarie wants to cling to it. For Lahna's father to say something so hurtful to his daughter . . . well, Avarie can relate to that. And she wishes she could tell Lahna just how much—wishes she could tell the entire truth about herself.

In a flash, Avarie grabs Lahna's hand in earnest, unable to ignore how much she craves the innocent connection. "No, Lahna. I don't want to be your friend."

"Oh." Lahna's gaze lowers. Her hand, the one Avarie is holding, goes a little limp, wilting like a dying flower. But that's not what Avarie meant to say at all! She mentally kicks herself. Why can't she say things right the first time?

"That—that didn't come out how I meant." Avarie takes a deep, calming breath, and tries to exhale whatever it is that's making her speak so nonsensically. "You weren't reading into things. I like you, Lahna. I've enjoyed your company a lot these past few days. But I have something important I must do—the reason why I left my home in the first place. I want to spend all my time with you, but I can't afford to be distracted. I told you, there's something inside that Corridor that I need to find. It's important to me, my family."

My kingdom.

Avarie doesn't want to address the latter half of Lahna's statement. She hardly knows how to address her strained relationship with Bruinen. She digs deep for words so that she can offer some form of solidarity. "And . . . your father's wrong. Your stories are so imaginative, and they've been a guiding light through some very lonely moments. Don't let him ruin your passion, something you're obviously so amazing at. Okay?"

"Oh." Lahna pauses for a moment, a mixture of emotions appearing on her face. "I'm glad to hear that it wasn't all in my head, and . . . thank you. For your kind words. I still don't understand what you hope to find in the Corridor, but I can assure you there's nothing good there."

"I know. What I'm looking for, it's not . . . good." Avarie tugs Lahna closer, as if she's afraid she might scare the taller girl away. "But I must find it. The truth. It's the only thing that will help us—my family to move on. So *I* can move on. My twin . . . passed recently. Someone took him from me . . . and I believe the truth behind his death lies in that Corridor, just out of reach.

"It was my fault. I'm the reason Aalto's dead."

Avarie feels sick. Like she's eaten seafood left in the sun for too long. She remembers the way Aalto looked as he laid on the floor, stripped of his scales and cradled in their mother's arms. The memory is the only thing she can see, until she can't see a thing at all. Avarie's vision narrows. Her throat constricts as she breaks apart in Lahna's arms. Lahna's lips are moving but she can't hear a thing.

She's going to pass out again.

"I'm so sorry. I'm so sorry," Avarie says weakly.

Lahna leads Avarie safely to the floor. "Don't apologize,

Avarie. Ava—do I need to get you to a physician? What's happening? Let me know what you need me to do." Avarie's eyes flutter close, but her grip remains wrapped around Lahna. There's a chilly breeze battling with the flare of Avarie's feverous skin.

Avarie remembers how to breathe while Lahna holds her. After a moment, she's able to speak again. "I'm alright. I think I just need a moment to breathe. I've never said that aloud. I've never said that my brother is dead. That it's my fault."

"And I'm sure that it was very difficult for you to say." Lahna pulls her close, her breath hitting Avarie's ear as she speaks. "I don't know what happened, but I'm sure your brother wouldn't want you to blame yourself. Now let me take on some of this weight for you. What else do you need?"

Tears are falling freely from Avarie's eyes. Lahna's soft thumbs brush them away.

"Just sit with me, please." Avarie's throat must be full of gravel, the way it scratches out those five words.

"I'm not going anywhere." Lahna huddles close, forming a protective embrace around Avarie. She hasn't felt this safe in what feels like a long time. Her brother is gone. Her home is falling to pieces. It feels as though she's lost everything, like all she has left is Lahna's calming embrace.

Lahna's smile is beyond charming. But her embrace is to die for.

She doesn't know how long they stay like that. She doesn't care about the passersby, glimpsing their quiet moment. Avarie doesn't care. She lets Lahna hold onto her like her life depends on it.

And in some ways, maybe it does.

"I'm so sorry, Avarie. No one should have to go through that. I hope the Corridor gives you the peace you need. And one day, I hope you'll forgive yourself."

Avarie cannot consider it peace. How can revenge bring

peace? Yet again, Avarie wishes she could tell Lahna the truth. How the Corridor's answers will only lead to a knife being driven into the heart of her brother's murder; that she is a mermaid on borrowed time, on a quest to deliver her Goddess's justice. But she can't.

"You couldn't have known." Avarie's voice returns from a whisper to an almost normal volume. "But I appreciate your kindness. Now I hope you can understand my insistence to learn that card game."

Opening her eyes, Avarie realizes that Lahna's face is red, worry tearing apart her expression, a single tear trailing down her face. Avarie reaches up without thinking to wipe it away. When she leans back, her hand hovers over Lahna's cheek, wanting to touch her face again.

Lahna smiles, no teeth, but still sincere. Then she grabs Avarie's hand and presses her lips to it, her mouth lingering there, their eyes connecting in a new way.

"We're going to get you into that Corridor. We'll practice all day, and tomorrow, and the next day if we have to. Under one condition."

"Wh-what condition?" Avarie scoots backward, eager to save energy by resting on the wall of the inn. Lahna follows suit, holding the hand she just kissed.

"Allow yourself to find peace. I don't think your brother would want you to keep blaming yourself."

Unable to find the words, Avarie lets go of Lahna's hand so she can pull her into a hug. Her arms wrap around Lahna's neck. Somehow, Lahna manages to pull her even closer, as if she fashioned glue and stuck them together. Avarie feels tears prickling in her eyes, but she blinks them away. "Thank you. You've been a great help, Lahna. I could kiss you right now."

"You could kiss me? I might let you," Lahna's voice is the softest Avarie has ever heard it. She peers down at Avarie, searching, searching for something in her eyes. And Avarie isn't sure what she finds, but Lahna's hand lightly grabs the back of her neck, bringing their lips just inches from meeting.

Avarie's eyes widen. Could this be her real first kiss? Sure, she'd kissed a mergirl when they were children, but this feels different. Plus, the moment lacks the strangeness from her kiss with Mai. Lahna's presence is energetic, exciting. Even her soft, measured breaths as she gazes into Avarie's eyes has a power of their own.

Enchanting.

But their lovely moment doesn't last, Avarie can't let it. She hasn't told Lahna the whole truth. Lahna still thinks she's from Adahy, that they might be able to see each other regularly. She doesn't know that Avarie belongs to the sea. She doesn't know that Avarie must become a murderer too. It's just lie after lie after lie. Avarie doesn't deserve whatever happiness Lahna could give her.

Disappointment hits Avarie square in the chest as she removes Lahna's hand from her neck. "Perhaps we should just focus on getting me inside the Corridor." Hurt flashes across Lahna's face, but it's gone in an instant.

Silence bathes in the wide rift created between them before Lahna speaks again: "Your wish is my command, princess."

Chapter Seventeen

The urge to tell Lahna that she is a mermaid is overwhelming.

An insatiable itch that Avarie's well aware should *not* be scratched.

Yet all their interactions so far tell Avarie that Lahna would keep her secret as if it were her own.

A secret for a secret.

Avarie knows that Lahna is L.H. Sirene. It's only right that she shares a secret of her own. Yet at the back of her mind, Avarie can't help but think her secret has more dangerous consequences. Avarie's secret could endanger her entire kingdom.

What if Lahna is not as kind when she learns about the 'Real Avarie'?

The Avarie who loathes public speaking, even though it's her duty as royalty. The Avarie who loves reading romance but lacks real experience. The Avarie who is lying through her chattering teeth because she's just a nervous stowaway.

Avarie shakes her head. This is not what she should be wasting her time on.

She fidgets with the sun ring on her finger, having almost forgotten its existence as she ruminates on futures that may not come to pass. It spins round and round, a reminder of the sunsets she has left to 'take the heart.' But what exactly does that mean? Is she meant to literally rip the heart from the chest of Aalto's murderer? Or is it more symbolic? Like in the books she reads, it could be a metaphor. Take the heart by killing what the murderer cares about most. Avarie shudders at both options. One feels worse than the other, but also a tad cathartic. She lets go of the ring and reaches for her necklace. If Avarie has to live without her brother for the rest of her life, why should she offer his murderer mercy? Why should they get to keep living with the one they deem most precious?

Knock knock knock . . .

Avarie's fingers pause on the ring. She walks promptly to the front door of her rented room. Who could it be? She wasn't expecting anyone. She doesn't know anyone in Deniz. The door lacks a hole to peek through, so Avarie cracks open the entrance an inch and asks, "Who is it?"

"Who else would it be?" the voice says with friendly sarcasm.

Avarie rolls her eyes, but a smile comes to her face. She opens the door wider. "Lahna? What brings you here?" She could question how Lahna knew what room she resided in, but sometimes the simplest answer is the correct one. The innkeeper must have told her. After all, she did drop her name to get this room in the first place.

"I took the day off from writing. Figured we could practice playing cards a bit more. After, if you'd like, I can show you a place that's special to me." Lahna voices the last part with an air of shyness Avarie has not seen before.

Avarie tilts her head to the side, pondering. What could this special place be? Most of Deniz is just woodlands. A vast expanse of trees . . . and nothing else. Other than the market and the collection of shops that surround the mermaid fountain, Avarie didn't think there would be much else to see.

But Avarie will eagerly grasp any alone time with Lahna. Just as friends, of course. Friends and nothing more. It's inevitable that Avarie must return to the sea. She must marry Mairya, and she must fulfill her duties as queen. As Merelani's queen, her heart's desires matter less than the wants and needs of the kingdom. When Avarie returns home, it will likely be forever. She could dream of returning to Lahna after ten years, but what of the price the Enchantress will demand for one oarfish potion? With Mai as the new Enchantress . . . that dream seems laughable. How could she ask her wife to return to the surface for a human? And even if she returns to Deniz, who's to say Lahna will not have forgotten her by then? Or found someone else?

Who's to say whether Lahna will even *want* to remain friends. Will she condemn Avarie? Sentence her to pay in blood for the life she must take? Avarie is beginning to think that the cycle of vengeance is never-ending. But she can see no other way.

"Hey, Ava. Can I come in, or are you planning to leave me out here alone? Unaccompanied."

"Solo."

"Abandoned."

"Friendless."

"Single." Immediately, Lahna winces at her quick retort. "S-Sorry. I didn't mean it like that. Got carried away with the word game. Can I come in, Avarie?"

Avarie's eyes trail to the ground as she opens the door to let Lahna through. Does Lahna resent Avarie's assertion to only remain friends? She didn't say it to be cruel. There's a lot Lahna doesn't know. And unfortunately, Avarie can't tell her.

Lahna and Avarie shuffle, flip, and deal cards until Avarie feels as though her fingers will fall off and her eyes will fall out. She doesn't know how long they play. But the sun's perfectly in the middle of the sky now, signaling that the morning is a thing of the past.

With legs crossed underneath her, Avarie has been practicing this move for a couple days now, and arms straightened behind her, she stretches forward, pushing her chest out to alleviate some of the tension in her body.

"Lahna, I appreciate your help but—" A stomach growl cuts Avarie off.

"But you're hungry. It's time for lunch." Lahna relaxes into an easy smile.

"Yes," Avarie admits with a laugh. "We could go to the market?"

Lahna averts her gaze, breaking eye contact in such a way that makes Avarie wonder if she had said something wrong. She isn't a fan of this newfound awkwardness. Everything with Lahna had been so easy. There was an eagerness between the two of them that usually pulled them together, squishing away any awkward situations because they enjoyed each other's company so much.

Maybe Lahna didn't want to spend the full day with her. Why did Avarie assume Lahna would? Sure, she had mentioned taking the full day off. But maybe she had plans. With someone else. And that was fine. Yes, that was perfectly fine. Avarie asked for distance because growing more feelings for Lahna will hurt tenfold after Avarie's trapped under the sea. She can't help if it stings to think of Lahna spending time with someone else.

"I'm sorry," Avarie says. "I didn't think you had other plans. I didn't mean to be presumptuous. I'll walk with you to the door, then we can part ways. It's really no problem! I-I can find my own food." Avarie unfolds her legs and scoots off the bed. She can't help but think about how this morning went. How Lahna's gaze somehow lingered too long on Avarie's lips. How each time they brushed hands, a little jolt passed through Avarie. Friends don't give you jolts, she knows that much.

Lahna hops from the bed and rushes to Avarie's side. Grabbing her hands, she says, "No. I'm sorry. Again. I'm being weird, aren't I? I—I have something planned. Uh, I just don't know if it's too much. I don't want to be too much. But there's a special place I'd like to show you. That is, if I haven't scared you off with my horribly crafted words."

Her hands.

Avarie does everything she can to not pull and squeeze those hands to her chest. To let them feel how fast her heart flutters. Like a sailfish rocketing through water. Instead, she goes for a more playful approach: "Wow, writer, you sure do have a way with words. Yes, I'd love to see what you have planned. I'd be honored." Avarie smiles encouragingly and gives Lahna's hand a light squeeze.

Lahna's face lights up, extinguishing her rising anxiety. She intertwines their hands, dropping them to their sides but not letting go. Avarie doesn't think friends hold hands like this either. But she will allow it. "Great. Let's get the rest of our day started then."

Lahna leads Avarie away from the room. They traverse down the stairs and out the inn's front doors. The unknown awaits Avarie, and she eagerly waits for it as well.

AVARIE FINDS HERSELF WITH A WOVEN WICKER basket in one hand and Lahna's fingers clasped in the other. Something must be in the air, the way their hands fit together with a perfection she thought was only reserved for her omnipotent Goddess. They did visit the market. But only to grab a basket full of food and a blanket just large enough for them to sit on.

Avarie watches, sitting cross-legged, as Lahna unpacks the basket's contents across from her. Lunch in Lahna's favorite spot in the forest. Instead of rocky paths and a dense cluster of thickets, it opens up to a clearing blanketed by soft grass the most marvelous shade of bluish-green that Avarie has ever seen. Overhead, the sun is shining through a thick canopy of leaves, enough that it's warm and bright, but not overbearing. It's cool under the shade, and the rows of trees around them seem to be funneling a constant breeze through the clearing. They're alone in the woods with only the forest's creatures for companions. Small animals rustle through the trees, jumping from branch to branch in some sort of chasing game. Acorns fall soundlessly to the forest floor.

Avarie watches Lahna's slender fingers remove fruits, veggies, and some sort of fragrant meat. Avarie's mouth begins to water at the enticing scent. It's a feast—a casual one—but carefully crafted all the same.

"That smells wonderful, Lahna." Avarie dares to interrupt their comfortable silence. "And this place is beautiful. How do you know about it?"

Lahna's dark eyes meet Avarie's. She can just barely imagine the memories existing behind Lahna's gaze. Indeed, this place seems special to her. Shyness once again breezes into the conversation. "Let's eat first, then I'll tell you all about this place. Deal?" Lahna arches an eyebrow, awaiting a response.

"Deal."

Even if Avarie had not skipped breakfast—a bad habit that even her human-presenting self cannot shake—the food would've exceeded her expectations. Lahna describes the meat as veal. Although it had a bit of a neutral taste, there was a sweetness to it too. That sweet aftertaste is what Avarie will miss when her plate is finally cleared.

Then her brain jumps to Lahna's lips, wondering if they also offer a lingering taste of that sweetness.

Avarie brushes a hand down her locs. Why did she think that? They're friends. She can't keep thinking this way about a friend. She needs a distraction.

"Lahna, what's so special about this place? It's charming. Quiet. And what convinced you to bring me here? After all, we could've had lunch at the pier or near the sea."

Lahna seems thoughtful, still with that undertone of timidity from earlier. "I guess it felt right to bring you here. No one else knows about this place. And honestly, I wouldn't touch the pier with a ten-foot pole on a windy day. One swift blow, or even a feeble sneeze could knock that thing clear over." She laughs for a brief moment. "My mother often took me fishing. But she also brought me here. This . . . this was *our* special place. Not even my father or his many ex-wives know about it."

Lahna shoots a wistful look around the forest. "At night, once the sun went down, we'd stretch across the grass and gaze up into the small circle in the sky the trees didn't block out. We'd count the stars. During the day, we'd have outdoor lunches like this. There used to be a garden here too. But it's long gone now.

"And I brought you here because . . . I don't know. I just had a feeling that this might be something you'd appreciate. You seem so curious, interested in exploring the unknown."

Avarie beams. "I appreciate you showing me. I love plants. What grew in the garden?"

Lahna returns the smile. "Moonflower. We loved to watch the white petals unfurl slowly in the evening as we waited for the stars. It was—" She hesitates for a moment. "It was magical. And the smell? Enchanting. Just like lemons."

"Why did you stop growing them, if you don't mind me asking?"

Lahna sighs. "After Mother died, my father didn't let me leave the house. He refused to even let me near water. The way she died . . . maybe that was his way of protecting me. But it was suffocating. He took me out of school and hired the best tutors to teach me instead—my first teacher became my stepmother. The flowers didn't have anyone to take care of them, so they died out. And now, the seeds are hard to come by. I haven't seen a starter plant at the market in years. Since I've moved out from underneath my father's hold, I visit here more frequently. I just don't have the resources to revive the garden."

How did her mother die?

A weighty sadness hits Avarie. She understands Lahna's pain. Memories of Aalto chasing her around the Royal Garden flash in her mind. Though they outgrew chasing one another, it stings knowing they will never have a chance to do so again. "I'm so sorry, Lahna." Avarie moves the wicker basket out of her path and scoots closer, pulling Lahna into a tight hug. The other girl relaxes into her embrace. "Thank you for sharing with me. If you don't mind my asking, how did your mother pass?"

Avarie feels Lahna's shoulders droop. "I know the reason. Yet I don't know. Does that make sense? It's a bunch of hearsay. Father claims that sirens lured her into the sea. I think he's just looking for someone to blame. Sirens don't cause harm unless necessary. Mother was gentle, kind. She'd never hurt anyone." Lahna's gaze drops to her hands. "The more realistic rumor is that she fell from the pier while fishing and bumped her head on some rocks. An accident caused by a turbulent breeze. By the time someone noticed her absence, her spirit was far gone from this world." Lahna clears her throat before continuing, "I keep her with me though. My first ever inkwell pen, she gifted it to me. Now, all my first drafts are written with it."

Avarie's shoulder feels damp. Is Lahna crying? Avarie hadn't meant to upset her. Guilt knocks at the door of her heart. She pulls away to gaze into Lahna's red-rimmed eyes. "I'm sorry, Lahna. I wouldn't have asked if I'd known it would make you sad." Avarie grabs a nearby napkin and dabs away Lahna's tears. "I think it's meaningful that you still write with the pen she gave you."

"No, no . . . this is good. I never get to talk about her to anyone. My stepmothers never want to mention her. And my father treats her name like it's a curse word. I can't say 'Katalina' without earning his vitriol. So, thank you. Thank you for letting me talk about her." Lahna runs a hand over her eyes. "Now, do you mind if I ask you something?"

"Sure, anything." And Avarie means it. At this moment, she feels as though she can tell Lahna anything. It's been a while since she's felt so close to someone. Avarie holds her breath, waiting for Lahna's question.

"What happened to your brother? It must have been tragic since you're traveling all the way down to Deniz."

Avarie bites her lip. She should tell her the truth. Everything. But how can she ease Lahna into the truth? How can she explain without bursting into tears? "I only know that the person who's responsible is here in Deniz. I'm here to learn who."

"What will you do when you learn this information?"

"I—I don't know. I'm undecided. But people are counting on me to . . . to do something that twists my stomach. I've never been this . . . scared. I'm here in Deniz, all alone, scrambling for answers and not knowing what I'll do when I find them. But I can't let my family down. I can't disappoint my p —my parents." *I can't disappoint my people.* "I'm on limited time, and on top of it all, I just really, *really* miss my brother."

Avarie's vision goes watery. Damn, she did *not* want to cry.

Lahna grabs both of Avarie's hands, an understanding in

her eyes that makes Avarie feel seen, heard—without Lahna even knowing the full story. Wow, she's so considerate.

"Whatever you do, Avarie, I hope it brings you and your loved ones peace. I can't condone violence, I've seen the pain that it causes. But I support your search for answers.

"I regret not looking into my mother's death more. I was too young when she died. I couldn't push for answers—my father forbade me, forbade anyone from talking to me about it. I haven't forgotten that day . . . but my memories have grown hazy with time. I hope you fare better than I do, Ava. I hope you find your answers." Lahna rubs a circle onto Avarie's hands with her thumbs. "My boundaries about the Corridor remain the same, but you have my support in everything else. If there's anything I can do, just ask."

Avarie appreciates Lahna's support. That she's offering help even though Avarie's actions might conflict with her beliefs. Though she wishes things could be different, Avarie has no choice. She has to bring Aalto's killer to justice now or else wait another decade for a chance to do so. That is, if Merelani even survives the seaquakes—and she can't let her people suffer for her failure.

Avarie is overflowing with gratitude. Unthinkingly, she pulls their joined hands to her face, her lips crashing into Lahna's knuckles.

Lahna closes her eyes as if she's savoring the moment. When Lahna is finally looking at Avarie again, there's a longing in her gaze that tempts Avarie to give in. To lose herself in Lahna. Even for just a moment. Can't she do both? She *wants* to do both. Why can't she make her kingdom *and* herself happy?

"You're going to make a liar out of me, Ava."

Startled, Avarie says, "What do you mean?"

Lahna loosens their hands and shifts to a new sitting position, her right hand flattening against the blanket and her arm straightening to prop her up. Avarie follows Lahna's motions so that they're both leaning on one palm, legs tucked to the side and facing each other.

Lahna continues. "I told you I was okay with friendship . . . but the more I spend time with you, the more impossible it feels to stay true to that." She scoots closer to Avarie, and her fingers land on Avarie's chin. Tilting it upward, she says, "I fear you might ruin me."

Entranced, Avarie asks, "Ruin you, how?" She licks her lips and tries to look down, but Lahna's fingers beneath her chin prevents her from doing so. It's as though Lahna is silently asking her not to run from this moment, to face it head on.

"Because I feel like I'd do almost anything for you, and we haven't known each other very long. And that scares me. It's irrational to like you this much, but I feel like my heart is safe with you." For a second, they just stare at each other and the small space between them feels charged with lightning. A storm Avarie wants to run directly into.

Lahna continues, "The truth is, helping you with Drowner was an excuse. Today was an excuse. I just want to spend more time with you. I don't know how to be productive when all my thoughts are about you. I try to write and all I can think of is wanting to get to know you better. I have this notebook full of ideas, but none of them matter because the story I'm most interested in is the one I'm creating with you. I don't know . . . *can't* know what the future holds. But however our story goes—however long it may be—I want to experience it with you."

Avarie's stunned. Lahna doesn't seem like the type to mask her feelings. Still, hearing her speak so candidly, so freely . . . Avarie can learn a thing or two about using her own voice the same way. And to be honest about her own feelings.

Avarie is hyperaware of their closeness, the positioning of their bodies on the blanket. For what feels like the thousandth time, her eyes dive down to the human's lips. Avarie wants to kiss Lahna so, *so* bad. Not her hands, but her aggravatingly plump lips. The desire doubles when Lahna moves her fingers from Avarie's chin to her cheek. "Lahna—I-I don't really know what to say, I'm not eloquent like you. You are truly the best part of my time in Deniz, but there's so much hanging on my shoulders right now, I…"

Lahna releases her physical hold on Avarie, but the one she's placed on her mind remains. "I'm not going to ask you to choose, Avarie. I just want you to know that I'm interested. That I'm willing to wait—wait for you to finish whatever it is you need to do, for you to return to your family with your success, and grieve your loss . . . I will wait for you until you can return to Deniz. I'm a patient woman."

Avarie doesn't doubt that, but how can she explain to Lahna that—if all goes well—she might have to wait a decade for Avarie? That their reunion will only ever last for a fortnight every decade?

In a perfect world, they might be able to make it work. Lahna the reclusive writer, and Avarie her Ten-Year Maiden. A happy ending for the both of them. That way, neither of them is *ruined*.

But in this world, Avarie is not as free as she would like to be—because Avarie is no ordinary girl. She is a queen. It's easy to forget while she's on land, masquerading as some village girl from the north. But Avarie's return to the sea involves duty— duty and marriage.

Avarie brushes a stray curl from Lahna's face, her hand shakily caressing her cheek. She longs to bottle this moment, store it for reopening for years to come. Instead, she clasps Aalto's shell, letting it warm her hand.

The words floating in her mind are beyond selfish, so Avarie keeps them to herself—*Please wait for me.*

AVARIE FINDS HERSELF RESTLESS. SHE STARES OUT into the sea, waiting for Mairya to appear. She promised not to miss another meeting, but she'd much rather spend her free time with Lahna.

While waiting, she reflects on her afternoon with the human. It was one of the best afternoons of her life. It's hard to talk about Aalto. His death. But looking into Lahna's eyes makes it easier somehow.

With a lazy finger, Avarie scratches an image in the sand, something that looks a little like a mermaid gazing up at a girl on the pier looking down into the water. It's rudimentary. Avarie doesn't draw. But these silly stick figures somehow give her hope.

"Queen Avarie? Can you hear me?"

Avarie's head pops up. She quickly erases the picture she drew, mortified that Mairya could see her heart's desire drawn in the sand. "Mai. I wasn't expecting you to appear so soon. How's everyone? How's the palace?"

Displeasure sours Mai's guarded expression. "Are you playing in the sand? At a time like this? What progress have you made?"

Avarie notes that Mairya does not respond to her questions.

"Tomorrow, I will challenge the men to the card game. I'm going to win then make it into the Corridor. My necklace grows warm each time I pass it. The answers Merelani needs are hidden there."

"Great," Mairya says. But her expression suggests that things are far from great. "Now if you'll excuse me, I have some palace business to attend to." Avarie ponders what sort of business that could be, wanting to be properly informed before her return to Merelani. As Mairya prepares to leave, she pauses, her eyebrows knitting in confusion.

Avarie prepares to ask what's wrong. But then she *feels* it. The sand vibrates, almost like it's humming. Maddened whispers. A warning. Like the ground is about to split open. Avarie digs her hands into the wet sand, attempting and failing to absorb the shakes.

"I'm running out of time," she whispers to herself.

Mairya's face twists in concern. "I have to return to Merelani. I hope you have a more productive update for us soon, Avarie. The future of our kingdom depends on you."

She descends below sea without another word.

Avarie pulls her legs up to her chest, squeezing her arms around her frame. She has even less time than she thought. The potion gave her two weeks, but the Goddess is working on a timeline of her own. Guilt hits Avarie. Suddenly, lunch in the forest feels like a waste of time. She could've used that moment to practice Drowner instead, make sure she really knew the ins-and-outs of all the cards. Maybe she could've gone back to the library to do more research . . .

How could she be having fun when her brother is dead?

When she has no idea what's happening back in Merelani?

She needs to focus.

Lahna is only meant to be her guide to Deniz.

Nothing more. She needs to stop forgetting that.

Chapter Eighteen

varie's hands brush across the cool spot on her bed where Lahna had sat yesterday when they were practicing. Her mind jumps to their afternoon in the woods, the privilege of having been taken to a place that used to belong only to Lahna and her mother, and the courage it took for Lahna to be so vulnerable with Avarie. Yet again, the urge to share her own secret itches like an incessant bug bite Avarie wanted to scratch.

Maybe *after* she wins the card game.

Her thoughts travel to the shuddering shore. The Goddess's anger is reaching new heights. She's left with no choice but to challenge the men today. Winning the game doesn't guarantee that she'll get what she wants. But she has no clues left. Avarie is as ready as she can be with time running out.

Only six days left to find her brother's murderer.

Only six days left to spend with Lahna.

But she pushes that out of her mind.

She must focus.

AVARIE SLAPS DOWN A DECK OF CARDS ONTO A TABLE crowded with four men. That's what Lahna told her to do anyway. Her exact words were to 'act confident and be sure of yourself,' and Avarie figured slapping the cards down would assert her dominance the best.

"I hear you all play cards. I'd like to join." She raises her chin and shifts her shoulders back, like Momma Cordelia often does. If Avarie can muster a sprinkle of the regal confidence possessed by Merelani's former queen, that should be enough to get her through this game.

"Who are you?" a man asks, the scar across his eye grimacing just like his mouth does.

"Avarie of Adahy. I'm new here, but I've heard a lot of things in Deniz. *Unspeakable* things."

Scar Face narrows his eyes while another one with a gap between his teeth retorts, "A woman—an outsider—asking about the Unspeakable." The table breaks out into a series of admonishing laughter.

Avarie continues, keeping her chin held high. Indignance courses through her veins. "Yes, a woman wondering about the Unspeakable Corridor. I'd like to gain entrance."

"Tell you what," A third man with eerie, ice-cold eyes, speaks up. "If you can survive three out of four games, I'll personally give you the information you seek."

Avarie wants to jump for joy, but she knows that's foolish. So, she only locks eyes with the third man, offering a firm nod.

"She can't play with us! It's not allowed!" Scar Face's outburst almost sends Avarie reeling backward.

"Says who?" asks Ice Eyes, frowning.

"No one says that." Came the immediate response and an eye roll from Gap Tooth.

"Well, I have no desire to play with a woman." Scar Face, the first man, huffs.

"Bayron's not here and we need a fifth person," pipes up the fourth man; he hadn't spoken until this point. "I say let the wench play," he says with a sinister grin, running a hand through his gnarled red hair.

The word 'wench' from the red-haired stranger sends a maddening anger pulsing through her blood, it mingles with her indignance, coagulating into some sort of hearty tenacity. Albeit the sexism, Avarie notes, it seems as though the majority of the men are on her side.

Scar Face shoots her a glare that could send children crying, but eventually he says, "Fine, let the girl play." He stands up, pulls an empty chair out from the table, then motions for Avarie to sit. "Quickly. Before I change my mind."

With an air of dignity that rivals her mother, Avarie settles into the worn, cushioned chair. She scoots up to the table, leans forward on her elbows before saying, "I've brought cards. I can deal them out."

"No," Scar Face says. "We'll play with our usual. Don't want any funny business from the likes of you."

A woman? Or an outsider? Avarie wonders which one he's referring to. But she doesn't ask. She'd rather get started before her nerves talk her out of it. A quick glance at the door tells her that Lahna isn't here yet. She promised that she'd come watch Avarie play. But her final dose of morale has yet to arrive.

No matter, the warmth of her necklace spurs her forward.

"Fine," she says firmly. "We'll play with your cards. Makes no difference. I'll still win."

THE MEN REEK OF ALCOHOL AND FISH, AND AVARIE surmises they must be fishermen. Scar Face deals out the role cards with such experienced precision that it quells some of Avarie's apprehension.

"We'll play best out of four games," Scar Face says as he's shuffling the deck of action and salvation cards. The cards are crinkly and smell of old paper; many oily hands have held these cards throughout their lifetime. "If missy here manages to impress us, she gets the password. If not, then tough luck. How 'bout it?"

Scar Face quirks an eyebrow.

"Fine by me."

Avarie turns her role card over.

Baker.

Seems simple enough. She'll just need to make sure that she doesn't get eliminated before figuring out who the Mermaid is. The first round passes by easily, her dealt hand working in her favor. Scar Face must be the Mermaid, Avarie observes. He is defensive when questioned about his action cards.

It turns out Avarie—and the other players—guessed incorrectly, and Scar Face, the Blacksmith, is mistakenly removed from the third round of the first game.

"I accuse you." Avarie points toward Ice Eyes.

Avarie makes her case as to why she believes Ice Eyes is the Mermaid. *How ironic.* The rest of the men look like they want to disagree—whether because she's an outsider or a woman, Avarie doesn't know—but their desire to win takes over. Begrudgingly, they follow Avarie's lead and vote against Ice Eyes.

The Mermaid drowns without a salvation card to save them. One game down three more to go.

Avarie wonders about the probability of finding a salvation card. Her two-person, two-role games with Lahna allowed them to pull more cards each turn. It doubled the chances of drawing a salvation card. She doesn't have the time to consider statistics since the game is so fast-paced; the cards in her vicinity are already being scooped away, and their next dealer, Gap Tooth, shuffles them quickly.

New roles are assigned, the cards slapping the table with a crisp *fhwip, fhwip* sound. Next, each player receives a random hand of five cards. A mix of mostly action cards and, if one is lucky, the rare salvation card. As always, the first two silent rounds pass without incident.

When her turn comes during the first verbal round, Avarie pulls the 'Star Gazing' action card from the center pile. As the Vagabond, she knows she's hit the jackpot. This is the perfect card to play for her role.

"There's nothing my role loves more than spending a night alone under a blanket of stars," she says confidently, placing the action card in the discard pile.

"I'd venture to see that my role would enjoy watching the stars too. Perhaps with a special someone," Gap Tooth says mischievously.

Avarie rolls her eyes. This wouldn't be the first time she's gained unwanted attention from a man, whether it's a land dweller or a fin. "A special someone like . . . their mother?" She counters. Gap Tooth frowns, a humiliated red darkening his cheeks. He says nothing else but slaps an action card down.

As more cards are added to the discard pile, Avarie's confidence in the Mermaid's identity falters. The other players seem so secure in their roles. Thus, she sides with the majority and eliminates Ice Eyes, who reveals his role as the Baker. So, one more round it is. This time, the majority is correct, and Gap Tooth is eliminated.

Go figure. The thinly veiled flirtation was merely a tasteless distraction.

Before Avarie can even celebrate this success, Gap Tooth

says, "Careful not to play too safe. You won't impress anyone that way. Remember, a lackluster performance means no code."

She shoots him a sarcastic smile but says nothing. Her left foot taps a pattern into the floor.

For what feels like the thousandth time, Avarie's eyes travel to the inn's entrance, squinting at the tiny brass bell attached at the top and wishing for it to ring, to reveal Lahna on the other side of the door. She'd been doing well, but with two more rounds left, Avarie's growing weary of playing with these men alone.

What could be keeping Lahna away for so long?

No matter. The clockwise rotation indicates that it's her turn to deal out the cards now. This round needs to be perfect. She has to survive, and not only that, she has to impress them.

Unfortunately, Avarie gets a bad hand. No way around it. The Milk Maiden doesn't match well with most of the action cards she has. 'Swimming in the Sea' is definitely a Mermaid card, and they'd accuse her almost instantly if she plays it. 'Haggling in the Market' is one of the more generic cards . . . but is it too vague? Avarie supposes she could play the 'Branding Cattle' card, given that milk maidens also work with cattle, but what if the Blacksmith thinks she's the Mermaid?

She's hesitating. Can the men see her hesitation? She looks at them looking at her. Their eyes seem like they're gleaming with satisfaction, that no matter what Avarie does, she'll lose. If only she had the 'Churn Butter' salvation card as a precaution, but she's got nothing. Again, she looks at the door, hopeful that Lahna will whisk through it, sparking her imagination to find a solution. But no, she's not there.

Lahna's not coming.

The acceptance settles in her bones like an anchor on the seafloor. Avarie tries to steel herself when it's finally her turn to play an action card. Since she dealt the roles, she's the last to put down a card. She 'haggles at the market' and the round concludes. But Avarie lacks her confidence from the previous round, and the men pounce at her weakness. She's eliminated.

There's not much you can do about the role you're dealt, it's all about how you play it, how you 'sway the mob.'

Lahna was right. Avarie needs to keep those words in mind for the next game. With a downtrodden huff, she scoots away from the table, desiring a small break while they further investigate who the 'real' Mermaid is.

Avarie stomps over to the abandoned front desk. The inn attendant is nowhere in sight. A headache pounds feverishly at her temples, knocking like a demanding visitor at someone's door.

Just calm down. You have one more round to prove yourself, to survive.

To get that code word.

She rubs her forehead, desperate to make the acute pain disappear. Suddenly, a ring echoes in her ears. Has her anxiety worsened to the point where she's hearing phantom bells? Avarie throws both hands over her ears, trying to block out the sound. She needs to focus. To think of ways she can win no matter the cards she's dealt the next game. She has to be confident like her mother . . . bring the confident part of her to the surface. It's there. Avarie just knows it's there.

To her surprise, long slender fingers brush across her back. Avarie stiffens for a second. How dare those men touch her? But when she looks to her left, the fire in her eyes dies down instantly.

Lahna.

"Hey there, champion." She beams. "How are you faring?"

A smile threatens to break on her face. Goddess, she's so glad to see her. "You're late."

Lahna rubs the back of her neck. "Had another unexpected visitor. I'm sorry. I hope you weren't waiting too long for me, Ava."

"I started already. Three games in now."

"Look at you! That's great—"

"I just lost Lahna. If I don't win—if I don't impress them in this next game, I'll lose my chance to get into the Corridor."

Lahna purses her lips. "Let's stick to the bright side, okay? You'll win this next game. And afterward, we'll go out to celebrate. As good friends. How does that sound?"

Avarie isn't too fond of the 'good friends' part, which is infuriating. Wasn't that what she asked for? Friendship. Just ignore the lingering gazes and touches. Her mind and heart are huge contradictions at this point. Nevertheless, going out after such a stressful situation seems promising.

"Sounds like a deal."

"I love the sound of that."

Guffaws of laughter erupt from the card players. The round must have concluded.

Lahna rubs Avarie's shoulder in encouragement, sending thrills of electricity through her touch. "Get back in there. I believe in you."

Avarie's hands tremble as she prepares to flip her final role card.

Mermaid.

It brings her some joy to finally play as . . . herself. But this joy is closely followed by skepticism. Can she avoid being caught?

Can she avoid being caught by humans?

Can she truly avenge her brother?

All these questions pile onto her like heavy boulders in an

unanticipated rockslide. But she mustn't succumb. Merelani demands her success.

Her five action cards are vague enough to help her pass the silent rounds, hopefully without incident. No salvation cards make an appearance. She draws another card to replace the used action card and places it face down on the table without looking.

Clockwise, the game continues, the men slapping down cards with proficiency, hooting and hollering in between.

Gap Tooth is quick to point a finger at Avarie when the accusation phase begins for the third round. But Avarie manages to throw off his argument by pointing out that Ice Eyes had played the 'Going to the Shore' action card.

It's one of the trickier cards that the Vagabond could play because it's just as associable to the Mermaid. To Avarie's relief, and Gap Tooth's displeasure, they eliminate Ice Eyes, who throws his cards face down with a huff, and they all move on to the next round. Avarie's got this. There's no way she can be accused; this is the most strategic she's been.

"Avarie of Adahy, I say you're the Mermaid," declares Gap Tooth, almost predictably.

"What warrants that assumption?" Avarie holds her chin high, embodying every bit of her mother for once.

Sure, she's the Mermaid. But all of the cards she's played so far makes it plausible for her to be at least two other roles. Based on the facts of the game, she could either be the wandering Vagabond or the dreamy Milk Maiden. Does Gap Tooth really suspect her of being the Mermaid, or was he simply angry that she rebuffed him earlier? Avarie's face remains stoic, but behind the mask a grimace sharpens itself. How dare he try to jeopardize her win because she refused his flirtation?

What a repugnant man.

Gap Tooth catches the gaze of his friends at the table,

learning forward with spiteful eyes. "Everyone's been the Mermaid here except for you. It's your turn. Must be," he says, confident in his ignorant argument.

"That means nothing. That probability can't stand on two legs."

"And neither can you, Mermaid." Gap Tooth sneers.

Avarie stiffens behind her mask. Does he know her true identity? He can't. How would he? She takes a subtle, calming breath. No, he's still talking about the game.

Whether Avarie wins or impresses them is moot. They're going to do everything in their power to keep her from whatever's in that Corridor, and there's nothing she can do to stop them. But she's not going down without a fight. Avarie eyes her face-down card while sending a silent prayer to the Goddess. Her mask feels ready to tear itself apart, exposing a multitude of haphazardly concealed emotions. But she must hold on for just a bit longer.

Merelani depends on it.

"You'll be removing an innocent player from the game," Avarie bluffs.

Scar Face joins in. "I think you're worth taking that chance."

"You're the Mermaid," Ice Eyes agrees with a shark-like smirk. Which sends a shock of irritation through Avarie. He has already been eliminated. His opinion doesn't matter.

"I'm siding with the majority," Red Hair says stiffly, unable to look Avarie in the face. His dark-brown eyes don't have the same evil, mischievous glint like the others do. He is a fish in a school full of other, more intimidating fish, just going with the flow. But that doesn't make Avarie feel any less disheartened.

With a deep breath, she flips over her role card, revealing the undeniable truth. She looks over her shoulder to Lahna leaning on the inn's counter. Avarie can't help but think she failed multiple people just now: Her parents. Merelani's citizens. Mai. Even Lahna.

Yet Lahna doesn't look disappointed, if anything, a determined fire fills her, bright as her auburn hair. Her lips move without sound, but Avarie knows what she's trying to say: "Turn the card over."

That's right. Avarie has one more card to unveil before the other players can 'drown her.' Avarie drops her right pointer and middle fingers on the card then slides it toward herself. With a quick flip, she reveals it. Behind the mask, her eyes sparkle with anxiety-induced tears, but in reality, she only purses her lips.

Upturning the card sends an uncomfortable, incredulous air around the table. Avarie holds her breath, staring in abundant disbelief.

The worn, yet beautiful 'Goddess of the Sea' salvation card watches her with a commanding elegance that confirms her belief in an instant.

Avarie never felt closer to the Mother of the Sea until this moment.

"Hold on, you haven't won yet." Gap Tooth thrusts a ten-sided dice into Avarie's palm. "You still need to roll an eight or higher before you can use that card."

Avarie takes the dice, throwing a silent prayer to the Goddess before rolling it on the table. The dice spins and rolls and lands . . . exactly on an eight!

"I won," she whispers. With a heaping pound of confidence, she repeats more loudly: "I WON!"

The men stare at her and the card with overarching shock, their voices seemingly swallowed by the sea itself.

Then there's an outcry: "Cheater! You cheated. We don't take kindly to cheaters 'round here," Ice Eyes says.

"No—no I won fair and square. How could I cheat?"

"You did something to the cards!"

"Yeah!" Scar Face and Ice Eyes chime in. Red Hair looks between his comrades, stunned into silence yet allowing their tirade to continue.

"These are your cards and your dice. We didn't use the cards I offered, and I brought no dice with me. I won fairly."

Scar Face snarls. "To hell with that, we're not giving the code to some outsider!"

"You think you're better than us because you're close with the Harts?" Ice Eyes slams his hand on the table.

Abruptly, the men stand from the table, knocking their chairs over in the process. Red Hair takes several steps backward, it's evident on his face that he wants no part in what's transpiring.

Scar Face tips the table over, sending cards and glass mugs to their deaths below. The fragile mugs break on impact, spilling their contents and seeping deeply into the rug like dark, rusty blood.

Gap Tooth swiftly pulls a knife from a hidden jacket pocket.

Avarie knows she should retreat. But she can hear her mother's voice telling her to never allow common men's fear of their own inferiority affect her. And she can feel her father's fierce, hot-headed pride coursing through her veins.

"Your loss says more about your gameplay. Your reactions say more about your lack of honor. How does it feel to lose to a woman? An outsider? A *mermaid*."

A Gap Tooth lunges toward her, and Avarie's mask breaks away instantly. A scream builds in her throat like bile as hands crash into her shoulders and lurch her backward.

Avarie doesn't need to turn around to see Lahna tugging her away from the danger. Scar Face and Ice Eyes reach into their jackets as well. She already knows what's concealed within their pockets. Onlookers begin to flee, the inn's doorbell clinking in a distasteful rhythm as residents exit with newfound urgency.

Lahna's hand shifts down to firmly grasp Avarie's left wrist. Then glass breaks behind them. Who else plans to join this one-sided brawl?

"Everyone out! Grab your things now. You're all banned for the month!" the innkeeper roars with an authority that shakes Avarie to her core. She bends at the knees, but Lahna holds her upright. Grumbling, and with their eyes still solely trained on Lahna, the men file out. Red Hair is the first to leave yet gives her the longest, most apologetic look.

"You too," the innkeeper directs his tired eyes at Avarie.

Still leading Avarie's body, Lahna pulls her upstairs in a rush. "Let's grab your belongings. Quickly. You can stay with me."

Avarie only nods, her broken mask leaking freely now, her hands trembling in Lahna's grip, and her heart crushed at how awesomely she has failed.

Chapter Nineteen

Feelings of failure coat Avarie's skin like a slick, slimy substance. She won, and yet she has nothing to show for it. She wasted a week. She got kicked out of the Siren's Rock. What will she do now?

Lahna lays a sympathetic hand on Avarie's shoulder, the warmth attempting to penetrate through her increasingly negative mindset. "I still think I should take you out. I think you deserve it."

Avarie doesn't think she deserves anything right now, but she has nothing to do besides wallowing in her greasy failure. So, she nods, a curt shake of her head at Lahna's request.

"Come on. Let's go to The Fin—a new eatery on the outskirts of Deniz. I've been hearing a lot about it lately. My treat."

Avarie recalls passing by The Fin on her walk to the library. Still engulfed by her somber mood, Avarie does not bother to ask if the things Lahna has heard are good or bad. She'll find out soon enough.

With an uplifting smile, Lahna moves her hand from

Avarie's shoulder to grasp her fingers. The sludge of failure sticking to Avarie seems to melt away from the contact.

Their entwined fingers foster a warmth that Avarie wishes to remember forever. But then, she remembers how she failed Merelani and the warmth fizzles to a weak ember, not completely gone, but its presence is so feeble that Avarie must focus to keep it.

Lahna leads Avarie into the night, their hands like a glowing spark illuminating the dark path ahead.

AVARIE FEELS A LITTLE UNDERDRESSED IN HER TAN knit tunic, black leggings, and weathered dark boots. Fifteen to twenty land dwellers are lined up outside the door. Most of them look dressed to party, to celebrate some sort of success. Unlike Avarie. But looking at Lahna puts her at ease. Lahna's clothing is plain, the fabric worn and comfortable like her own. An attendant standing in front of the brick-and-mortar building motions for them to come forward then whisks them inside, handing them off to a server who places them at a secluded table.

The attendant's enthusiasm reminds Avarie of the innkeeper's sudden change in tone when he learned that she was Lahna's friend. Avarie knows a thing or two about powerful families, and she wonders if the 'Harts of Deniz' are comparable to the royal family of Merelani.

They are ushered to their table so quickly that Avarie didn't have time to take in her surroundings until now. The low, warm lighting from the candles and the overhead chandeliers cast an intimate glow over the two of them. Their round table is draped with a maroon velvet cloth; on top of it are polished golden utensils surrounding a stacked saucer and a black marbled plate.

The sturdy backing of the seats seems to be made from gold-plated iron, and the seat cushions match the tablecloth. Live music—a harp—breaks up the nervous silence of first dates and clinking cutlery.

Awe grips Avarie. The scenery around her is reminiscent of the banquet parties held back home. Then she remembers she's not alone in this experience. Her eyes gravitate to Lahna, who's perusing a papyrus menu.

"This place is nothing short of astounding," Avarie beams.

"It is lovely. Did you get a chance to look at the menu?"

Avarie's eyes travel to the menu placed precisely on her left. She'd forgotten that this was a place for eating, not just for gawking.

Her fingers trail down the menu, tapping potential items she'd like to try. "Maybe a crustacean? I love shrimp." Then her eyes catch the words 'Oarfish,' and she nearly jumps out of her seat. An asterisk accompanies the word, denoting that the dish is seasonal. Still, it's unnerving to see. "They . . . they serve oarfish here?"

"Hmm . . . maybe. But I doubt it's in season. I haven't tasted oarfish since I was a little girl. I bet it'd be served on a tiny, gratuitous plate. A pint-sized hors d'oeuvre garnished with a heaping of herbs to make up for its minuscule size."

"Those were a lot of words, Lahna."

"I am a writer, after all. Would you expect anything differently?" Lahna takes her gaze hostage before winking and returning to her menu. Avarie just about falls out of her chair onto the dark gray and black marbled flooring.

She winked at her.

SHE WINKED AT HER.

Avarie's heart feels ready to fall out, but her feet keep her grounded in more ways than one. She briefly puts a hand to her neck, trying to calm her breathing. But it's like her lungs have been hijacked by the innocent flirtation.

Was Lahna flirting? That was flirting, right?

She clears her throat, training her focus on the menu. Avarie loses count of how many times she's reread the sides The Fin offers before a light touch on her forearm shakes her out of it.

"Are you ready to order? The waiter's here."

Avarie looks up to her right and there they are: a waiter wearing cleanly pressed pants, shiny shoes, and a collared shirt. The eatery's name is stitched onto their breast pocket in curly black lettering. They have a quill in one hand and a small notepad in the other.

"I'm Arrow, are you two ready to order?"

Lahna takes the lead by saying, "Hi Arrow, I'd love to try the Water Nymph Tonic and the baked sea scallops. Plus, water with lemon." Done ordering, she looks up from the menu to Avarie.

Avarie hadn't even considered the drinks yet. Her crush on Lahna had sent her into a sort of distracted panic. She scours the menu, in search of refreshments. Finding nothing, she flips the double-sided menu over, a new sense of anxiety settling in at having to make the server wait.

She settles for the first beverage her finger lands on: "I'll take the Velour Enchanter, please."

"And what dish?"

"Oh yeah, um, how about the blackened shrimp?"

"Of course, and that comes with a side of your choosing."

"Right, right. Maybe the sea salt roasted potatoes?"

"Perfect! I'll get this order in, and your dishes will be ready soon." Arrow nods, as though assuring Avarie that she did a good job ordering, and they disappear through a set of black double doors that must lead to the kitchen.

Lahna chuckles and puts her menu face down on the table. "Do they not have eateries in Adahy? Seems like you've never ordered before."

Avarie would be offended by the teasing, had it come from anyone else. But Lahna's kind, playful dark eyes yield only feelings of delight.

"Things aren't as fancy in Adahy. I've never been on a date like this." Or a date at all. Then Avarie cringes. Why did she say 'date' aloud?

Lahna shows her no mercy, her lips curling up into a smirk. "A date, you say? We're calling it a date, now? I was under the impression that we were both ignoring our feelings for the sake of our friendship."

Avarie looks down at the napkin splayed across her lap. Why can't she shut up when she needs to shut up? "I'm sorry. I didn't mean to say—"

"No. I was only teasing. I don't want to make you uncomfortable again." Lahna leans forward, her hand nervously tapping the table.

Avarie takes a deep breath. "I don't mind calling it a date. If you don't mind calling it a date."

Relief washes over Lahna's face, easing her furrowed brows. "Let's call it a date then."

"Deal."

Arrow returns with their drinks. An ornate glass with a thin stem and a triangular opening is placed in front of Avarie. The liquid is sweet, seafoam green, and garnished with glittery specs. It slides down smoothly, just like an octopus skirting across the seafloor. Velour Enchanter calls to mind her obsession with Moon Goddess cake, a delicacy reserved for special occasions—like Aalto's coronation, had it not ended so catastrophically. Avarie gulps down more of the drink to wash down her rising thoughts.

"Woah, you might want to slow down. I don't think you've eaten much today, and I know that has spirits. Matter of fact . . ." Lahna picks up the menu and scans it quickly,

"Yep, vodka and melon liqueur. Why don't you wait until your food arrives? Here, take some of my water."

Lahna scoots the water closer to Avarie. She playfully rolls her eyes before taking a sip. She won't deny that she needs water. Already, a strange giddiness is building inside of her. She'd had alcohol in Merelani before, but only sparingly.

"It tastes like my favorite hard candy," Avarie says between sips of water.

"I'd rather walk you back to my place than carry you." Lahna gives her a pointed look.

Carefree laughter spills out of Avarie. "What about your drink? How is it?"

Lahna samples the drink, briefly swishing the liquid around her tongue. A thought creeps into Avarie's mind that the liquid is certainly lucky to explore Lahna's mouth like that. A mixture of shock and embarrassment leads her to stare down at her lap. Maybe she should lay off the Enchanter.

"Tastes like a pine tree and a little like the sea." Lahna grimaces. "I thought I'd take a break from my usual red wine, but I don't think I'll order this again."

"Can I give it a try?" Avarie starts to reach for the stem of the half-moon-shaped glass.

Her date quickly flicks her hand away. "Absolutely not. Drink that water."

Avarie's lower lip jokingly puckers out for a moment. She swallows a swig of the Velour Enchanter before returning her focus to the unflavored water. She squeezes a lemon into the glass for dramatic effect.

"You're stubborn." Lahna swallows some of her own drink, her gaze never leaving Avarie.

Once the food arrives, they dig in. Only sounds of clinking forks and harp notes can be heard. Avarie hadn't truly realized how hungry she was until now. The blackened shrimp is yummy, though not fresh like in Merelani. The sprinkling of salt on her potatoes is exquisite and filling. She doesn't think she'll ever trade Merelani cuisine for anything, but The Fin's food is a close second.

"That was so damn good. I could eat this every day," Avarie says.

"Glad you enjoyed yourself. My scallops were tasty too. Do you want dessert?"

Dessert? Avarie hadn't considered that. She was stuffed, but maybe she could fit just a little more. Honestly, she'd do anything to prolong this moment. As soon as they leave The Fin, she'll be thrust back into reality. She doesn't want to think about failing Merelani. Failing Aalto. Not just yet.

Avarie wipes her mouth with the cloth napkin then nods. "Sure. I'll try whatever you want."

Lahna beams before signaling Arrow to their table. "We'd like to end the night with the Mascarpone Sea Foam Cake."

"Absolutely. I'll let the chefs know. I'll bring your payment ticket promptly." Arrow scribbles in their notebook then disappears again behind the double doors.

"Thank you, Lahna. Really. I've been having the best time."

"I wanted to do something nice for you today." Lahna takes Avarie's hand. "You deserve nice things. Don't let the world's bullshit make you think otherwise."

A pleasant, tingly feeling races up Avarie's arm. It's definitely the alcohol, bolstered by Lahna's words. She can't help but think that she doesn't deserve Lahna. Especially because she still doesn't know her secret.

All of a sudden, Avarie's heart weighs a ton.

"I—I need to run to the toilet. Too many liquids." She laughs, but Avarie knows Lahna can see that it doesn't reach her eyes. Avarie scoots from the table to stand, scanning the room for signs to the restroom.

"I'll come with you. I need to go too."

Avarie sighs but doesn't protest. The farther they get from the tables, the quieter it becomes. Lahna links arms with her as they walk. Their bare skin brushes together, sending chills down her spine. It's inviting, magnetic. A feeling she's yearned for. Eventually, they end up in a narrow T-shaped hallway. It's dim, but around the corner to the right, a light crawls onto the path's darkness.

"What could that be?" Avarie inquires.

"Surely it's something extravagant."

"We'll find out soon enough."

The two turn the corner and are bathed in a hollow, artificial light. Avarie's legs tremble. She gapes at the horror before her. Her dinner curdles in her stomach. She clutches her midsection desperately for relief. Aalto's shell burns her flesh with a fiery vengeance, so much so that Avarie debates removing it.

"Oh, my Goddess . . ." Tears brim in Avarie's eyes.

"I had no idea this would be here." Lahna looks between Avarie and the hellish sight, her features showcasing her shock and disgust.

"I think I'm going to be sick. Take me out of here. Now."

With haste, Lahna wraps an arm around Avarie's waist and steers her away from the horrific scene.

But the image is seared into Avarie's mind. It is a moment she will never wash away.

There, in the room they left behind, was a gigantic fish tank filled with rocks, sea plants, and various fish. In it was a shackled mermaid, beaten and bruised for the amusement of land dwellers. Her eyes were devoid of hope. Her tail was patchy, as if her scales had been ripped away. The whole time, her mouth seemed stuck in a weary smile. Out of place. Wrong. The tank's artificial waves made wisps of her hair move in the water. But it's unnatural, a facsimile of what mermaid tresses do under the sea. There were land dwellers staring at the tank in awe, stabbing their fingers at the trapped creature. They had a real, living mermaid on display.

Lahna dumps a handful of coins onto their table. They move wordlessly toward the exit, only Avarie's sniffles and the harp can be heard. All of a sudden, Lahna stops, digging her heels into the marble floor.

Disgust runs rampant across her face. She shifts to grab Avarie's hands and says, "I should say something—we should say something. I'll find the owner. I'll make this right." Her brown eyes are wide, earnest, filled with a determination that Avarie wishes she felt instead of the fear and the hopelessness.

"I don't see the point," Avarie says, voice almost a whisper.

"What do you mean? We should say something." Lahna stares at her in confusion.

But suddenly, Avarie's no longer at The Fin. She's in the palace foyer, broken coral falling all around her. She's watching Aalto walk past her. She feels the words bubbling on her lips again. Words to help her brother. But she doesn't say them.

She didn't speak up then.

And she can't speak up now.

"I just don't see the point. Nothing will change. We can't fix this."

"We can't just sit idly, Ava. This is wrong. Evil—" Lahna tilts her head toward her shoulder, hoping that Avarie will finally agree.

"Humans are evil. They do what they want. They don't listen. Please, just get me out of here."

Lahna purses her lips but says nothing, the fire dying in her eyes. She relinquishes the hold on one of Avarie's hands, squeezing the other as she leads Avarie away from The Fin.

Chapter Twenty

To the dismay of The Fin's outdoor attendant, Avarie bursts into tears as she and Lahna cross the threshold. She just can't keep them in anymore. The horrid image of the enslaved mermaid flashes in her memory. Lahna holds her close, attempting to quell the tremors without much success.

"I'm so sorry, Ava. I had no idea. If I had known, I—I would have never taken you here." Lahna rests her chin atop Avarie's head. She scuttles them a few feet away from the entrance to avoid getting hit by passersby. "This was supposed to be a good thing. I fear I've only made your day worse. I feel as distraught as you do."

But she can't be, Avarie thinks. Because Lahna didn't see her brother's lifeless body when she looked into that tank. An innocent Merelani citizen trapped, and Avarie can't do anything about it without revealing too much of herself. "You couldn't have known," Avarie says, though the last word lodges itself in her throat. She blinks away the remaining tears and takes a calming breath.

Lahna pulls back to look at Avarie's face, revealing that her own is weighed down by tremendous guilt.

"But I still feel horrible. I only wanted to take away some of the pain I glimpsed in your eyes. I just wanted you to have something good today."

Avarie chews her bottom lip, searching for words. "I did have something good today. It was great, actually. Before we saw the trapped mermaid. And—" Suddenly, Avarie realizes something. "I appreciate you wanting to ease my pain. But I think I'm starting to understand that that's my responsibility. It's not your burden to bear. I don't know how long it'll take, but that's an hourglass only I can flip."

Lahna pulls Avarie closer, their foreheads lightly touching. "That was quite insightful. Could I borrow that for my next novel?"

Avarie opens her mouth, a much-needed laugh escaping out.

"Only if you give me credit," Avarie sniffs, the remaining sadness melting away.

"I'll be sure to let everyone know in the acknowledgments that a beautifully complicated girl named Ava inspired me."

"Beautiful? Beyond measure. Complicated though?" Avarie jokes.

"You are a riddle. A tiny, little, teasing conundrum." Lahna smiles.

"You make it sound like I'm too much." Insecurity seeps into Avarie's voice.

"Something leads me to believe that I can handle you." Her smile remains, though it shifts into a sort of rakish delight that makes Avarie's stomach flip.

Avarie doesn't think the words, she just *feels*.

"Then handle me."

That damned smile of Lahna's enchants itself into a wicked smirk.

Her mouth moves in response, but Avarie is distracted by the short distance between their lips. Lahna's voice fades away almost completely.

Avarie ogles the perfect heart-shaped pink lips before her. They part, a tongue briefly running across them. Lahna cradles Avarie's face in her hands and the noise of their surroundings returns, breaking the spell. Sound pours in like the evanescent moment after breaching the water's surface.

And their lips finally meet at last.

Avarie's eyes flutter shut, her arms reaching to wrap around Lahna's waist. Her heartbeat dances in her chest. She marvels at the softness of Lahna's lips. Then she notices that her date's heartbeat is mimicking hers, similarly entranced by their amorous exchange.

As Lahna deepens the kiss, she moves a hand, trailing a finger down Avarie's neck and making her gasp in delight. Avarie's skin is aflame, burning with a frenzied yearning that she has yet to experience until now. She grips Lahna's tunic, wishing to be closer than humanly possible.

In response, Lahna adorns Avarie's chin with slow kisses, dipping lower and lower to the curve of her heated neck. What could be better than this? Avarie wants to live in this moment forever.

Someone clears their throat, the sound of it brings back the awareness of where they are and draws them apart.

A familiar, expressionless face watches them. "I thought that was you, Avarie of Adahy." Red Hair stares them down, taking in Lahna's hand still caressing Avarie's face, her lips just a few inches from Avarie's neck. With the utmost regret, Avarie removes the warmth from her face, returning the hands to Lahna's side. But she doesn't let go completely, clasping three fingers clumsily with her own.

"I never got your name," Avarie says slowly, still reeling

from her trance moments ago. Then the daze fades, replaced by fear.

What does this man want?

Does he intend to hurt them?

Are the other men waiting, hiding in the dark to attack?

"Elias of Deniz," the man says.

"How can we help you, Elias?" Lahna assumes a protective stance, shielding Avarie behind her.

Elias throws his hands up, palms facing outward. "I mean no harm. I wish to apologize on behalf of my friends. The game was fair, and you won. I believe in fairness, so I will keep our end of the bargain." He tentatively takes three steps forward, but Lahna simultaneously walks three steps back, lightly pushing Avarie along in the process.

Avarie appreciates the protectiveness, she revels in the safety Lahna provides for her. But something in the man's eyes makes her trust Elias. She places a palm on Lahna's back; the girl relaxes under Avarie's touch. "I think he's telling the truth. We should hear him out."

A long sigh flows from Lahna's mouth, but she doesn't object.

Elias walks forward again and motions the duo out of hearing range from those waiting outside of The Fin. "The code that will grant you entry into the Unspeakable Corridor is *Siren's Oarfish*."

That's it? *That's* the elusive answer that's worried Avarie for a week? She could scream and tear at her locs in annoyance.

"But that's not all," he continues. "Make sure to arrive at sunset, lest you not be allowed through . . . I should go now. I wish safety upon you, whatever you're seeking in the Corridor cannot be good." Elias backs away slowly, then disappears into the starry night.

"Well, that was awfully kind yet strange." Avarie catches

Lahna's eye as she looks over her shoulder. They share a mutual look of confusion.

"Maybe his conscience got the best of him. Whatever his reasoning is, nothing can be done now. You must endure the night so you can reach tomorrow," says Lahna.

"That was awfully poetic," Avarie jokes.

"Never completely explored poetry. Although, I'm imagining I could write a sonnet about someone."

"Oh really, who?" Avarie can't help herself, rising to the tips of her toes to kiss Lahna.

The smile that Avarie never tires of, appears on Lahna's face. "Eh, probably the nice lady that always gives me discounts at the market."

"Of course, I couldn't imagine anyone else."

"She has my heart, what can I say?"

Avarie's cheeks warm. There was just something about Lahna. She lays a hand on her warm necklace. Something comforting. Something enticing.

Something that will break her heart when she returns to Merelani.

But for now, she'll relish the moments wholeheartedly.

AVARIE SETTLES CROSS-LEGGED ON THE SHORE. Alone. She dropped off her few belongings with Lahna before excusing herself, stating that she needed some time in solitude. They'll be back together soon enough. The thought sends a thrill through Avarie's midsection. But right now, she needs to update Mairya.

Avarie hadn't forgotten the tinge of jealousy she detected from Mai the last time they had conversed. Foolishly, she did briefly forget their impending marriage. And she has every intention to forget again.

Lahna consumes her thoughts.

"Mairya of Merelani, I need your presence."

Mai doesn't magically appear. About five minutes pass before Avarie detects any disturbance in the sea. Mairya's head pops above water. Avarie senses the worry behind her eyes.

"My queen. You called?" Her expression lacks the warmth and comfort of Lahna's smile.

"I won the card game. I'll visit the Corridor tomorrow. I'm so close to finding out who killed Aalto." It seems odd to condense her eventful day down to just three sentences, but Avarie can't reveal too much.

"That's great news, Avarie. I trust that you've ended contact with the land dweller now that you no longer need her?" Mai arches an eyebrow, her hands tightening around an ornate plate with pastries that Avarie only notices now.

"What? I—"

"Yes? I've been working on my marriage oath. It's nearly perfect now. I can't wait for you to return home."

Alarms sound off in Avarie's head. Vows? Mai has already put together her vows, and they're perfect? Avarie's hardly been able to wrap her head around Merelani's loss. "You must have a lot of time on your hands. This is . . . quite unexpected, Mairya."

"Your time on land is fleeting. We both know that. I thought it would be a nice 'welcome home' gift."

"Vows. Vows are your gift?" Avarie runs a hand through her locs. This is not at all how she anticipated this conversation going.

"No, my queen. Our wedding. Palace workers are preparing an altar, deciding a menu, making a guest list. It'll be a great way to reunite our kingdom after such a tragedy."

"And my parents approve of this?" Avarie feels as though hives have popped up on her skin, she scratches her forearm uneasily.

Mairya hesitates for a moment. Immediately, Avarie senses that what she'll say next is a mixture of the truth and a fabrication. "Of course! Bruinen and Cordelia are thrilled. They suggested we have a public wedding for all of Merelani."

Avarie can't remember the last time her father was 'thrilled' about anything her name was tied to. How peculiar. Seems like there's some misinformation she'll need to combat once she returns home. Despite her bargain with the Enchantress, Avarie can't jump into a marriage so quickly. Not when she'll be grieving her parting from Lahna.

There's no need to deny the intricate bond between her and Mairya, but her budding feelings for Lahna feel so much more natural, organic. On the contrary, her relationship with Mairya seems riddled with secrets and deceit. Weighed down by history—a past that's somewhat embarrassing, and a present that's too painful to think about. Though she and Lahna are short on time, she wants to see where they could go. And when it's inevitable, Avarie will tell Lahna the truth.

And Mairya.

"A public wedding sounds wonderful. Merelani will love that." She desperately hopes Mai doesn't hear the crack in her voice.

Avarie has read plenty of land-dweller romances to believe that Mai is not her true love. Kissing Lahna made that even more apparent. Nevertheless, Avarie accepts the plate of Moon Goddess cake from Mairya. Because Mai remembered it's her favorite and she'd feel guilty otherwise.

Her walk back to Lahna's cottage is slow, silent. Avarie squints her eyes to see in the dark, peering through her glasses and shoveling down cake so Lahna won't find the evidence.

When she finally arrives, Lahna leads Avarie to the guest room. They don't discuss their kiss. Avarie purposely does not reflect on the day at all. She curls into a ball on top of the duvet, throws her glasses a safe distance away, and crosses over into a dreamless slumber.

THE HUMDRUM OF AVARIE'S EIGHTH DAY ON LAND IS welcome. She's done all she can—prepping her satchel with essentials, reciting the code in her head until it's seared into her thoughts. Now all that's left to do is wait for nightfall.

Avarie spends most of the day by herself. Lahna is locked away in her writing room, only emerging from it to procure snacks and liquid sustenance. They talk in passing, sharing brief kisses, making Avarie long for the sound of the writing room door creaking open. Each time, she puts a finger in the book she's reading and looks up eagerly, ready to hear a few words from her favorite author.

"Time for a celebratory snack!" Lahna nearly shouts.

"Oh yeah? What are we celebrating?"

"I finally finished this chapter I've been dreading." Lahna crosses over to the couch and collapses right next to Avarie. She wiggles closer, sliding her head onto Avarie's lap. The way they have grown comfortable with each other still astonishes Avarie.

"That's definitely a reason to celebrate." Avarie places a curious hand on Lahna's scalp, her fingers lightly massaging the hair and skin there. Lahna closes her eyes and sighs in appreciation. "Why have you been dreading it?"

"I've been wanting to do a retelling of 'The Ten-Year Maiden' for the longest time. But I wanted the ending to be happy, you know? And not too cliché." She puts *cliché* in air quotes. "And instead of a prince, maybe a princess falls in love."

"Okay, I'm already sold. Let me know when it gets published," Avarie says. Her laughter catches in her throat.

She'd forgotten that, by time this story gets published, she'll be long gone.

Lahna's eyes pop open. "Everything alright, Ava?"

"Y-yeah. I'm okay. I just can't keep my mind off these eventual snacks."

Lahna sits up, squinting, as though saying she doesn't buy Avarie's response. She tugs Avarie from the couch. "You'll get the first copy, I promise. Now let's discuss snacks. I'm in the mood for rice crisps. I'd love to know your thoughts though."

Avarie allows herself to be pulled from her seat. But as Lahna loosens her grip, Avarie tightens her hold. She wants to cherish this connection for as long as she's able. "Rice crisps are great, but I'm in the mood for something else."

Once in the kitchen, Lahna disappears into a pantry. From there she calls over her shoulder: "Let me guess . . . you want your favorite."

She reappears, nearly hopping on her toes like a rabbit, her auburn curls bouncing with excitement. In her hand is a thin, paper packaging, and inside it, Avarie sees what looks like seaweed.

Astonished, Avarie says, "Lahna Hart, I dare say you've gotten to know me perfectly in such a short time. How did you know seaweed is my favorite snack?"

"When I was mending your torn bag, I noticed you had seaweed in there." Avarie thought that was it, but Lahna continues. "You seem to have a fondness for the sea, a great respect for its depths.

"Your reaction to the mermaid in the tank . . . anyone compassionate would have been upset. But you—you were distraught." Lahna's face grows more serious. "Avarie, why did I also find a knife in your bag?"

Avarie's eyes widen, her mind scrambling for some sort of truth—because she's tired, so tired of lying.

To Lahna.

To Mai.

To herself.

Her gaze drops, hands finding her sun ring and twirling it for the first time in days. "It's for protection. My brother got hurt, who's to say that I wouldn't?"

Lahna considers her words for a moment. "That makes sense." Sensing Avarie's shift in tone, she continues with, "I'm sorry I asked. I know you'd never hurt me."

"I wouldn't dare to," Avarie responds almost breathlessly.

As the promise lingers in the air—it feels ironclad to Avarie—they kiss, the action feeling more desirous each time.

"Why don't you go back to reading? I'll put on some tea."

Avarie tucks her bare feet underneath her. She's leaning on the settee's pillows when Lahna emerges from the kitchen, teacups in hand. With only a thigh-length tunic on and thick socks that stop mid-calf, Lahna's long brown pigmented legs catch Avarie's attention. She rests the book on a cushion, promptly losing her place in the novel.

Lahna looks her up and down before setting a teacup within Avarie's reach. She doesn't leave. Her gaze holds Avarie hostage. Behind her eyes are unspoken words that Avarie is certain will make her body melt with longing. All of a sudden, Avarie feels flustered in a way she never has before. Euphoria makes her breath hitch in her throat, making her deliriously ache to touch Lahna. From the curls on her head to every part she'll allow Avarie to. Avarie sucks in a sharp breath. She falls back onto the cushion, not realizing that she'd been leaning forward.

What was this feeling? Why did she want to do everything to explore it?

But before Avarie can do anything, Lahna steps away, walking backward to her writing room. "I-I-um—I should get back to writing." She fumbles for the doorknob.

Her hand hits the door twice before managing to grab the

knob. Still, she refuses to look away, holding Avarie's gaze until the last possible moment. The door shuts behind her, a barrier intervening between the growing desires on either side.

Avarie thinks back to all the land-dweller books she has consumed. *Oh.* Now she understands. She knows this feeling. *That feeling.* Avarie finally releases the breath she was holding. *Oh, Goddess.* There is no way they are stopping at just a kiss. The tide is too strong, and Avarie yearns to drown in it.

Chapter Twenty-One

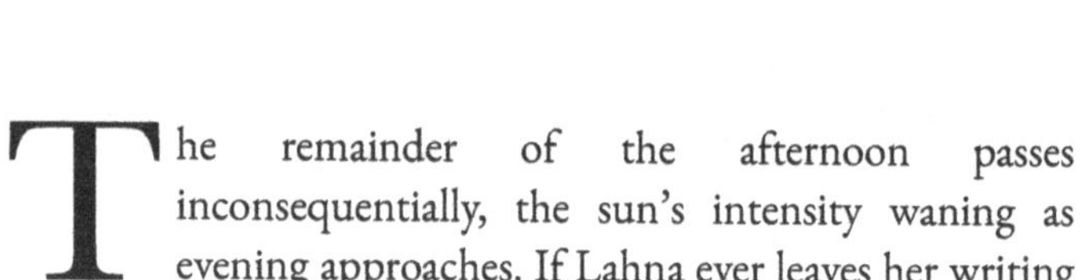

The remainder of the afternoon passes inconsequentially, the sun's intensity waning as evening approaches. If Lahna ever leaves her writing room again, Avarie doesn't notice. She spends most of the time napping.

Unchaste dreams—wishful thinking—play in Avarie's head. She awakens with a start, hands and forehead clammy. She retires to the guest bathroom to wash herself. She wasn't prepared for her mission on land, and she certainly isn't ready to resist the enigma that is Lahna Hart—with her kind and protective nature, her intelligence and her way with words.

Avarie doesn't stand a chance.

For now, she'll distract herself. She splashes her face with cool water, washing away the sleepiness still clinging to her eyes. Time to visit the Unspeakable Corridor.

Deniz wears dusk amazingly. The tapestry of

purple, orange, and yellow in the sky is unlike anything Avarie's seen under the sea.

The setting sun signals most of the merchants to pack up and go home to whatever is waiting for them. But a darkness clings to the farthest parts of the market, and shiftier merchants linger there, waiting for unsavory deals to be made.

Avarie's mind wanders to the last few hours as her boots trudge forward. She thinks of her newfound closeness with Lahna, the way her heart grows fonder of her with each setting of the sun. Less than a week left before she returns to the sea.

Goddess, there's so much more to see, to experience.

Rounding the Corridor, Avarie's met with a rugged-looking man. He stares her down and she does the same. Though similarly gritty, he is not one of the four men that played her in Drowner. This relaxes her for the moment.

She recalls the first time they met, the painful shove to the ground. This time, she won't be leaving without the answers she needs.

"Password." His utterance is gruff and curt, more of a demand than a question.

Avarie's reply mirrors the stern tone of the man. "Siren's Oarfish."

The man narrows his eyes, holding her gaze, waiting, expecting for her to squirm. But she doesn't. Avarie stands firm, sure that she's finally gotten something right. The cloaked man eventually recedes into the shadows, engulfed by the Corridor's secrets. Avarie's surprised he doesn't hiss on his way out.

Before a smug smile can reach her face, a rush of fetid air hits her as she descends farther into the Corridor. Torches overhead just barely fills the narrow space. She pulls her tunic up to cover her nose. *Goddess, it smells like months-old sea urchin in here.*

With her sense of smell momentarily blocked, Avarie can now inspect the Corridor. It seems to stretch on forever. As she treks deeper into the unknown, her necklace becomes warmer, almost to the point where she wonders if it will scald her skin.

She passes by merchants selling imitation oarfish meat, gaudy jewelry, and various poisons. But none of these are what she's searching for, so she continues on, trusting her necklace to guide her.

Avarie passes another table before pulling to a stop. This table is almost pretty, covered by a faded red tablecloth long enough to obscure the seller's feet and anything lurking beneath it. The owner took some care laying out their stock. She seems to be selling a variety of plants and herbs. Some herbs, Avarie notes, seem deadly. But they offer a nice reprieve from the stench wafting from the mouth of the Corridor. One smell in particular makes her inhale deeper through her nose.

Is that moonflower?

Avarie replays Lahna's description of the flower in her head: *We loved to watch the white petals unfurl slowly in the evening as we waited for the stars . . . and the smell? Enchanting. Just like lemons.* The plant in front of her matches that description perfectly. Avarie inhales again. Yes, that's definitely a moonflower, no questioning it. It was a small thing though. Only a tangle of leaves leading up to a single cluster of petals. But the stem was strong, launching the flower fully upward, no wilting whatsoever. This isn't what she's looking for. Not at all what she came for.

"How much for that moonflower?" Avarie points to the plant.

The woman with tired gray eyes coughs out a reply, phlegm moving around in her throat: "Sixty coins. No bartering. No exchanges. No returns." Avarie wasn't a hundred percent sure that the one flower was worth that much, but imagining the look on Lahna's face when Avarie gifts it to her is worth emptying out her purse. Avarie pulls the bag of coins from her satchel. She counts slowly so as not to make any error. Avarie frowns. *This can't be right.* No way is she this low on currency. But she did lose quite a few coins when her satchel got torn. She counts again. The seller's foot is audible against the cobblestone, signaling her impatience.

Nope. Avarie was right the first time. She has exactly sixty coins left. It would be wise to save it for her true purpose here. Or even to get her through the last few days on land . . .

Today, impulsiveness wins.

She drops the purse on the table, sliding the coins back inside. Her mind is already visualizing the joy on Lahna's face. With a sigh only she can hear, Avarie pushes the coin pouch toward the seller. The woman smiles, revealing her plaque-covered teeth.

The woman counts the coins for herself before gesturing toward the moonflower. Avarie picks up the cracked ceramic pot, cradling it like an infant, and backs away from the table. She only hopes that her spontaneous decision doesn't catch her by the metaphorical fin.

Avarie continues deeper into the Corridor. It's so dimly lit that she finally gives in and throws her glasses on. Eventually, she approaches a merchant selling some items that look shiny and rectangular. She can't really see what they are just yet, but her necklace is burning, as though affirming that this is the merchant she must talk to.

Her chest tightens in anticipation.

She coughs, trying to relieve the nervousness in her throat. Avarie tries to speak, but when she finally sees what the merchant is offering, she staggers into a resolute silence instead. Avarie rushes to the table, anger so hot in her chest it could boil the sea. She wants to scream. But instead, she bites the inside of her cheek, drawing blood.

On the chipped and dusty wooden table is an assortment of polished mermaid scales, each placed in velvet-lined boxes as if they were an engagement ring or some other fancy jewelry. Her shocked silence prompts the merchant man to speak: "Authentic mer scales. Take yer pick. These are the best you'll find in all of Deniz. Perfect for grounding into powder to restore your youth."

"Authentic?" Avarie wonders aloud.

Restoration of youth?

Is that really what humans think their scales do? Avarie would laugh if her shock wasn't gripping her by the throat.

"Yes." The merchant studies Avarie. "Not satisfied? Well, I have something special. Wasn't supposed to sell for a couple weeks, but I think you'll like it." The merchant briefly disappears underneath the table before popping back up with a closed velvet box in his hand.

The box is similar in size to the other ones on the table. He carefully extends it with both hands to Avarie. After a moment's hesitation, she accepts it. The box is soft as expected, and it barely weighs anything.

She opens it with her right hand.

Inside is an onyx merscale—a scale that could only belong to one merperson. A lump blossoms in Avarie's throat as she moves to touch it.

The flood of memories is instantaneous. Avarie easily recognizes that they are not her own. The dreary scene is all-consuming, transporting Avarie away from the Corridor.

She is staring down at Aalto's deep-black tail and fin, they were dusted with the sands of the Denizian shore. She tries to look up but she can't do anything, stuck seeing the memory through her brother's eyes. There is a shadow looming over Aalto, and then his head is jerked backward. His eyes stare up at a man hovering over him with a sickening grin. The man's dark skin is almost luminous against the sun's rays, his muddy eyes taunting. He stalks around Aalto until he is mere inches from the end of his fin.

He meets Aalto's gaze with a sickening confidence before brandishing a knife from his coat pocket. He stabs the knife into Aalto's lower half, plucking a scale from his body. The howl of pain that follows sends Avarie reeling and gasping for air.

She's back in the shady Corridor. Suspicious, the man peers over the rickety table to stare at her on the ground. "If you're not going to buy it, put it back."

"Wait, wait . . ." she pleads. Shakily, Avarie stands up and reaches in desperation for a different scale. The same thing happens—she is transported into the merperson's body moments before their scale is removed from them.

Again.

And again.

Avarie is transported by another scale, sometimes whimpering at the violence inflicted upon her through the memories.

"Stop touching all my merchandise! You scratch, you buy," the merchant scolds.

She places her trembling hand on Aalto's scale again, her body almost frozen with grief. She studies the man from the scene again.

Black hair. Slicked back.

Tan coat. A broken oyster with a missing pearl sewn on the collar.

Sturdy black boots.

This is the man who murdered Aalto. A near self-destructive rage fills Avarie from head to toe.

"If you're not going to buy anything, you need to leave. Now."

"S-sorry. I'll take this one."

"That's forty-five coins," the man says impatiently.

Avarie hesitates, knowing full well that she shouldn't have spent all her coins on the moonflower in her trembling left hand. Could she return it? No, no . . . the woman said no exchanges or returns. *Damn it.* She looks longingly at the scale in her right hand. Avarie needs it. How else can she have proof of her brother's death?

"Hurry up," the man says, now irate. He stands up from the table. Avarie backs away in response. She closes the box and tightens her grip around it. She's going to be impulsive again. She's going to do something so stupid and dangerous that she might regret it.

Avarie takes another step back from the table. The man's hand shoots out, clawing at the scale, but she leans just out of reach. Eyes wide, legs jittery, Avarie turns over her left shoulder and runs.

She clutches the moonflower and the scale to her chest, ignoring the man's shouting as best as she can.

She's a thief. But for a good cause. Avarie feels no remorse for the man's loss, only anger for the merpeople who fell victim to the cruelty he was complicit in. Avarie tells herself this over and over as she dashes through the Corridor, brushing by people, knocking items from tables, and eliciting indignant shouts from merchants. But she doesn't care, all she can think about is Aalto. Aalto and his scale. Aalto and that damned poacher. Aalto's last moments.

Avarie runs and runs and runs until her chest is hollow and only the trees surround her. Avarie touches her temple, anticipating a headache. She wipes the tears from her cheeks; there's no time for crying. She must share the news with Mairya. She carefully drops the moonflower and scale in her bag and resumes running again. Night has fallen all over

Deniz. The beach will be empty. There will be no one there to witness her grief except for the waves.

Avarie collapses onto the sand, its gritty texture cutting into her knees. But she's too numb to care.

"Mairya!" she screams, the despair in her voice mimicking Cordelia's from all those days ago.

Chapter Twenty-Two

"Good news, my queen—" Mairya's voice dies when her eyes focus on Avarie.

"I know who killed Aalto." Avarie's tears fall freely. Her eyes burn. Her head aches. Her gut is struck by nausea. It's like it's happening all over again, and she's feeling the force of Aalto's death a second time, yet with the same intensity, if not more.

"Who? How do you know?" Mairya whispers, her voice barely rising above the waves.

"Deep in the Corridor, I found a merchant selling merscales." Avarie's hands fumble for purpose, frantically searching for the velvet box in her bag. Avarie intentionally omits the part about stealing it. "I didn't know we had this power, Mairya. Why did no one tell me this?"

"What power do you speak of?"

"The scales," Avarie stammers. "Touching an extracted scale shows you the merperson's last moments before the scale was removed."

"Preposterous. I've never heard of that." Mai folds her arms, looking every bit in disbelief.

"Have you ever touched an extracted scale?"

"Absolutely not! How could I? Only vile humans extract scales."

"Then you'll need to touch this." Avarie drops the bag at her feet and slips out of her boots. She rolls her pants up past her ankles. With bare toes, she inches forward past the shoreline and into the sea. The water licks at her ankles and she stops there, not wanting to venture further since swimming remains an unmastered skill for her. Avarie crouches down to meet Mairya at eye level. "Take this box. But I warn you, it will not be pleasant to see."

Mai stares down the box, like she's willing it to open on its own accord. When that doesn't work, she reaches out cautiously, wet but soft hands clenching the object and touching Avarie.

Avarie feels a small, magnetic pull when they accidentally brush hands. It's nothing compared to simple eye contact with Lahna. The sensation fades.

Mairya toys with the box, turning it in her hands until she asks, "Whose scale is this, Ava?"

" . . . Aalto's. Open the box. Please."

Mai mouths a few words, perhaps a prayer, but it's difficult to read her lips despite the moonlight. With a deep breath, she lifts open the top, revealing the scale.

"Mother of the Sea . . ." Recognition shines in her eyes. She knows. No one else in all of Merelani had dark scales like Aalto. Their father's are dark too, yet with a red undertone. Aalto's scales were the same inky black as the night sky. Mairya touches the scale and her face goes blank. Her eyes look faraway, seeing nothing and everything she is meant to see at the same time. Is this how Avarie had looked to the merchant? No wonder he had wanted her to leave his table.

Five seconds is all it takes before Mairya returns. She backs away from the shore and bursts into tears. Avarie understands completely. Watching a loved one in danger with no ability to save them is gut-wrenching.

"He suffered. He must have suffered so much," Mai weeps. Avarie's mood further wilts, like a flower starving for water. They both love Aalto, there's no mistaking that.

A stupid idea ventures into Avarie's head, since before there was a crush . . . they had been good friends. She wades deeper into the water, walking on her toes to remain above sea level. But Avarie's still too far away. She continues moving forward until she's gasping frantic and struggling on her toes with the water at her neck.

"What are you doing? You're going to drown!"

"Shhh . . . I won't if you hold me. If we hold each other." Avarie extends her arms to Mairya, waiting for her to accept the invitation. She wishes she'd comply quicker. It's a frightening feeling to have water caressing your neck when you can't swim.

A humorless laugh runs from between Mai's lips as she wraps her arms around Avarie. "This won't last long. I can't hold you forever."

"It'll last however long it's meant to last, Mai."

"Find him. You have to make him pay. Make him regret what he did. Go back to that Corridor and demand to know who the merchant's vendor is." Mairya's words are cold against her ear. But when Avarie shivers it's because she's confirmed what she must do.

The only way to stop the pain, the seaquakes, the only way to end her guilt, is to kill the man.

Something pinches at the back of Avarie's mind, but she ignores it. Revenge is the answer, and she's finally made her choice.

"I *will* kill him, I promise. But I can't return to the Corridor, Mai."

"And why not?" Mairya's lips curl at her ear. "Don't tell

me you're too scared to finish the job, Avarie. You'll be queen soon. I'll be queen soon, and I will *not* be the consort to a coward."

Avarie sucks in a breath, simultaneously shrugging out of their embrace. She increases the distance between them. *Consort to a coward?* "You cannot speak to me like that. You *will not* speak to your queen like that."

Maybe it's this human body. Or maybe she's found the confidence in herself that she had admired in Lahna. Maybe it's her brewing rage at witnessing Aalto's last moments. Whatever it is, she's not going to let *anyone* disrespect her again.

Avarie returns to the shore, drenched and hot with indignation. Out of respect for Mai and the friendship they shared, Avarie had tried to dismiss it, but it's clear her entitlement knows no bounds. Bargain or no bargain, Mairya has no right to claim Avarie as though she were merely some tool to get the crown. Mai's desperation for the throne isn't settling well in Avarie's stomach.

"Apologies, my queen." Mairya's head bows low, feigning respect, but Avarie swears she can just barely glimpse the mermaid's hands curling into fists beneath the water.

With a deliberate tone of annoyance, Avarie says, "I can't go back to the Corridor, Mairya. I stole the scale. I'd be an idiot to show my face there ever again."

"What if he comes after you?"

"He can't. He prematurely sold Aalto's scale without his supplier's permission. Plus, he doesn't know where I'm staying."

"Then what are you going to do? Actually, why didn't you just buy the scale? I gave you plenty of currency."

Mairya's questions are rapid-fire. Avarie tries to keep up, but her resolve is slipping. She can tell by way her shoulders fall, the way her gaze seems magnetized to the sand instead of

Mairya. The way her hand is itching to spin the sun on her ring finger.

Avarie *cannot* share that she bought Lahna a present. Watching the unamused squint on Mairya's face, she knows that's absolutely the wrong path to venture down.

"Maybe . . . maybe the card players will know something." Avarie gives in to her urge to spin the sun ring.

"So, you're relying on the candor of shady men?"

Avarie looks into Mairya's eyes, instantly saddened by the doubt in them. "Lahna Hart is well known around here. I'm certain she'll know something."

"Hart? Your land-dweller friend," Mai states dryly.

"I'll get him. No matter what it takes," asserts Avarie.

"Just promise me you'll be careful." It would have warmed Avarie's heart to hear those words if she hadn't just heard all the doubt and displeasure Mairya threw her way.

"Yeah. Show the scale to my father. Keep it from my mother. I don't want to break her heart again."

"I'll share it with my mother too. Maybe she can explain why we're seeing these memories." If the Enchantress couldn't explain it, Avarie doesn't know who can.

"Take care of yourself, Mairya." Avarie can't describe it, but this time their parting feels final.

Like something had *broken*.

Trust.

Friendship.

Something.

Whatever happens between them the next time they meet, Avarie's certain it won't bring them closer. They will only drift further apart.

Avarie leaves the beach with a sense of purpose, and an overarching feeling of ominous confusion and fatigue.

Chapter Twenty-Three

L ater that evening, after she'd given her clothes a
chance to dry, Avarie knocks on Lahna's door. Not
even a full second passes after she opens the door,
and Lahna is already pulling Avarie into a tight embrace.

"How was your evening? Is it embarrassing to say that I
missed our time apart?" Lahna's smile is so hopeful, so
genuine.

Avarie doesn't have to question whether she believes her
at all.

She drops an appreciative kiss on Lahna's lips.

"It brought clarity. And no, I missed you too." Avarie reci-
procates the tightness of the hug. She holds on to Lahna like it
might be their last one.

"I'm glad. Alone time is important. Now, come in. I've got
some hot water going. The kettle should be ready to burst into
song any minute." Lahna takes her hand and leads Avarie to
the kitchen.

The kettle's voice rings in her ears, and Avarie welcomes
the association with Lahna's home, the noise somehow
calming her. She settles into a chair with a teacup in her hands,

watching Lahna pour water inside. They had grown unimaginably closer in such a short time. The unsung knowledge of Avarie's fleeting presence in Deniz produces a frown on her face.

"What's wrong? Not in the mood for tea?" Lahna gestures to the tin canister full of herb-filled sachets resting on the table.

"No . . . I'd love some tea. Can I try the chamomile and lavender blend tonight?" Her frown deepens, not that she wishes for it to do so. She just can't stop thinking about the Corridor. About her conversation with Mai. Avarie grabs a tea sachet and drops it into her mug. Lahna places the kettle on a thick towel then quietly sits beside her in the other chair.

"You saw something in the Corridor. Maybe I should have never told you about it." Lahna blows a gust of air over her steaming beverage.

"I'm thankful you told me. I'm just reeling from the memory of it all." Avarie does the same, blowing her tea, wishing to blow away all her problems.

"Do you mind sharing what you saw with me?" Lahna puts a comforting hand on Avarie's shoulder.

An internal debate develops within Avarie. How much can she tell Lahna without revealing who she is? Would it be a bad thing to tell her the truth? Lahna has compassion for the sea creatures she writes about. She became outraged when she saw the mermaid trapped in the tank. She has been every bit supportive of Avarie, even the stuff she disagrees with—playing the card game with those men, entering the Corridor.

Avarie resolves to tell her as much of the truth as she can.

"I saw the face of my brother's killer. I can't unsee it. I feel haunted by him."

Avarie's fingers drift to her shell necklace. It's blessedly cool right now. Despite this, she feels as though the pendant is searing her skin. She can still see Aalto's last moments playing before her eyes, his body in the foyer . . . the crack in the dome.

My fault.

Lahna's eyes widen. "Well, we must do something! Talk with Denizian lawmakers. They'll make sure the man is caught."

"I'm not from here, Lahna. I need to do things my own way."

Silence expands between them like a rift. Lahna meets Avarie's gaze with worried eyes of her own. For the first time, it seems as if she's run out of words.

"Tell me about your family, Lahna. I don't know much about them." A change of subject seems best at this point.

Lahna looks away, casting her eyes over to the wood-burning stove. "My mother died when I was six or seven. It was just me and my father until I couldn't stand it anymore. We're not close. His lifestyle . . . the family business—let's just say he disapproves of my writing just as much as I hate what brings him money. After selling a few books though, I can confidently say that I no longer need his dirty money." She chews on her lower lip before eyeing Avarie.

Avarie ruminates on her words. All she had were palace riches bestowed upon her. She knows nothing of working hard, paving a new way for oneself through rock-solid foundation. Lahna truly is amazing.

"And your stepmother?"

"Which one?" Lahna cackles. "I've had a host of surrogate mothers that hate me but love my father's money. The latest certainly wins *world's worst stepmother.*"

"Why do you say that?"

Lahna's lips curl up. "She keeps trying to fix me. She gave me bleach to even my skin tone. As if my vitiligo is contagious and not simply something that makes me unique."

Avarie's jaw drops. "I'm so sorry, Lahna."

"Not your fault. My father told her to never say things like that to me again. So, there's that . . ." She shrugs, but Lahna's face looks ready to crumble.

Avarie can't stand it. "I have a gift for you," she blurts out. Before Lahna can reply, Avarie races to the living room, nearly clipping her ankle on a table as she dives onto the couch for her bag. With care, she removes the tiny moonflower plant and speedwalks back to the kitchen. When she nears the door, Avarie shouts, "Close your eyes!"

As she passes through the door, Lahna says, "They're closed." Her long fingers cover her face. Avarie pulls them down with one hand and places the potted plant into them.

"Open." A giddy anticipation hits Avarie like unruly waves crashing ashore.

Her brown eyes open, and Lahna cries out in surprise. "This—this is a moonflower! How did you find this Avarie?" Her appreciative gaze grows tearful.

"I bought it in the Corridor. I didn't mean to make you cry." Avarie returns to the seat next to Lahna, worried.

"No, no, Avarie. These are happy tears. Thank you. I love it." Lahna blinks away her tears before saying, "You're amazing. I haven't had a thoughtful gift like this since my mother's inkwell pens. I can't even fully explain how much this means to me. Who—who are you?" Eyes shining, Lahna carefully places the moonflower on the table. "I'm starting to wonder what I did to have the privilege of meeting someone like you."

"And *I'm* grateful to have met someone like you. And pardon my language, but your stepmother fucking sucks. You deserve so much more." Anger flares in Avarie's chest at the pain she cannot wipe from Lahna's being.

"My father thought it was a misguided but nice gesture. The bleach, that is." Lahna's joke falls flat. Her attempt at a smile wobbles until it completely flattens. "We still argue from time to time. I'm *'hurting his business,'* he says."

Avarie almost slips up, ready to ask if the man she saw storming away from Lahna's cottage is her father. But that would expose her as a liar. She had already mentioned seeing no one at the time. Sensing that Lahna's returning to a less saddened state, Avarie ventures forward with her inquiry. She asks, "What business is your father in?" Maybe he can help find Aalto's killer.

"Illegal things. Shameful things . . . What about your family?"

The change in subject doesn't surprise Avarie. Lahna doesn't seem fond of her father, or the things he does for a living. Lahna possesses a moral compass that Avarie wishes she had, rejecting wrongs and welcoming rights with open arms. Maybe she can catch her father the next time he visits. Though, it's glaringly obvious that time is dwindling away.

"My father, Bruinen, I suppose he's a lot like yours in some ways. He's stern and he doesn't approve of a lot of things about me. I know he favored my late twin more than me, but I've accepted that long ago.

"My mother, her name is Cordelia, she . . . possesses the confidence of a queen and she loves immensely. I had never seen her break down until the day Aalto died. Aalto—" Avarie stares down at the mug of tea she's hardly touched. "I think we all lost a part of ourselves when Aalto died. My brother was . . . the perfect blend of our parents. My best friend.

"Our mom and dad were very protective of us. We grew up isolated, like you did. We didn't really have any other friends except Mairya. That's his . . . widow, I suppose you can call her. I think she's waiting for him to return. She's still clinging to . . . what could have been. And I suppose I understand that. Goddess—I miss him. It feels like there's a gaping hole in my heart sometimes."

"I'm sorry, Ava."

"Not your fault," she echoes Lahna's words from earlier.

"Still, I don't wish that pain on anyone. I hope you find your brother's killer. I hope he gets everything he deserves and more." Lahna leans over to hug Avarie. And like usual, Avarie melts against her.

"Thank you." For a moment they just stare at one another. Not ready to leave this moment behind. Avarie reaches up to remove the remaining moisture from Lahna's cheek. Then Lahna yawns, and Avarie realizes how tired the girl is. "Bedtime?"

"Bedtime. I'll see you in the morning, princess."

Avarie smiles, watching Lahna move from the chair and exit the kitchen. A yawn catches her too. She covers her mouth, drained from today's agenda. As Avarie heads to the guest room, her troubled feeling returns.

She needs to get in contact with Lahna's father. Given what she knows about him—his business, the way people in Deniz seem to fear him—Avarie figures he's the man she needs to talk to. She doesn't want to pressure Lahna into setting a meeting between them. She needs to find another way.

She settles under the duvet, heart weary and eyes drooping.

These are questions for the morning. She'll stress about them then.

Now accustomed to the sun waking her, Avarie is shocked when her eyes open to pitch blackness. Tiny, frantic knocks echo against the closed guest room door. Avarie sits up in bed but doesn't bother fumbling for her glasses on the nightstand. They wouldn't help much anyway. She can just make out the fuzzy outline of the door.

"Lahna?"

The door opens a crack but no light filters in. A dark shadow squeezes through the entrance.

"Lahna, is that you?" Her heart begins to pound as she grips the duvet cover.

"Avarie. It's me," the familiar voice speaks calmness to her rising urge to flee.

"What are you doing up so early?"

"I had a bad dream. About my father. Can I stay with you the rest of the night?" Though phrased as a question, Lahna is already moving across the room, sliding under the covers, and scooting next to Avarie.

Fatigue still has its claws in Avarie, so she awkwardly drapes an arm over Lahna and transitions back to sleep. The return to unconsciousness is easy, Lahna's warm body serving as a sleep aid stronger than any herb Avarie could ever take.

Chapter Twenty-Four

Avarie wakes up again, this time from Lahna lightly snoring. Each breath is accompanied by this musical trill that has Avarie nearly bursting into a fit of sleepy giggles. The fireplace only contains glowing embers. She's certain it's freezing out there though she's untouched by the cold. She snuggles closer into Lahna, basking in her warmth. They breathe in sync with the same ease as Avarie's tail treading through water. Cuddling with Lahna feels like a relaxing day in the Royal Garden.

A smile appears on Avarie's face. She could get used to this. Avarie wants to stay in this moment for as long as she can, to remember this feeling forever. The warmth between their bodies is a fire unlike anything Avarie has ever experienced; a heat that spurs her desire to protect Lahna. To hug her, and to kiss her. To be with her for as long as she will have Avarie in her life.

Avarie trails a curious hand down Lahna's thigh then back up to her ribcage, entranced by the patterns on her skin. She wonders what it might look like if Lahna were to have a tail.

What color would her scales be? Would they also have the same, mesmerizing patterns? Lahna's breathing hitches. She snuggles closer to Avarie.

Avarie's skin puckers up like gooseflesh, though not from the cool morning air. Uncertainty swells inside her as Avarie ponders what to do next.

"Good morning," Lahna says, voice thick with sleep. She twists over to face Avarie. Their eyes meet. The air between them seems to come alive. Avarie forgets how to speak as her gaze travels from Lahna's eyes, down to her nose, and her full lips.

As if reading Avarie's mind, Lahna murmurs, "You have beautiful lips, Avarie."

Avarie nods slowly, as if agreeing that she, in fact, does have beautiful lips. Something she'll agonize over the embarrassment later. But for now, her own eyes lock onto Lahna's.

Their lips meet, banishing what little distance lay between them. The kiss is easy.

Natural.

Avarie's hand goes to frame Lahna's face. Her lips feel softer than the duvet, and Avarie could melt to pieces being kissed by them—especially when Lahna places her fingers on the side of Avarie's neck, her touch light but sure, her thumb brushing across Avarie's chin.

Lahna pulls away for the briefest of moments. Avarie manages to resist the urge to pout, stopped short by the look in Lahna's eyes. Like she's seeing Avarie clearly for the first time, or like she's wondering how she could ever believe they were only destined for friendship. Avarie's beginning to wonder the same thing . . . because the simplest connection, the lightest of touches between their lips feel enough to burn Deniz to the ground.

Lahna leans forward again, kissing Avarie more deeply this

time. The emotion behind it seems to stretch further than the vastness of the Merelani Sea. In response, Avarie grabs a fistful of Lahna's curls. She doesn't know what being struck by lightning feels like, but she imagines it's a lot like this. Avarie doesn't dare to extinguish this divine, prickling heat.

Lahna rolls over, carefully pressing Avarie's body into the pillows and sheets below them. The linen smells exactly like Lahna. The human is *everywhere* and holding Avarie's senses hostage—something she doesn't mind at all. Her knees push Avarie's legs apart, creating a home for herself between them. Almost instinctively, Avarie invites Lahna closer.

Their kisses transition from sweet to feverish.

Avarie finds herself caressing the supple skin beneath Lahna's clothing. And Lahna expertly rakes her fingers up Avarie's thigh, one hand pinning Avarie's right wrist to the pillow beneath her head. Avarie forgets how to breathe when Lahna leans in again, her mouth trailing featherlight kisses down Avarie's neck.

Avarie's eyes flutter closed in pure bliss. They remain unopened as she struggles between kisses to speak. "Lahna. Lahna I—"

"I know, Ava. What do you want to do?" Avarie's not perturbed by Lahna's interruption at all. The breathy whispers against Avarie's neck make her long for more attention to her lips.

Lahna pulls away, breathing heavily and searching Avarie's face.

All the words that Avarie wants to say gets caught in her throat. Oh, how she wants—wants to know what happens in the stories after the scene fades to black, wants to experience the in-between before the two characters wake up wrapped in each other's arms—but she doesn't know how to ask for that.

"I need to hear your words, Avarie," Lahna encourages. "What do you want? I'm fine with whatever you want to do."

Lahna slips her hand from Avarie's wrist to interlock their fingers. Her gaze is kind, doting. It relaxes the tension in Avarie's throat.

"Lahna—I want ... to experience you. All of you." Did she really just say that? She did. Avarie is changing, a boldness she never had before finds its way into her vocabulary with a swiftness she never expected. She doesn't regret it either. Nothing could make her regret her impassioned plea.

Lahna smiles, her eyes darkening in such a confident, assertive fashion that Avarie shivers; a newly heated yearning swells inside her, ready to engulf her entire being.

Neither of them says another word, speech transforming into a writhing melody of tender sounds and whimpers Avarie will never forget.

"MY BROTHER WAS RIGHT ABOUT YOU," AVARIE SAYS while nestled into the crook of Lahna's neck. Avarie notes that this is the first time she's joked about Aalto, and it's liberating.

Lahna trails her pointer finger along the length of Avarie's spine, pulling her back to their conversation. "How so?"

"L.H. Sirene did end up leading me down a path of debauchery."

"Is that a complaint?" Lahna's hand pauses, tapping her spine in a teasing manner.

"No. Not at all."

Her hand continues its achingly slow venture down Avarie's back. "Good. But I will say that L.H. Sirene is rather tame. It's Lahna Hart that needs worrying about. Because when I set my eyes on a girl, and I know that her eyes are set on me, there's no limit to the debauched actions I'm willing to commit."

Avarie's stomach lurches with anticipation.

Lahna pulls away to meet her eyes. "Can I show you my favorite?" The human's hands travel suspiciously close to Avarie's thick, inner thighs.

"Yes—" Avarie interrupts herself, smashing her already swollen lips to Lahna's.

Lahna laughs against her mouth, giving Avarie pause.

Wait, did she come on too strong? She's desperate. She must look *so* desperate right now. Avarie squeezes her eyes shut, hoping to disappear into thin air. Instead, she attempts to shrink away.

But Lahna clutches her tighter. "Don't run from me. I love the confidence. I just want to ask you another question first."

Avarie's body relaxes but she still won't meet her gaze. "Ask away." The response sounds muffled since Avarie refuses to remove her face from Lahna's chest.

"How was it for you?" *Oh.* Well, it was one of the best things Avarie has ever experienced. It was like cracking open oyster after oyster until finally discovering one with the perfect pearl inside. The thrill, the *satisfaction* is unmatched.

"Um, it was good. Great. Fantastic. Couldn't ask for a better f-first time."

"I'm glad." Lahna caresses the side of Avarie's face. "I could tell."

She could tell? The seaquakes might as well take Avarie out now because the mortification coursing through her veins is far too much.

"You—you could tell?"

"Just some first-time shyness. Different from your regular timidity."

"I'll be candid, I had no idea where this conversation was going. I'm glad it turned to something good before I catastrophized my mind away . . . how was it for you?"

"Amazing."

"No complaints?" Avarie says with an air of hopeful jest.

"Every box checked."

"I could tell that *wasn't* your first time."

"No"—Lahna admits, and before Avarie's mind tries going to war again, she finishes with—"but I'm certain that it was my favorite."

Hours later, with the rising sun as a witness, someone's stomach growls, causing the two lovers to break away in a fit of laughter.

"Sounds like it's time for breakfast," Lahna muses. She rips the duvet from their bare bodies, earning a surprised shout from Avarie. Frigid air swiftly usurps all the warmth they had built up overnight.

"It's cold! Put it back," she begs.

Lahna chuckles but replaces the blanket back on Avarie as she slips out of bed. She plants a kiss on Avarie's forehead, her face screwed up in pure amusement.

Avarie's eyes hungrily graze Lahna's bare frame, drinking in every beautiful patch of multi-hued melanin. Was Lahna truly hers? Could such temptation even be claimed? Avarie desperately wants to be hers as well. Should she say this aloud? Or is it obvious that their once linear paths are now entwined and twisted together, for better or for worse?

Lahna walks to Avarie's side of the disheveled bed and drops a tender kiss onto her lips. "Stay warm here. I'll deliver breakfast to you momentarily."

Avarie pulls the blanket up, so that only her eyes and forehead are visible. Her muffled, "Thank you," is caught in the covers, but Lahna manages to understand her.

Lahna throws on her discarded tunic then opens the bedroom door. Avarie watches her walk out barefoot to greet the rest of the coldness in the cottage. She has no idea how Lahna's feet can withstand the chill.

Once Avarie hears the familiar cacophony of ingredients becoming a meal, she rolls over, thoughts immediately on the last few hours. She touches a finger to her lips in wonder. So that was what a real kiss—what *it* felt like. She could do that again, over and over, in this lifetime and the next. Avarie cannot even begin to reimagine what happened shortly after their lips touched. She smooshes her face in the duvet in a fit of timid glee. The latter part of their morning surely would have left Avarie with regret, had it been with anyone beside Lahna.

Not wanting to waste time away from her, Avarie jumps from the bed, eager to get dressed as quickly as possible. But something about the idea of being wrapped in Lahna's scent entices her to pull open the armoire and slip on clothing from there instead. After, she rifles through her bag, tugging on a pair of socks and slipping into her jacket. Her fingers graze against a sharp object—the knife meant for her brother's killer. Her elated mood sours. She will have to use it soon . . . her kingdom demands that she does.

She drops the bag to the floor. Although she's wearing socks, brisk air encircles her toes. She wiggles them to shift more warmth there. The knife remains in her hand. Its sharpness spurs a flutter in Avarie's chest.

Could she do this?

Could she kill a man?

What exactly will this revenge solve?

A loud, uncharacteristic banging sends Avarie's focus to the closed bedroom door. Something must be wrong. Whatever early morning post-coital brain fog she's experiencing lifts. She walks to the door, though her legs shake a little. Did

Lahna break something? If anything, Avarie was the clumsy land dweller, not Lahna.

"Get out!" Lahna screeches at the top of her lungs.

Avarie's hold on the knife tightens as she rips open the door, running toward the noise at a breakneck pace.

Chapter Twenty-Five

Avarie follows the sound of screaming to the living room. Her necklace burns her skin, so much so, that a hiss slips from her mouth. From the hallway, she sees Lahna struggling with a large man at the front door. His clenched hands dig into her shoulders as he directs a stare at Lahna, thus shielding his face. Though tall, Lahna's strikingly shorter in comparison to the intruder.

Anger pulsates in Avarie's heart as he shoves Lahna backward and she falls onto her backside and hands. Then the man locks eyes with Avarie and the world and its surrounding chaos stills to a dull, inconsequential hum.

It's him.

Slicked-back black hair.

Muddy eyes.

Brown skin.

Woven, tattered strings at his coat's collar resemble the dreaded symbol she has been searching for this whole time: a circle encompassing a broken oyster with a missing pearl.

Aalto's murderer.

In a fit of rage, instinctive, rivaling her father's, Avarie runs forward with the knife clutched in her hand. She sidesteps Lahna on the floor and sinks the weapon into the man's shoulder blade. She wanted his heart. But anger makes her graceless, imprecise. The man roars, an anguished pain that would have unsettled Avarie had her own blind rage not taken over. Blood blooms like a moonflower, spreading across his white shirt.

This is what she was here for.

This is for Aalto.

Before the man can remove the blade from his shoulder, Avarie rips the knife away. They both shout. Her hand aches from how intensely she's clutching the knife. But she won't let go. She can't—not until he's lying on the floor like Aalto's lifeless body in the Grand Foyer.

His lifeless, scaleless body.

All she can see is Aalto.

She'd pluck every pore from this man's skin if she could.

Now, Avarie will aim for his heart, just as the Enchantress had said, and she will not miss. Ragged breaths escape her lips in short bursts. She raises her arm, ready to slash again.

Lahna's screams cut through the air. "Avarie, stop!"

Confusion stalls Avarie's attack, allowing ample time for the man to shove Avarie in the chest and run out the door.

Fury twists his face into a gruesome expression as he clutches his bleeding shoulder. "I don't know who you are, but you'll regret this. My men will not hesitate to hunt you down," the stranger says, spitting venom and saliva Avarie's way. He sizes her up before trudging off into the forest.

This isn't over, Avarie thinks.

With misplaced outrage, Avarie stares down at Lahna, rubbing the spot where the man had aggressively pushed her. "I should have killed that man. He deserves death." Avarie's conscience is overwhelmed by her burning wrath. She can't understand why in the hell Lahna would defend the man who attacked her.

Tears brim in Lahna's eyes, quelling the enmity ready to surmount all parts of Avarie's reasoning. She falls to her knees, eye level with Lahna. Avarie scans the girl's body for any cuts or bruises. Thankfully, she finds none. Even with an immeasurable anger pulsing through Avarie's veins, she needs to ensure Lahna is okay.

With unbridled agony, Lahna whispers, "It's like I don't even know you—h-how could you—you can't just kill him?"

Avarie scowls at her with indignation. She has one task in Deniz, and it has just walked away freely. But she won't let that happen again. No matter what Lahna says.

"Why not? Why can't I kill him?" Avarie responds, her words as sharp as the stained knife dripping blood on her hands and shirt.

"He's my father, Avarie."

Chapter Twenty-Six

A chilling mix of horror and dismay washes over Avarie. Her voice cracks as she tries to speak. "That man killed my brother. He must pay in blood."

Lahna's trembling lips part, "I-impossible, he—My father would never—he. . ."

"I'm not human, Lahna." Avarie looks to the floor, at a loss for words. She could have led this conversation in multiple directions, but she had a feeling that no matter where she steered, Lahna would've been upset. Telling the truth doesn't breathe any relief into their situation. If anything, it stifles it.

Lahna's brows scrunch up. She stares at Avarie for a long moment. It feels like an eternity. "Human? Then what—" She interrupts herself, eyes widening in steadily growing understanding. "*Oh.* The way you stated that Adahy is chilly year-round—I just thought you didn't want to tell me where you were really from. But Adahy is a desert, Avarie. Any human from that village would've know that." Lahna slowly claps a hand over her mouth. "The way you reacted to that poor mermaid in the tank—are you truly what I think you are?"

"Yes," Avarie responds, her voice barely above a whisper.

Lahna grows quiet, disbelief playing over her features.

"I'm sorry, Lahna. I really care about you. But I can't return home without taking what is owed to Merelani. I must avenge Aalto's death. Our kingdom could be destroyed by seaquakes if I don't."

"What? I don't understand. Seaquakes?" Lahna reaches forward to touch her, but Avarie stiffens. Lahna's hand falls.

"I have to take what is owed."

"If you do this, I'll never forgive you. Please, just—" Lahna stares at her pleadingly, her eyes begging Avarie not to kill the man that caused Avarie, her family, her people so much pain. "—don't."

Avarie's hands harden into fists. "So, you'd rather my kingdom be destroyed? That I spare a murderer who will undoubtedly jump at the chance to kill my kind again? That's what you want me to do? Your father doesn't deserve mercy. He deserves death. And now I feel so stupid wasting my time with you—"

Avarie winces, desperately wishing that she could take back her words. Because it's so far from the truth. Avarie cannot imagine her journey through Deniz without Lahna. She never would've learned what it felt like to be loved by someone she cherishes.

But the damage is done; no enchantment can wind back time.

Lahna's face collapses like a fallen stack of cards. Tears pool in her eyes and she looks away, refusing to meet Avarie's gaze.

"I didn't mean that. You have to believe me. You are not a waste of time."

In fact—Avarie realizes—they're inconveniently perfect for each other.

It is time and circumstance that is being unfair to them.

Lahna meets her gaze now, and her quick words are sharper than Avarie's bloody knife.

"I have to *believe* you? You used me. Was sleeping with me just something to check off your list of land escapades? I told you about my mother. I never talk about my mother. Did you consider my feelings in any of this? Or does nothing matter, as long as you get what you want?" Lahna rakes a section of hair out of her face. Avarie worries that her hands will take strands with them.

Lahna continues, "And what you want is to take away the only parent I have left in this world. You want me to feel the loss of a loved one—just like you—you want me to be miserable and be out for revenge." Her dark eyes are daggers. "Just. Like. You."

Lahna's words sting, but they ring true. What did Avarie expect? That Lahna would still want her after she learned the truth? After Avarie married Mai? That Lahna would have settled for only seeing her from a distance every ten years, if at all?

Avarie desperately wishes the world would stop turning, for their differences to fade away. "I didn't mean to use you. And I wasn't plotting for us to sleep together. That moment is so special to me," Avarie admits, her eyes burning with tears.

"Intention versus impact," Lahna says curtly.

"What?" Avarie's voice is nothing more than a pathetic squeak.

"You can have all the best, naive intentions in the world. But that doesn't absolve you of the negative impact you leave on others. You're still responsible for the outcome, Avarie. Good or bad. Do you not get that? Do you not understand?" Shakily, Lahna stands, fists balled and hands vibrating with indignation.

For a second, Avarie braces herself to be hit—and immediately, she feels horrible that she did. After all, she's the violent one. *She's* the one with a knife.

"Do you think this is easy for me? Lying to you? Taking a

life? Do you think this is something I would have chosen to do on my own?" Avarie rises to a standing position as well, eyes locked on the open front door.

"You're playing the victim again. Take responsibility for the shit you've brought into my world. I keep to myself. I haven't liked a girl in so, *so* long. All I wanted was to live peacefully and write books about the sea—not to develop feelings for a mermaid who's fine using my heart as collateral to fulfill her murderous plans."

Avarie's stomach twists. Is this what it feels like to be seasick? She clutches her abdomen and swipes a tear away with her free hand. Her voice is warped, like she's swallowed jagged coral. But she pushes through to say, "I'm sorry. I didn't think about the impact. I wish things were better, that neither of us was caught up in this. But I swear to you, my feelings are real. I —I just don't have a choice in any of this." Thoughts of pulling Lahna close sprint through her mind. Then she remembers the blood on her hands. The knife at her side.

"We always have a choice." Lahna glares at her.

"As a queen who has the needs of Merelani on my shoulders, I don't get to have a choice."

"Get out, Avarie. Get out of my house." Lahna refuses to look at her, shoulders shaking with what must be anger and grief.

Avarie reaches for Lahna, one final time. "Please—"

But Lahna jerks away, her tears falling freely. She says, voice broken, "Just get out. I don't want to see you ever again."

Less than an hour ago, they were entwined in bed, laughing, cuddling. And now, Avarie and Lahna are absolutely nothing.

Stumbling and barefoot, Avarie takes the escape Lahna offers her, rushing into the thick fog outside as sobs stab her chest.

It's all so unfair.

Her kingdom is falling apart.

Lahna hates her.

And nothing she does will bring Aalto back.

Avarie's impaired vision leads her down a twisting and distressed path to the shore. She doesn't know where else to go. She shakes with heartache and a host of other emotions she has no time to process.

Lahna's father is a murderer.

Aalto's murderer is Lahna's father.

Lahna will never forgive her when she kills him.

Avarie must speak to Mairya. To return a semblance of order to her day's sickening start. The dense fog functions as a shelter from prying eyes. The heavy mist clings to her bare skin like wet sticky paste. Avarie's toes dig into the sand for refuge, slowly rediscovering the early morning chill now that her breathing has slowed. She realizes the knife is still clasped tightly in her hand.

"Mairya, Mairya . . . I need you." Tears fall from Avarie's eyes like drops from storm clouds as her hands land on the pier's wooden floorboards. The wood fastened into the ground sways haphazardly with the breeze. There's a rumbling —an anguished rumbling rising above the water that can only belong to the Sea Goddess.

In the distance, what must be Lahna's voice carries to Avarie. Just as she's about to look over her shoulder, Mairya pops above the surface with wide, concerned eyes.

"What's wrong? You only call to me at night. Something has happened." Mairya's dark eyes try to search Avarie's but she won't meet them.

"Everything's wrong. I don't know if I can do this anymore."

"Wait, wait, wait," Mairya coos. "Tell me. Whatever it is, we can fix it. I promise."

Avarie rubs her eyes and finally meets Mai's gaze. "I didn't mean to develop feelings for Lahna. I tried not to. But I did. And her father. Her father . . ."

"Yes," she says with an impatient undertone.

"Her father is the man that killed Aalto. I can't kill him. She'll hate me forever." Avarie doesn't need to be underwater to drown. She is already drowning in the bleakness of this entire situation. "And what will his death solve anyway? How could the Goddess ask us to spill blood to wash away a tragedy? What will that do except inspire more humans to hunt us?"

"Oh Avarie, never fall in love with a land girl." Mairya looks disappointed. Which isn't at all what Avarie expected to see—and it doesn't match her next actions.

Mairya pulls herself onto the rickety pier, a pained expression taking over her features as she sits beside Avarie. She bends over, holding herself and shaking a little. Gasps escape from her mouth. But she sits up, spine straight and tail flicking in the open air.

"What are you doing Mai? You're hurting yourself."

"Don't worry about me. Though it feels like my scales are on fire. Matter fact—" She plucks a loose scale from her right side and throws it into the sea. "That should buy me a few more minutes. I think you could use a hug." She tries to smile through the discomfort. Before Avarie can respond, Mairya reaches over to hold her close.

Avarie leans into the touch. "I just don't know what to do."

Mai leans back to kiss Avarie on the cheek before returning to the hug. "It'll be alright."

"How?" Avarie croaks. She drops the knife, pushing it away from them. A violent wind picks up, blowing their hair in a frenzy.

Mairya's right hand opens, and a tiny black bottle rests in

the curve of her palm. She says between ragged breaths: "Come home early."

Mai rubs where her left thigh would be if she were human.

Avarie should stay on land to think this through, figure things out. She can't run. Flee. That's all she has done her whole life. Too afraid of anything. Too afraid to speak up. Just, too afraid.

"I think I need to stay. I don't know what I'm going to do, but I can't run anymore, Mai. When things get tough, I flee. I can't do that anymore."

Mairya's expression clouds for a moment. Then her eyes become almost hollow, unfeeling. She flicks away the bottle's top and shoves Avarie down on the pier with a strength Avarie never knew she possessed. Before Avarie's mind can even form a response, the mermaid pries her lips open, pouring the liquid into her mouth. The taste is vile. Avarie gags, and to her dismay, Mairya throws her lips onto Avarie's mouth.

But it's not a kiss. It's not kind or loving. It's cruel. Peculiar—like the one in Avarie's reading nook days ago—and like it did previously, a fatigue tries to strangle away Avarie's awareness. Her calves begin to tingle, the feeling crawling its way up to her thighs. With heavy-lidded eyes, she stares at Mai.

"What the hell did you—"

"Avarie! Where are you?" Confusion racks her tired mind. Is she losing it? Lahna cannot be calling out to her.

"Lahna?" With a lot of effort, Avarie whips her head over her shoulder, searching. And afraid. Afraid that she'll never see Lahna again after parting on horrible terms. Then a bright, blinding light emanates from her legs. Avarie squeezes her eyes shut at the same time she feels Mairya shoving her off the pier. She sinks, the light guiding her way down as her hair plumes upward in the opposite direction.

Where is Mairya?

The brilliant light fades, leaving Avarie with a tail and

ripped pants that continue their journey to the seafloor. But she fights through her fatigue, swimming to the top with urgency. Where is Mairya? She grasps onto the pier like Mairya did moments ago and lifts herself up halfway, just enough to see but not enough to cause any pain. Her chin collides with two legs instead of a tail. Avarie's arms give out, no match for whatever enchantment Mairya's placed on her.

She falls back into the water just as Mairya is peering down at her. She upturns the now empty black bottle and flashes Avarie a devious grin.

"You can't do this . . ." Avarie's voice fades. She's weakening. But she doesn't need an answer. She knows exactly what has happened.

Mairya saved some of Avarie's potion. She's going to use it to find Lahna's father. But how long can she remain on land with the amount she took?

"I'm the daughter of a sea witch. I can do anything, my queen." Mairya scoots backward awkwardly, grabs the bloody knife, then comes to a wobbling stance. She saunters inexpertly on the pier, eyes on the shoreline.

"You can't kill him!" Avarie shouts, but she feels miles away from Mairya. Her voice sounds strange to her, and she can hardly keep her eyes open.

"I won't kill him." The determined look in Mairya's eyes does little to inspire confidence in her words.

"You won't?" Avarie's head is racked with heavy confusion.

"I won't. I'm going to take his heart instead."

Avarie marinates on her words for a moment until realization hits her like a loaded wagon. Her heart sinks to the depths below.

"Don't do this . . . I'm the queen—I forbid it." Avarie's demand is full of desperation. Her limbs are growing heavier, and she has to fight against slipping deeper into the sea.

Mairya peers into the depths of water behind Avarie, ignoring her outright.

"Guards, please escort Queen Avarie back to her chambers. She's had a trying time on land and deserves rest."

Avarie doesn't look behind to see the quickly emerging guards. She jerks in their grasp, but it only manifests as a slight twitch of her arms. Her vision grows dark. Her skin heats up. And suddenly, Avarie realizes that she never had a chance. Because even without Mairya's damned kiss, her anxious heart will have pushed her into unconsciousness anyway.

As she's pulled closer to the ruins of the palace, her head slumps to the side, her breath ragged, but she swears she hears Lahna say, "Avarie, where are you?"

Unease settles into Avarie's bones when she hears— "Lahna? I'm right here"—knowing for certain that she had said nothing.

Then she faints.

Chapter Twenty-Seven
MAIRYA

Her vision is dreadful. She can scarcely make out the shapes and shadows before her. Somehow, it seems to amplify the rest of her senses.

Mairya's nose wrinkles in disgust. Deniz smells vile. A vast contrast from the lovely, familiar scent of Merelani. It must be the stench of humans. But another smell invades her nostrils, something pungent, musky. Perhaps the fur from an unwashed animal? The latter scent seems far away. Good. There is no way she can outrun any land creature.

Oh, how she loathes this human world.

Mairya can't conceive the smallest bit of understanding for Avarie's obsession. Nothing about it seems worth leaving the sea for.

The wooden floorboards of the pier dig into her heels, scratching against her tender skin. The biting wind makes her shiver. She wraps both of her arms around her chest to seal out the cold, and to somewhat cover her nude body.

A lingering fire still exists where she plucked her scale off. Mairya grimaces. She had always prided herself in being pure, never marring her body by hopping ashore. Until now. Though unsteady, she walks with the dignity of a queen.

A true queen.

Unlike Avarie.

Avarie was too kind. Too meek. A precursor to Merelani's downfall, if Mairya allows it. Their home is already in ruins. The market and palace have remained closed for days. She knows who Avarie gets her delicate nature from. Her mother. Mairya can't recall the last time she had a coherent conversation with Cordelia. The few words Mairya was able to speak only resulted in tears and the former queen sealing herself away in her chambers.

She has grown tired of Avarie's little crush on the land dweller too—she was willing to look past it, if only Avarie could have done her damn job. It's one thing for her eyes to wander to another merwoman. But a human? Insulting beyond measure. Ava let her feelings get the best of her. But this all works out in Mairya's favor. She'll bring honor to her kingdom *and* rid herself of the human nuisance in one fell swoop.

Their shared kiss in the reading nook sowed the roots of her plan, giving her the opportunity to sample Avarie's voice. The original plan took a turn. She did not administer the full potion to Avarie, hoping that she'd transform while still on land. Avarie would have never made it home then. Mairya would reign as the sole queen; she and her mother would fix the 'lack of an heir' part later. They would have to. No merperson in Merelani is eligible to be her mate.

But things rarely go as planned.

Sand slips between the crevices of her toes, the strange sensation making one of her eyes twitch. And why aren't these walking appendages the same length as her fingers? Seems like a disadvantage. Mairya huffs, all of this is so overwhelming—the weather, the sounds, her new body. But also *under-*

whelming . . . what does Avarie love about any of this? For a brief moment, she is astounded by the way Avarie so easily adapted to this world. But the feeling is fleeting.

Avarie had one job—kill Aalto's murderer. Though others have been taken before, the Mother of the Sea determined his death was the last straw. What remains puzzling is how Avarie was chosen to avenge him. Why wasn't she, his wife-to-be, asked? Because they deem Mairya as a nobody until she marries into royalty? . . . Yet she knows the power in her blood can make more than just Merelani's ground tremble. She is so much stronger than Avarie. So much more determined. How the hell could an omnipotent Goddess not see that? The whole situation is vexing, but perhaps Mairya is just not meant to understand the whims of a Goddess.

Still, Avarie was a horrible choice. The Mother of the Sea should have chosen someone who wasn't afraid to spill blood. Like Mairya.

She wasn't always this way; her malice did not grow overnight.

Mairya had always felt like an outsider—only important because her mother tricked the queen and king. No one truly wanted her in the palace. She could tell by the way the servants' mouths took on a displeased curve when she breezed into a room. By the way merchildren flinched with fear when she had attempted to make friends outside the palace. By the way her and her mother's living quarters had been shoved into a hidden area for few to see. It's their prejudice that shaped her into the merwoman she is today.

That's why she grew to love the Room of Enchantment; the potions were her friends. And there was a hidden passageway connecting their quarters to the Grand Foyer. Mairya used it many times as a child, peeking around the stairs to glimpse Cordelia playing with her twins. She hadn't needed to know about her mother's deal with Merelani's rulers to take a liking to Aalto. And the little glimmer in Avarie's eyes every time they looked at each other, amused her.

When she *did* learn of her betrothal to Aalto, she had hoped attitudes would shift. That merfolk would welcome her and her mother with open arms. But only in Aalto and Avarie's presence did things change. People were kind, they smiled. But when alone, everything was the same. Everyone looked at her like they did not want her to exist.

Mairya faces the woods, naked, a chill deep within the marrow of her bones. There is no way she'll be able to get close looking like this. Yet Mairya knows she lacks time. The drops of oarfish potion she ingested will only last a few hours, if she's lucky.

"Avarie?" Lahna calls out into the void again.

Mairya remains silent, trailing the voice like a trained hunter. She needn't strain her eyes, the human will lead her.

"Avarie, can we talk about this . . ." The voice shrinks, losing confidence. The blanket of fog troubles Mairya's vision, but she finds a tall moving shadow to careen toward. This must be Lahna.

The shadow recedes deeper into the forest, and Mairya follows silently. The rocky, uneven forest floor hurts her bare feet, but she pushes through. They pass a dilapidated cabin, eventually making it to an elaborate cottage.

Mairya sneers. It's a shame that, after today, the cottage's owner will be sacrificed to the Sea Goddess. Worry wades into her stomach. Avarie will hate her for this, but that is something she will deal with later.

Lahna enters through the cottage's front door and slams it behind her. Mairya searches the perimeter for another door or an open window. She peers into the kitchen but cannot see what the long hallway she finds will lead to. Creeping along, Mairya discovers an open bedroom window. She jiggles the windowpane up and slips inside with barely any noise.

The room was used recently. There are embers in the fireplace though it now lacks warmth. Bed covers and pillows are strewn about haphazardly. Mairya stalks toward the armoire and tugs it open. All the garb inside looks as though it will itch and constrict her sensitive flesh. She rejects the clothing inside, instead opting for a discarded heap of pants and a tunic near the closed bedroom door. Fully dressed, she searches for footwear. Peeking from underneath the bed, she spots a familiar pair of boots.

Avarie's.

Do these clothes belong to Avarie too?

Was the queen living here? For how long?

Mairya's ichor boils. Avarie is supposed to be hers now that Aalto is gone. She promised. Thinking of them sharing a bed makes her angrier than she has ever been. Sure, her heart will always belong to Aalto . . . but Mairya could have made it work with Avarie. For their kingdom, Avarie is the next best thing.

Avarie could have transformed while still ashore and died. *But* now that she has survived, a small, hopeful thought embeds itself in Mairya's head about them ruling together. Will Avarie be surprised to learn that Mairya hadn't actually bothered planning for their wedding since she didn't expect her to return home?

Sure.

She had burned the vows she had composed for Aalto, and Mairya couldn't find the energy to write new ones for Avarie. Those vows would have been diluted, dull like counterfeit Merelani jewels.

Cordelia was too sad to notice the lack of wedding preparations. When she wasn't locked away in her own chambers, she was wallowing in Aalto's. Meanwhile, Bruinen's intense anger flared like the seaquakes, roaring about his favorite child being gone. Ranting about what he'd do if he were still in charge. He would rage around the palace with uncontrolled fists, sometimes beating their Sea Goddess to the literal punch.

It was so easy to distract them from the truth. Neither of them had asked if she were sad, or angry. Her lies grew in number like a massive school of fish.

Mairya slips on Avarie's boots. They're a perfect fit. She moves through the house with as much strength and certainty as her new legs allow. Sobbing from the main room leads her forward.

A girl, facing away from Mairya, is crying into her hands on the floor with her feet folded underneath her body. She has curious-looking skin. Mairya's hand wielding the knife tightens. She stalks forward on tottering legs.

This is it.

It will all be over soon.

Without warning, Lahna stands up, eyes wiping furiously at her face, then disappears behind a swinging door.

Whoosh. Whoosh. Then the door's movements still.

Mairya frowns. She wants this over quickly. She can't imagine how painful it will be transforming back to her true self in this dry cottage, only to die an awful death as hundreds of her scales pop off one at a time. Mairya makes her way to the swinging door. She raises a hand to push the door open but an alarming bang on the front door nearly separates her spirit from her temporary human body. She stiffens, flattening herself between the wall and the door.

"Hello?" Lahna calls out. She pushes through the door and steps a few feet out.

"Open up. We're here. Where is she?" Orders a deep male voice. Her father?

Without much time to think, Mairya lunges through the swinging door, clasping a hand over Lahna's mouth and affixing the knife to her throat. Muffled screams try to escape through Mairya's hand, but that only makes her dig the knife deeper. A drop of blood runs down Lahna's throat.

Her larynx goes silent as her body freezes.

The man pounds on the door again.

Lahna's heartbeat pounds loud enough for Mairya to feel her pulse against her hand on the girl's throat. She shoves Lahna toward the backdoor.

Mairya clears her throat once before transforming her voice into one she is certain will further confuse the girl.

"Make any noise, Lahna, and I'll kill you."

Chapter Twenty-Eight

LAHNA

Lahna's fear intensifies at the sound of Avarie's voice. Why does she have a knife to her throat? It's the same one she plunged into her father's shoulder earlier. Mixed emotions flutter through her head, like the plot for unwritten manuscripts that rouse her in the dead of night.

But the hand around her throat feels different, and so devoid of the tenderness it had possessed during their intimate morning together . . . one that now seems like a lifetime ago, like an ancient fable instead of a real story. She walks to the backdoor, not wanting to upset this strange version of Avarie that is wobbling like she has noodles for legs and is gripping Lahna in the roughest of ways.

She wishes to call out to her father; this could be over in minutes. Lahna is certain he has the manpower and the cruelty to end whatever is happening. Yet a sinking feeling whispers to her that he'll only make things worse.

Despite all the harsh words they shared, Lahna could never hurt Avarie.

So she walks forward, stiffly, deep into the forest until the oppressive hand falls from her mouth onto her shoulder.

Avarie guides her forward and Lahna has a dreadful sense that they are heading to the shore.

The early morning fog thickens, it hangs low, hungry, wrapping them both in mist. The biting air nips at her exposed skin. She shivers in response. Avarie pushes her forward.

"Why are you doing this?" Lahna risks speaking, trying to appeal to the humanity she knows Avarie possesses. What her captor says next chills her blood.

"You're the one. You're the heart. I will kill you for my kingdom."

It is not only the unnerving words that give Lahna pause, but the sudden unfamiliarity of the voice. This can't be Ava. She never sounded like that. Not even during their intense conversation earlier this morning. Nausea brews in her stomach. Who is this woman holding her hostage? And why does Lahna get the impression that she and Avarie are after the same thing?

The Denizian shoreline comes into view. A fleeting memory of fishing with Avarie pops into Lahna's brain. She should have known this woman is not Avarie. She simply doesn't *feel* the same. The stranger pushes Lahna toward the old pier, a place she actively avoids since it's unsafe, and likely the spot where her mother had perished. But Lahna is already in so much danger that it no longer seems to matter.

Lahna's naked foot gets caught in one of the pier's many holes. She trips, falling forward, pressing the knife deeper into her skin. Blood flows freely from her neck as she cries out. The woman sighs heavily like she's annoyed, as if Lahna's injury has inconvenienced her.

Anger surges within Lahna and she uses it to swat the woman's hand away from her. She stumbles again but puts distance between them. Lahna turns around to view her captor.

Stranger she is indeed. Lahna had grown up all her life in Deniz. She knows when someone doesn't belong. Like Avarie, the stranger sticks out like an ethereal sore thumb. Lahna watches her willowy black hair blowing in the breeze and her manic eyes. She is wearing the clothing Avarie had worn . . . before Lahna had removed it.

Her eyes land on the stranger's hand still clasping the dripping knife and her shaking legs.

Lahna presses her fingers over her throat, attempting to staunch the bleeding. Her chest heaves, but she cannot catch her breath, and her exposed limbs grow increasingly colder by the minute.

Lahna manages a feeble string of dialogue. "Who are you?"

The girl laughs, haughty. "The future queen of Merelani. Any last words, land dweller?"

Merelani? She's a mermaid too?

Lahna takes an additional step backward, her heels teetering on the pier's edge. She is so close to slipping, but she can't think about that now. "And Avarie? Where is Avarie?" Lahna coughs into her other hand, glancing at it she sees her palm spattered with more red. Her legs feel like lead, she hunches over, lungs desperate for air. But she makes sure to keep her eyes on the girl.

"Does it matter? You'll never see her again. She was never yours, you know."

Lahna detects jealousy. She will use it to her advantage. In the distance, Lahna can see torches breaking up the compressed fog. A mob? Her father and his mermaid poachers are close. But they remain out of earshot. She needs to buy time. "I disagree. She gave me permission to hold her, to kiss her. And I offered the same in exchange. I think it goes without saying that we belonged to each other, even during our short time together."

The girl glowers, lowering the knife and closing the space

between them to get in Lahna's face. "She will love me. Only me. Like her brother did."

"You're Aalto's widow," Lahna digs further.

The woman's breath hurls in her face. "She—she talked about me?"

"Not by a long shot. I hardly know your name."

"My name's Mairya, you pathetic land dweller." Spit lands on Lahna's cheek.

The mob grows closer, the dancing fire from their torches become brighter. Lahna can make out the oval heads of the crowd, but the distance makes it difficult to discern facial features. She knows her father will be among them. He will choose violence, something Lahna has always disdained, but she has no other options at this point. If she can get Mairya to drop the knife, maybe, just maybe she can save them both.

"Avarie will never forgive you if you hurt me. You know that. Besides, do you truly want her, or do you just want what she has to offer?"

"What she has to offer is my birthright. Something you, a measly human could never understand." Mairya glares at her, pure hatred in her eyes. But Lahna can glimpse the smallest bit of regret too. Mairya blinks it away.

"If it's your birthright, why do you need Avarie to be queen?" Lahna coughs, spitting blood to the side. The wind picks up. It's sharp. Biting. Angry. Lahna and Mairya's voices strain to new heights, trying to be heard above it.

"You talk a lot for someone about to die."

"You talk a lot for someone threatening the life of a mermaid hunter's daughter," Lahna counters. She doesn't want to play that card, but it's the truth. For all their disagreements and fights, Lahna knows for certain that her father will protect his only daughter, whether or not he knows that Mairya isn't human. "It doesn't have to be this way. Humans and merpeople can work together. We can make a truce that benefits both groups. No one has to die. You have seaquakes, right? Maybe we can find a way to stop them. But that can't happen if you kill me and Avarie wants nothing to do with you. Let's stop the violence. Maybe this is just my stupid humanity trying to appeal to the kindness in you, but I really, *really* don't want to be without Avarie. I don't want to hurt her. Do you?"

Mairya pauses for a moment, chewing on Lahna's words. She lowers the knife. Tears brim in her eyes. And suddenly, Lahna can only see a desperate being clinging to a revenge that will destroy her future with a girl they both care about.

"I don't know how to be anything else but be the bride to Merelani's heir. That's my purpose." The woman looks at the knife, drawing an invisible circle with her wrist. She laughs, but it's not a happy one. "Do you know what it's like to grow up and have your entire life determined for you—and then it all sinks into the void? It's not freeing. It's *terrifying*." Mairya inhales sharply, as if she is the one that cannot breathe. "I don't want Avarie to hate me. We've been friends since we were merkids, and she's the closest thing I have left of Aalto—"

A cacophony cuts Mairya off. The mob is here wielding nets, torches, and weapons of their own. The ruckus sends Mairya looking over her shoulder for a brief moment.

That's all the time Lahna needs before staggering to a straight position, she swipes the knife away from the distracted Mairya and points it at her.

Through coughs, Lahna manages to say, "I think you should return to the sea. Never come ashore again."

Mairya turns back around and Lahna is gripped by the panic in her eyes. Then those eyes harden like molten volcanic rock. "You tricked me. You talk about peace with the knowledge that this approaching swarm of humans has every intention to hurt me." Mairya slaps the knife out of Lahna's hand.

Lahna lacks strength to resist. The weapon flies through the air, landing blade first into the wooden pier, out of reach from both of them.

"Can you swim?" A cruel, frenzied smile spreads across Mairya's face, ready to split her mouth in half.

Lahna acknowledges her own heels digging into the pier. Her heart drops to her stomach. Her father never let her go into the sea. She'd sink like a waterlogged ship. Still, she only glares at her captor, silent, revealing nothing.

Somehow, Mairya's smile widens even more. As heavy feet land on the pier, the treacherous mermaid pushes Lahna. Her arms grab blindly at the air, then *whoosh*, water floods into Lahna's ears and mouth. Her eyes burn from the salty fluid. She thought the frigid air was undesirable, but below the sea lurks a coldness Lahna has never experienced. It shakes her senses.

All at once she's flailing, air bubbles escaping from her lips as water enters her mouth. Her lungs burn. She kicks her legs, circles her arms frantically. But she continues to sink. A ribbon-like trail of blood follows her. Dots form at the edge of Lahna's vision. She blinks rapidly to no avail.

Glancing up to the pier a final time, Lahna sees Mairya sitting at the edge watching her demise. Her legs swish back and forth like a child's. Fire illuminates the world behind Mairya, a red-hot backdrop of torches.

Mairya, eerily, is speaking in Avarie's voice. "Drown her, drown her. Watch her go. Down, down to the waters below."

Somehow the rhyme follows Lahna even underwater.

Chapter Twenty-Nine

AVARIE

The dead silence of the sea awakens Avarie. It's too quiet. No bustling servants, no skittering sea animals. Nothing. Almost like everyone and everything is in hiding.

The guards are dragging her through the doors of the ruined foyer when Avarie comes to. Her lungs are tight in her chest, as rigid as the vise grip around her wrists. She gasps for breath, whipping her head around in all directions to get her bearings, but the motion dizzies her vision. She forces her eyes shut. The familiarity of home sickens Avarie, knowing that right at this moment, Mairya is stealing Lahna from this world. Frustration surrounds her like an oppressive bubble. A heavy sadness hits her in the heart, and a silent sob breaks between her lips.

"Let me go," she moans, but just like her cry, no sound comes from her mouth.

The aforementioned foyer doors lack their majesty, broken at the hinges and unable to close, leaving the once jovial part of the palace wide open like a gaping mouth stuck in a permanent scream. How did Mairya figure out that Lahna was the *heart* well before Avarie did? Perhaps there's a minuscule part of Avarie that knew all along . . . knew that Lahna was more than just a stranger she had accidentally bumped into . . . knew the gravity pulling them together was more than just enticing happenstance.

Avarie's unsure what land goddess her Sea Goddess is in cahoots with, but surely this is a master plan orchestrated by them both. A cruel plan. Since Lahna holds a special place in that damned poacher's heart, but Avarie's as well. She begins to wonder what this all means, truly. Why would the Mother of the Sea allow such tragedy to happen, and yet not intervene? Again. Why would she allow Avarie to grow feelings for a human that she is meant to kill?

Avarie screams at the absurdity of it all, this time the sound successfully bellows out, mirroring the brokenness her mother displayed when she wept over Aalto's body. She knows Lahna won't hear her, but she hopes that she can feel a sense of connection. Avarie would let the entire kingdom crumble before she kills an innocent girl.

The girl who has her heart hostage but cradles it with such gentle hands.

Avarie screams again, her throat raw from the effort. Someone needs to hear her pain. Somehow the scream empowers her, fueling her body with a red-hot anger. Is this how her father feels all the time? It's a searing sort of energy but it's also invigorating.

"Remove your hands from me this instance!" Avarie orders the guards. She glances between the two of them, an anguished snarl twisting her features. But they hold fast to her wrists. She looks frantically around the once Grand Foyer. Right now, she can't process the crumbling palace, the lack of decoration for a wedding she never wanted.

Avarie should have realized that Mairya had been lying.

Who can prepare for a wedding when seaquakes start up without notice?

But right now, that matters little. She must save Lahna before it's too late.

With a resilient shake, she rips herself free from their hold, shoving both guards away, just as her parents float down cracked spiral stairs to meet her on the fractured landing.

One of the guards attempts to grab her again, but Avarie backhands them, her quick movement fueled by her rage. She fumes, her hand stinging and her scales flickering to the darkest hue they have ever been.

"Touch me again, and I swear to the Goddess, you will regret it." She narrows her eyes at both mermen. They slowly back away, hands up and eyes bewildered. They were just following the orders of the future queen, but Avarie doesn't care. *She* is the queen now, and she will see to it that Mai never rules beside her, bargain with the Enchantress be damned.

"My daughter, you're back. Is it done? Will the seaquakes cease?" Cordelia asks. The former queen wraps her sheer shawl around Avarie's arms with shaky hands. Bruinen follows behind Momma Cordelia, a look of tense fury on his face. But he says nothing. Her father rarely says *nothing*.

Avarie needn't respond. The seafloor trembles, and a crack in the ground opens so wide that the floor begins to cave in, taking tile, furniture, everything in its path. A worried expression etches over Cordelia's face. No, it is not done. The Sea Goddess remains unappeased which lends Avarie some hope that Lahna is still alive.

For now.

There's still time. She can save her. She can fix this. There must be a way.

"What is the meaning of this Avarie?" her father's voice strains with agitation. "We gave you one task, and you could not commit to it. Look at our kingdom. This is your fault. I knew you could never—"

"Will you just shut the hell up for once!" Avarie interrupts, matching Bruinen's fury. "I am in charge. Not *you*. You do not get to treat me this way, not anymore. You've hated me, wanted me to be someone I'm not, my entire life. And you know what, father? I don't care. And I won't give any more energy to this. Either accept that I'm not Aalto or leave me alone."

Avarie ignores her mother's wide eyes, but she doesn't miss the hint of pride in Cordelia's gaze either. She doesn't bother to spare a passing glance to Bruinen. Avarie swims through the Grand Foyer's doors with such speed that the shawl slips from her shoulders. If this were a race around the palace, Avarie would have beaten Aalto for the first time. But there's no joy in her rush to the barrier. There's only a recurring prayer in her mind, which sickens her. Because after all the trauma the Sea Goddess has put Merelani through, she is still praying to her to save them. Avarie casts expectant eyes upward. She can't —she *can't* handle seeing a body floating down to meet her. But as she passes through the barrier, morning light breaks through the depths of the water, illuminating a dark figure sinking slowly toward her.

Her explosive resolve is extinguished.

Avarie's parents come up behind her to the edge of the barrier, staying a safe distance within its confines. "Avarie? What's happening—" Her mother calls out, but her voice dies off upon seeing the body. Avarie doesn't care to turn around and see her father's reaction. Instead, Avarie swims toward the dark figure, hoping that she is wrong. Yet she knows with a sinking certainty what she'll see.

"A betrayal. One of the utmost high," Avarie whispers, her tail flicking with a deep, familiar sadness. One she can't help but think that she is feeling again much too soon.

Chapter Thirty

MAIRYA

Mairya feels the fire before she sees it. Heat singes the raised hair on her forearms. She flinches. This was not part of the plan, remaining trapped on land with an angry mob ready to kill her mercilessly. The shouts of unadulterated hatred curl her spine; she pulls her legs up from the pier's ledge and holds them with tight hands. She shudders, chilled to the bone despite the oppressive heat.

There is no escape.

She could jump, fall into the sea, drown if she doesn't shift back in time. She can't gauge how long it will take for the transformation to enact.

Which horrible outcome is more preferable?

Clinging to the small hope of survival?

Or standing her ground?

Mairya's eyes burn, but not from the heat.

A tear trickles down her face. She wipes it away in surprise. On her left ring finger, there's a shining star that spins, and spins, and spins. She flicks it.

A gift from Aalto. She wore it more than her engagement

ring. It meant more to her than the gaudy Merelani jewels that weigh her hand down. It was a symbol of simpler times.

Back when she, Aalto, and Avarie didn't have the glare of responsibility staring them down. Back when their predestined roles hadn't alienated them from each other.

Mairya looks to the sky, unable to face the truth that she endangered her underwater home. She never wanted to kill Avarie. She *had* to. Avarie's unsuited for the crown. She wasn't focused like Mairya, and she shied away from her royal duties like they were a plague. Killing her was the only way to guarantee that Mairya would have a claim to the throne. To set things back on the right course. Mairya clung to the sliver of hope that Avarie might have returned successful; that, when she did, she would honor the bargain she made with her mother for the potion. But here comes Lahna messing everything up. If Avarie's heart belongs elsewhere, where does that leave Mairya?

Alone.

Aalto is gone.

Avarie's focus is elsewhere.

Without the Merelani crown, her mother would never pass the Enchantress title to her. She'd apprentice someone else in a heartbeat.

Mairya inhales a shaky breath.

No.

This isn't her fault. None of this is her fault. The Mother of the Sea wants this to happen. She laughs bitterly. Mairya truly believed she was destined for greatness. In truth, she is just a pawn to fulfill the whims of an omnipotent Goddess.

Her faith breaks like pearls on a severed necklace.

More tears stream down Mairya's cheeks. She squeezes her eyes shut.

What has she done?

At least, she'll be remembered—for centuries to come—as

the girl who tried to commit regicide, poisoning her future and everything around her.

There is a desperate joy in her chest from the idea of being remembered at all. At this point, that's all that she can ask for.

With a slow nod, Mairya chooses her fate. Then the sun emerges from behind the clouds, casting light onto the pier and her shuddering limbs. It brightens her dark thoughts. She opens her eyes, smiling through the tears. There is a majestic beauty to her end, she thinks.

Suddenly, cloaked faces drag her from the wooden pier, her legs and feet meeting splinter after splinter from the friction. All the while, their shouts of anger ring in her ears like an explosion.

She is dumped on the ground; the gritty taste of sand meets her mouth. Mai spits it out, a long sliver of saliva trailing from her mouth to the shore.

This is where she will die.

A man approaches her slowly. He is larger than the rest and his shoulder is caked with blood. Mairya watches him, imagines what's going through his mind.

There's no need to rush. She has nowhere to flee.

He crouches down to her level. "Where is she? What have you done with her?"

Mairya has never felt more terrified in her life—but she mustn't show it. Royalty should never do so, even in their final moments. So she lifts her chin, just as she has seen Cordelia do many times, and meets his dark-eyed gaze.

"She belongs to the Sea Goddess now."

Hot breath and spittle greet her as the man roars. Mairya can practically see his heart breaking. She lays on the gritty sand. She still doesn't see the appeal in it. Just a bunch of crushed shells.

But perhaps she cannot see the beauty in things like she

used to, with her eyes and mind overshadowed by grief and her once divine purpose.

The man grabs Mairya by the neck and squeezes with unexpected strength. Her eyes widen and bulge from the force—but she doesn't fight him. Mairya continues to absorb her last moments in this realm in silence.

She forces her eyes shut, relishing in the smell of sea that wafts into her nose. It smells of home.

Comfort.

Then a searing light bursts from her two legs like a thousand lightning bolts striking at once. Pain thunders in her lower half. She cracks open her eyes to see her bright, yellow tail slapping the sand. This is when the real pain starts.

"Siren!"

"Monster!"

"Kill it! We must kill it!"

But Mairya feels numb to it all. The pain recedes as the poacher continues his strangulation with a renewed hatred. The others begin plucking off her shimmering scales. Her tail glows brighter, like the emerging sun above.

A scream—no—a final song erupts from Mairya's lips. It carries, fanning out through Deniz and far below into Merelani. She closes her eyes, waiting for the smell of fire to fade, for the pressure on her neck to wane. Waiting to return to her lost love.

In the end, all she truly wanted was a sense of purpose, of belonging—but it was something she wasn't meant to touch in this lifetime.

Chapter Thirty-One

AVARIE

Aalto's lifeless body resurfaces in Avarie's mind as she watches a different figure sink lower and lower toward her. A figure she has laughed with, and touched, and kissed with joy in what seems like a lifetime ago. Now, she is only filled with gloom and sorrow.

Avarie hoists her arms in front of her, in the same manner she imagines her ancestors had envisioned the Goddess reaching up from the sea when they designed the Merelani flag. Avarie is prepared to catch the body, but her mind is far from ready. Her limbs shake, so she squeezes them with laborious strength, freezing them to just a few tremors.

Lahna lands in her arms with a numbing silence that Avarie will never forget. The silence is underscored by a song, frighteningly similar to Mairya's voice, traveling through the sea and down into the void below. Nausea builds in her throat. So much death—and for what—to appease a Sea Goddess that allowed so much death in the first place?

Avarie could scream. At this point, she almost wishes to sing herself.

She visually examines Lahna's waterlogged body. It's frail,

lifeless; heavy with the ruined, impossible future Avarie wished to build with the human. Lahna's eyelids are closed, hiding the dull, lifeless stare that is likely behind them. Avarie descends back to the now quiet seafloor, breezing past her parents, refusing to make eye contact. Because what can she say? She had found her voice only for this loss to leave her speechless.

Avarie veers toward her second favorite place in Merelani. What's left of it, anyway. The Royal Garden looks devastated; every trellis is knocked over, plant stems are mangled in morbid angles like the permanent snap of a neck. Avarie bends down, laying Lahna's body with care on a bed of sea roses. Avarie isn't knowledgeable on how long it takes for a body to float. She can't bear to think about that. Not at this moment.

Her skin prickles, sensing eyes on her, but for once she is unbothered. This fleeting moment belongs to her and Lahna. All of Merelani could gaze upon her grief, like killer whales before a smaller shark. Avarie doesn't care.

Horror racks Avarie's chest at the sudden realization that three souls she cares about are now dead.

Aalto.

Mairya.

Lahna.

It's as if her throat is constricting from the weight of all the emotions building in her windpipe. She can feel the invisible heat of dread coating every inch of her, from head to tail.

Avarie throws herself over Lahna, sobbing without decorum, without the stoic facade of royal expectations. She doesn't care. She just doesn't care. She wishes nothing more than to go back in time and live in ignorance, having never breached that damned border.

Having never met this wonderful human.

Avarie buries her head in the crook between Lahna's neck and shoulder. She feels the exact moment life slips away from Lahna. Her body grows lax. Too lax. Bubbles rise from

Lahna's mouth as if she were exhaling during a deep slumber. As if she were snoring. Avarie leans backward and attempts to rein in her sobs.

Lahna is gone . . . and there's nothing Avarie can do about it. Perhaps that is what hurts the most, knowing her kingdom is safe and feeling no sense of relief.

Her shoulders remain stiff.

Her breathing remains ragged, which distresses her more —because Lahna is no longer drawing breath, but Avarie still is.

Avarie caresses Lahna's cheek. Regret fills her, overwhelming her rational mind.

She regrets that she agreed to this plan to appease the Goddess.

She regrets ever finding herself at that marketplace where she met Lahna.

She doesn't regret loving Lahna, but right now she wishes she had never known what it was like to do so.

She feels a firm tap on her shoulder, shaking Avarie from the ever-growing list of regrets her brain is concocting. It takes almost all her strength to look over her shoulder. She sees none other than that witch—the Enchantress—staring back at her.

Regret is replaced with anger. It's HER fault. None of this would have happened if she never suggested that Avarie go to Deniz. What does she know about the Goddess's will? How does *anyone* truly know that she is ordained to speak for the Mother of the Sea? And look what she has done to Mai . . . making her believe that the only option for her to thrive in life is to be queen. She never encouraged her to do anything else. And now she's dead.

The Enchantress is evil, malicious. Avarie's mouth twists into a scowl as she narrows her eyes. Her grip on Lahna's body tightens.

What in the hell could she want?

"I know what my daughter has done. And she has paid for it with her life," the Enchantress says with a sadness that boils Avarie's blood. She wants to feel sad right now? How dare she. She's only *sad* her direct connection to the throne is gone.

"Let me help you"—The Enchantress gestures to Lahna—"help her. It's the least I can do."

Atonement? She can take her atonement and shove it.

"Get away! You—your family has done enough." Avarie continues to cling to Lahna, but a tiredness inches forward, watering down her impassioned rage. She rubs a thumb over Lahna's cheek before sitting on her side to lend minuscule attention to Mairya's mother.

The Enchantress sighs. "Oarfish will give *you* legs. But it can also give *others* life."

Avarie's shrill voice cuts through the heavy silence. "What —what are you talking about? She's gone. Lahna is gone. *Gone*. Why don't you get that she's gone?" If anger truly is in her blood, then Avarie has never felt more like her father than this moment. Her first act as queen will be banishing the Enchantress. Utilizing her power always comes with a price— and for this 'favor,' Avarie knows that she'll owe a debt to grief forever.

The Enchantress meets her fiery gaze with cool patience. "There is time. But not much. If you stop resisting my help, we may be able to save her, Queen Avarie."

Avarie considers her words for a second. She said she would do anything to save Lahna. But to trust the Enchantress again . . . ? She clears her throat, trying to dislodge the despair stuck in there. "Okay. What needs to be done?"

"The meat of a freshly dead oarfish is known to restore life. If you can get her to swallow the flesh, then you may be able to revive her. Make sure she ingests it fully. Then we must wait. Either she'll awaken and need to be returned promptly to the surface. Or she'll transform." The Enchantress sinks down to Avarie and Lahna's level. "I couldn't stop thinking about the oarfish you mentioned appearing at King Aalto's funeral. It should have been at least a decade until one migrated to our waters . . . I have no explanation for its appearance, other than the seaquakes disturbed it from its home in the deep. I set off to capture it. I thought it would be good to have oarfish flesh at hand with the seaquakes endangering us all. I was right."

Avarie shakes her head with skepticism. Her mind drags to interpret the information thrown at her. Her grip tightens on Lahna's limp frame. In truth, she has nothing to lose. Lahna could live again. Or she can remain the same. But what of the cost? There's always a cost. The Enchantress can't be trusted. Avarie says, "I don't know if I can trust you. You do not lie, but you place an unbearable burden on everyone that you help."

The Enchantress sighs yet does not deny Avarie's statement. "My daughter is dead because of me. Because I pushed a burden onto her. I wanted to secure a valuable future for her. For me. So much so that she lost her way. This is my attempt at making amends. I will not gift an offer like this again, young queen."

The Enchantress snaps the necklace at her neck, beads exploding in every direction. Then she opens her hand to reveal a tiny vial. It's a dark, shrouded hue like the rest of her bottles, preventing Avarie from seeing its contents. Quickly, the merwoman grabs Avarie's hand and shoves the vial into it. With a sniffle that Avarie pretends not to hear, the Enchantress backs away, receding behind the now growing crowd of her parents, palace staff, and commoners.

With the seaquakes officially gone, the merfolk must feel safe enough to move freely around Merelani.

Avarie tugs the cork from the vial and empties three small jerky-textured pieces onto her free hand.

They're so tiny, so immaterial. But Avarie is not ignorant

to their Goddess-given power. If this is the only way to fix some of the wrongs that has transpired, she'll do it.

She will bring Lahna back; she has to try.

Avarie moves Lahna's head to rest near the line of her bare skin where her scales begin. Her fingers clumsily clasp onto the oarfish, her limbs shake as she uses her thumb to tug open Lahna's mouth. Avarie sprinkles the oarfish inside and promptly pulls Lahna's lips closed. She brushes hair from Lahna's face with delicate care.

She recounts the brief instructions given to her: feed in the oarfish, make sure Lahna swallows, then wait. The latter takes the least amount of effort. But to reach that point, Avarie must do everything perfectly.

Though unsure how helpful this will be, Avarie tries massaging the oarfish down Lahna's throat. Her fingers jerk when she grazes the wound on Lahna's neck. Avarie opens Lahna's mouth to make sure there is nothing caught on her tongue or teeth. Then comes the waiting.

Time ticks slowly, and Avarie feels each agonizing second like the removal of a scale. Finally, she looks up. The eyes of Merelani watch her. Their gazes are full of resolute concern. Her people are here with her.

They are no longer cowering from any seaquakes.

They are not condemning her for loving a human.

It's enough to make her lose her feigned resolve. Her assertion of indifference.

Avarie cares so much.

She wants nothing more than to see Lahna alive, even if that means she must return her to the surface. Who knows if Lahna will even remember Avarie if she were revived. The Enchantress mentioned nothing of salvaged memories. Avarie wouldn't be surprised if Lahna grew to hate her . . . to be trapped in a foreign world for ten long years, despised by her father for transforming into a creature of the sea.

Avarie waits.

And waits.

Nothing.

A sob builds in her throat, but she swallows it down.

She's too tired to cry. And she's tired of crying.

Lahna is gone.

She'll remain a painful memory. Just like Aalto. Like Mairya. An ache that will follow wherever Avarie goes.

She crushes herself to the girl, embedding her face once more between her shoulder and neck. Lahna doesn't even feel the same. Avarie pulls away. With a sense of finality, she places her lips to Lahna's cold forehead.

The kiss is not romantic.

It's a tortuous goodbye.

As Avarie pulls away, her shoulders shake like the sea did. She understands the Sea Goddess now. Her pain. Why she sought revenge for Aalto. The seaquakes . . . it's a last-ditch effort for control. What happens on land, she cannot control. But she can twist, turn, flip the sea into anything she desires. It's unfair, but Avarie supposes that's just what goddesses do when they are hurting. Avarie could throw her own fit if she wanted. Imprison the Enchantress for the rest of her days. Tell her father off. Refuse to marry, breaking all tradition and leading Merelani into ruin without an heir.

But she won't. She has to break the cycle of pain.

For the last time, Avarie caresses Lahna's face. Then she just rests there, eyes closed, inches from Lahna's lips with their foreheads pressed together. The coolness of Lahna's skin makes Avarie nauseous.

"I'm so sorry, Lahna. I would trade my crown. My life. If it meant saving you. You didn't deserve this. You are—you were so good. Too good for all of this mess. And falling for you put you in more danger than I could have ever imagined."

Fingers tap her, but she brushes the feeling from her mind. It's over. She tried. But it's over.

Why can't whoever is tapping just leave her alone. Leave her be.

Please.

The fingers tap again, this time on the hand touching Lahna's face. Avarie pulls away in annoyed confusion. She opens her eyes to see Lahna's hand trying to weakly hold her own. Avarie gasps in disbelief.

Lahna tries to speak, opening and closing her mouth, only for bubbles to fly out.

What is happening?

Is she alive?

Should Avarie rush her to the surface?

Before another thought can form in her mind, a familiar blinding light outlines Lahna's body to the point that Avarie sees nothing.

"Avert your eyes!" Avarie commands her merfolk.

A garbled scream releases from Lahna's mouth. She must feel so confused. Is she drowning all over again? Lahna thrashes in Avarie's arms.

But Avarie doesn't dare let go.

She can't. Lahna's on the other end fighting for her life. The light burns through her eyelids, allowing Avarie to see a phasing figure in her grip. She opens her right eye to get a sense of what's happening, but the intense burning sensation that follows makes Avarie close it promptly. Cries and shouts to 'turn away' or 'guard your eyes' ring out, but Avarie stays composed. She won't leave Lahna for a second, no matter the consequences.

"Lahna? Lahna," she calls out, even though she is certain of the weight in her arms. The thrashing has stopped, replaced with ragged yet steady breaths. Avarie's own breathing begins to mirror that of the girl in her arms.

"Ava?"

The outline of Lahna's body changes with a spark, then dies down, extinguishing itself. An unknown force flaps against the underwater current. *Woosh. Woosh.* Something fin-like, something new.

Avarie wishes she could see it. But her eyes open to reveal nothing but chilling darkness.

"Avarie? Look at me. *See* me. Avarie, are you okay?"

Epilogue
SOME TIME LATER

Avarie didn't marry right away.

The merpeople of Merelani had to rebuild first, until the seaquakes were a distant, somber memory. Avarie prioritized fixing the homes that were destroyed before moving on to the palace. The fragile coral ceiling of the Grand Foyer was replaced with impenetrable shells, like the sturdy shingles on a roof. The fractures in the palace floor and the walls were filled with sealant made from moray eel. The smell was horrible, but upon solidification, everything damaged looked like new.

Almost.

Today, the kingdom closely resembles its once pristine condition. But a pinch of fear still lingers. Fear that they all remain at the mercy of a tempestuous Goddess. Fear of what will happen the next time a poacher encroaches upon their peaceful home. It's not enough for merpeople to hide in the shadows, praying that a ship will continue past. Praying that their barrier functions properly. There must be protocols in place.

Thinking of these protocols and the potential peace

treaties with humans is what keeps Avarie awake at night. That, and dreams of Aalto. Not nightmares. Not anymore. She remembers him for the overly serious twin who loved to tease her, who could somehow always make her smile. Nevertheless, these dreams are sometimes more painful than the night terrors . . . especially when they venture into a hypothetical future that will never exist. At least the nightmares are truthful, merely reiterating the facts with no feelings involved.

Aalto was gruesomely murdered by a human poacher. A poacher that also happens to be Lahna's father. A lurid killing, a song no one anticipated to hear so soon. Through the adrenaline of it all—going on land, falling for Lahna, returning to Merelani empty-handed—Avarie acknowledges that she didn't have the proper time to grieve.

Between sorrowful dreams and brainstorming how best to protect her people, Avarie somehow finds a chance to linger, a chance to lay with her sadness. To meet her grief head on. To cry at the lost futures of her brother and the missing guards.

Mairya.

Avarie can't bring herself to hate the mergirl. The tether of childhood friendship chains them together, even in death. But the feelings aren't joyous either. They are a peculiar mix of melancholy and betrayal.

She cannot fathom the level of desperation that Mairya succumbed to when her route to the throne slipped from her grasp. Did she truly believe she was destined to be queen? Or was it the uncertainty brought on by Aalto's death that pushed her over the edge? It makes Avarie wonder what grisly deed the Enchantress did to climb her way into the royal court. What words did she whisper into Mairya's ears to make her ravenous for the crown? Avarie knows how she stayed there—she gave the rulers two heirs, dooming her own daughter in the process.

Perhaps there is an answer to this that Momma Cordelia

can supply. Avarie will add it to the list of things she needs to ask her mother. Maybe she's *almost* ready to talk about her own heir to Merelani. Yet the timing isn't right. All the regal attitude in the world cannot conceal Momma Cordelia's heartache. Avarie sees it anytime they lock eyes. Avarie and Aalto's near identical features are a burden to her mother.

And while Avarie's presence evokes sadness in Cordelia, Bruinen adopts a neutral face anytime they are in a room together. The disappointment in his gaze has vanished. But the neutrality doesn't feel *good*. Avarie thinks that her father views her as more of a *you'll do as queen* as opposed to a *I'm proud of the queen you've become*. Perhaps that's all she can expect right now. Bruinen grieves in his own, estranged way. But Avarie will accept that over his fits of anger and unkind words.

Momma Cordelia and Bruinen reside in separate chambers now. And sadly, Avarie notes, maybe that's the best 'happy' ending for them.

Then there's Lahna.

When Avarie's mind isn't consumed by her queenly duties or the merpeople she has lost, it nestles up to ardent thoughts and memories of Lahna.

"MY QUEEN. ARE YOU READY?"

"Just a second. Somehow, I always lose my sense of time in the palace library."

Avarie twists around, taking in her former chambers, now transformed into the new Royal Library. The old one was so damaged . . . it couldn't be saved. Her reading nook remains, except now it's the favored spot of the palace librarian. The merwoman enjoys maintaining the growing collection almost as much as her affinity for writing novels. Which is evidenced by the intricate mix of human and mer books lining the shelves.

"I should finish writing this chapter. Who knew I could be a successful writer, even *under* the sea?" Lahna adjusts the sea rose tucked behind her ear, gold ring glittering on her ring finger. The sea rose is no moonflower, but she seems to like them just as much.

"I did. But do you miss it, dwelling on land?" *Do you resent me?* Lahna's brow wrinkles, likely the result of Avarie asking this question for the thousandth time. Lahna puts down her pen carved from whale bone, exhales, then meets her gaze.

"When will you stop, Ava?"

Apprehension makes Avarie's heart skip a beat. She veers closer to the cushioned nook, twirling the sun ring that will forever remain on her finger, just like her golden wedding band. "Stop what?"

"Worrying about me. Feeling guilty. I'm okay, really."

Avarie only offers a concerned, arched eyebrow as her response.

Lahna shuts her notebook and pats the free space next to her. Avarie sits, their hands finding each other in an instant.

"I'm as okay as I can be. I'm certain my father and my cousin Keeya feel my absence every day. And I feel theirs. But I'm in good hands down here." Lahna squeezes their hands together for emphasis. "I didn't expect to fall for a mermaid, not outside of my novels. And while our story isn't perfect, I can't see myself with anyone but you." Lahna presses her lips to their joined hands. "None of the 'Ten-Year Maiden' variations end with the human falling in love *and* following her love to the sea. We have the best story."

Avarie's throat grows tight with emotion. "Do you really mean that Lahna? That you're not mad at me, that you've fallen in love?"

She did attempt to kill Lahna's father, after all.

Lahna offers Avarie her favorite smile before caressing both sides of her face and kissing her. "Don't get me wrong, being told I cannot see my family for ten years and the girl I have feelings for—who also stabbed my father—is not actually a *girl*, but a merwoman? And that I'm like her now too? It's not easy to accept on the first day, but thankfully, that day is long past." She leans in to kiss Avarie again. "And I've absolutely fallen in love. With each passing day. Maybe even since that wagon incident . . . which is a nice perk, considering that we're in a mandatory marriage. Did I really stand a chance though? Have you seen you?" Lahna marvels.

"Little old me?" Avarie's cheeks warm, her lips still tingling from their last kiss. "I'm falling in love with you too. I can definitely see our story as a plot in one of your novels."

"Oh, I'm definitely incorporating this."

"Well, make sure you change my name in your story." Avarie smiles.

"Hmm, what about Avree? A-V-R-E-E."

"Dear Goddess, that's literally the same thing!" Avarie collapses into a fit of laughter.

"Not quite." Lahna tilts her gaze to the ceiling in full jest. "It's one syllable shorter. No one will know."

"I may need to consider an annulment at this point." Avarie playfully narrows her eyes.

"You wouldn't dare get rid of me. I'm the perfect queen for you."

A queenly menace.

And that inner thought reminds Avarie of one of the last conversations she had with Aalto. But it doesn't make her tearful. If anything, her mood improves. She touches the warm necklace at her throat. Yes, her twin would have loved Lahna.

Not privy to Avarie's inner thoughts, Lahna continues,

"And to think I was calling you a princess the whole time when you're actually a queen. You should have corrected me."

"I should have corrected you on a lot of things," Avarie says as her chin dips to her hands, that good mood quickly sinking.

But Lahna lifts it back up. "You did the best you could with the grief you were carrying. I will never fault you for that. Plus . . . I didn't really lead with 'my dad turned evil after my mom died and he blames every merperson for her death' when we first met either. Just know that I forgive you. And I need you to forgive yourself."

"That's relieving to hear. If you had led with that . . . I think my trip to Deniz would have gone differently. And forgiveness . . . I'm trying. Some days are better than others. I keep telling myself his death isn't my fault. That I didn't kill him. But sometimes that mean voice in my head screams otherwise. And that doesn't excuse my behavior. *Intention versus impact* right? I'm going to make it up to you, no matter how long it takes," Avarie says. "I know ten years is so far from now, but I promise. I'll take you to see your cousin."

Avarie leaves Lahna's father out of the equation. He killed Aalto, and upon Lahna's recollection, led the mob right to Mai. There will likely never be a day she'll be willing to see the face of Aalto and Mai's murderer again. But Avarie knows that Lahna's heart aches at the loss. Just like she would if Bruinen passed away. Sure, their relationship is estranged, but that's her blood. Avarie would surely miss parts of Bruinen.

Lahna sucks in a huge breath. "A decade is a long time. But I appreciate you. At least I get to spend it with an immeasurably gorgeous queen."

What remains of the oarfish from Aalto's funeral is unknown. After rebuilding the witch's chambers, it was nowhere to be found. The Enchantress holds many secrets up her shawl, but her transparency on the depleted supply of oarfish was not up for questioning. Avarie wouldn't be surprised if the merwoman doesn't emerge from her potion room for ten years.

"Funny, I could say the same thing. There's a really gorgeous writer that I've been crushing on for a while. I hope I can muster the courage to talk to her." Avarie smiles.

"Something tells me you're brave enough. You've got this outspoken energy about you now. It's . . . really attractive." Lahna gifts her a meaningful look and runs a finger down Avarie's arm. Of course, as a result, Avarie's stomach somersaults.

"You know . . . I feel like we could delay the coronation for an hour or two," Avarie suggests.

"You can do whatever you want. You're the queen. Emphasis on, do *whatever* you want to *me*. Really, anything." Lahna smirks. "I trust in your royal judgment."

"I adore your propensity for debauchery," Avarie says, almost breathless.

A sudden burst of light flashes through the nook's window, the last remaining coral glass in the palace. Avarie rubs at her temple sensing that the unexpected light will bring forth a headache. Her eyes water in frustration not from the light, but from the permanent damage to her eyes.

Avarie's vision suffered because of her refusal to look away from Lahna as she transformed. It destroyed the vision in her right eye, though her left is mostly okay, if extremely sensitive to light. But she couldn't look away. What if Lahna had disappeared?

Avarie would do it again.

Before anymore sadness can leak into their conversation, Avarie changes the subject.

"Let me look at your adornments," she says. Avarie rubs her eyes as she pivots away from the window to face the ethereal merwoman next to her. Dots of black paint her periphery, but in a way, the tunnel vision allows Avarie to fully focus on Lahna.

Lahna's height was not diminished by her transformation. She remains tall, long tail flicking with learned precision to keep her afloat. But her scales make Avarie's jaw drop every time—akin to her melanin-speckled skin, the scales are varying shades of brown. Some are so dark, they're almost black. Others, a light brown the same shade as her auburn hair. A kaleidoscope of intricate wood, walnut, and cinnamon hues.

"You're captivating," Avarie muses.

"Enthralling."

"Alluring."

"Spellbinding."

"That's the one." Avarie ends their little game. Lahna smiles before rising to twirl in a circle, her waist beads sparkling like gems below her belly button. Her hickory brassiere boasts the same beads at her waist. The shawl on her shoulders is a crisp white. All that is missing is a crown atop her head.

"I look . . ." Lahna hesitates for a moment, looking around the huge room then finally at Avarie. " . . . like I belong here."

"You've stolen the words right from my mouth. Come, let's show the merworld just how much you belong. I know there is much for us to discuss, issues for us to work through. But right now, this moment belongs to us and Merelani."

"Show them how much I belong with you? Now that's an easy feat." Lahna tugs her queen from the soft cushions, cupping Avarie's cheek with a reverence that gives her chills. Lahna pulls her into a slow kiss, one full of warmth, security, and love. Avarie drags them closer, chest to chest, as she throws her arms behind Lahna's neck. Lahna smells just like a sea rose. Like Avarie.

Like Aalto.

She hugs Lahna even harder.

Emotions do not speak, but Avarie can easily feel their amorous exchange declaring their closeness, their everlasting bond. A soft but deliberate knock on the door pulls them away, but Avarie does not fret. They have time for their emotions to be as thoroughly expressed as the profound words that Lahna writes.

They have a lifetime.

Mrs. Clara, her mermaiden, laboriously pushes a library door open. "My queen—and queen-to-be!" She glances at both mermaids respectively. "It's time for Lahna's coronation. And the unveiling of the Royal Library! Such wonderful occasions to surmount so much loss. Merelani is thrilled. Are you two ready?"

Echoes of what Mrs. Clara said on the day of Aalto's coronation float into Avarie's mind that exact moment.

Love can ensnare you at the most unexpected, and sometimes inconvenient time.

Avarie's whole life, Mrs. Clara has yet to be wrong.

Lahna loops an arm through Avarie's. "Let me guide you," she says kindly. Her contagious smile returns, and Avarie can't help but smile too.

Avarie plants a chaste kiss on Lahna's right cheek, squeezes the shell necklace at her throat, then she nods at Mrs. Clara.

"We are ready."

Lahna leads them from the library, and the utmost confidence takes over Avarie. With Lahna at her side, and Aalto's memory beating in her heart, ruling Merelani will be a light sea breeze.

The Ten-Year Maiden

BY LAHNA HART

When the maiden washed ashore, it was the dead of night. Despite the darkness, she knew precisely where to go, inspired by a feeling of divine purpose. She was no simple merwoman. She was not chosen at random for this venture ashore.

Her tail transformed into a pair of lithe feet, new limbs that were as steady as a great seaquake. Her first steps were accompanied by the songs of nature; the crashing waves and the vermin skittering across the light sand. And there, in the forest before her, birds chittered and snakes hissed. Quietly, she headed toward the forest, to the cabin in the distance, wobbling on her new and still-unsteady legs.

Once she was safe in the cabin, the maiden fashioned the lingering seaweed on her body into a robe, covering the stark nakedness in which she arrived ashore.

Exhausted by her journey into this new world, she fell onto the bed, not bothering to drape herself with blankets, and drifted to sleep.

The morning comes. As soon as the sun made its first

curious look toward the sky, the maiden sprung into action, turning the abandoned cabin into a home.

She dusted every nook and cranny, and she cleaned the windows. She went to the garden behind the cabin, tilling and pruning and sowing new plants.

The maiden relished the solitude, for she was never granted this peace in her underwater home.

No soul came to bother her.

That is, until the third day.

The maiden was bathing in the sea, cleansing her dark-brown curls. The water warmed her skin, as did the sun, tanning her already deep-brown skin tenfold.

Satisfied by how the water revived her dry hair, she splayed out in the sea, relishing in the calm day. She was on her back, floating among the waves, eyes closed in bliss.

Then they snapped right open.

A noise tickled her ears. But it was far from irritating. It was lovely, a low hum that floated from the forest beside her cabin.

The maiden turned her eyes to the noise, in dire need of putting a face to the wondrous voice. Nearer it came, and she could just make out a slender figure strolling closer from the tree line.

Her eyes raked over the sight in a matter of seconds. Dark-brown skin. Fiery-red curls tossed into a tight top knot. A glittering suit of armor.

As much as the maiden was intrigued, her fear took over. She has never met a human before. The purpose of her journey is a rite of passage that does not involve human interference. Panicked, she ducked below the sea's surface. But the human had already spotted her and had called out to her.

The maiden's stark panic forced her back to her natural form, and she swam for home.

She returned to her mermaid duties. When questioned

about why she wasted a gift ten years in the making, she could only shrug at her family and friends.

The maiden vowed to move forward from this mistake and never speak of it.

HER THIRD NIGHT BACK HOME WAS UNDERSCORED by curiosity as she heard an ethereal singing that she knew no merperson was capable of.

The voice lured her back to the surface before she even realized it was doing so. Her head popped above the sea line and she locked eyes with the enigmatic stranger.

The maiden's breath caught in her heaving chest.

The stranger with fiery hair loose upon their shoulders was a woman.

Dark eyes met dark eyes.

Silence bloomed between them. And then the woman spoke.

"I've been calling to you. When you didn't answer, I thought I might've imagined you."

"I heard you—your voice is nothing short of enchanting —but I was scared to be seen by you," the maiden said.

"Why is that?"

The woman, devoid of her stiff armor, walked closer and sat at the edge of the shore where sand and water became one.

"I've never been seen by a human. I'm not supposed to be seen."

"But what a sight you are. Tell me. I must know your name." The woman leaned forward as if to caress the maiden.

And the maiden would have allowed it, had their infuriating distance been shorter.

In this moment, a shyness possessed the maiden. She ran

her fingers down the line of her bare chest, to the scales at her waist.

"No."

"Why ever not?" There was a pinch of indignance woven into her response.

Ignoring her question, the maiden said, "Show me that I can trust you. That you will not hurt me."

The woman nodded and accepted the request.

"I, Princess Anaphora of Adahy, will earn your trust."

For the next three nights, the pair met on the shoreline. They shared every detail about themselves and their lives until they felt like old friends venturing into the territory of lovers.

On the fourth night, the maiden beckoned Princess Anaphora closer.

"Come, Ana. I must show you something wonderful," the maiden said.

The princess rolled up the cuffs of her pants and waded into the water.

"No. You'll need to remove all your garments where we're going."

So, as the princess walked closer, she shed all her garments one at a time until she was as bare as the maiden.

The maiden smiled and tugged the princess underwater.

Their fingers intertwined and the heat between their hands felt as though it would boil the sea if they allowed it.

They find a cavern. It was a bowl of some sort in the sea that offered a coverage of water for the maiden and pockets of air for the princess.

Inside the cavern, the pair rose to let the princess breathe.

The maiden caressed the side of Princess Ana's face. "You are gorgeous beyond measure. And so kind as to show me this wonderful cavern."

"I can say the same about you. I am blessed to be the first mermaid you have ever met."

The princess pulled the maiden forward and their lips met with a satisfying sound. Again and again and again they kissed . . . until the cavern seemed ready to be lit from within by the fire they had kindled between them.

The princess sighed, content. "Will you finally tell me your name?"

But the maiden shook her head no.

"Why—why not?" Hurt filled Princess Ana's voice.

"Meet me tomorrow. I will tell you my mermaiden name then."

The princess agreed, though not without a note of defeat in her tone.

The maiden escorted Princess Ana back to the surface. They met again the following night.

Something about this night felt different. Perhaps it was the calm sea. Or the manner in which the moon and stars mingled together with an intimacy that matched the princess and the maiden.

They ventured farther into the underground cavern where there was a bit of land. It was the perfect spot for them to rest. The princess could recline fully on land while the maiden could remain half submerged in water.

And this time, as they kissed, they refused to leave the safety of their underwater nook. The separation between them vanished as they became one with each other. One with the rocks, the sand, the water . . .

It was dark in the cavern. So, they weren't aware of the time that melted through their smoldering grips.

But the princess grew faint . . . for as filling as it was to the mind and the soul to feast on each other, it did not appease the stomach.

The maiden led Princess Ana back to the surface. She watched the human redress before the princess asked, "—and your name? We've shared each other in the most tantalizing manner, yet I still don't know your name."

The maiden smiled and said, "My name is Korinna. Princess Korinna. When will I see you next?"

"I will look for you tomorrow evening. And the next day after that. I will uproot my kingdom and align it to the shore if it grants me more nights with you."

The maiden was overcome with happiness. She laid a hand to her lips in silent awe.

Princess Ana's face grew worried.

"Have I said something wrong? Was that uncouth?"

Princess Korinna gasped.

"No! I'm just shocked. Shocked that something as evasive as this amorous love has seized us, and that it exists only for each other. I've longed for this, begged the Goddess for just a taste of mutual affection. For it has been so, so difficult to know if someone truly valued me, or merely my status."

Anna collapsed upon the sand, unrelenting hunger forgotten for the moment.

"I love you, Korrina. Please say that I can see you tomorrow. And tomorrow's tomorrow. Until both our trials of life perish. Please say it could be so."

The princess wrung her hands, twisted her fingers in anticipation of Korinna's response.

"I love you too. Our lives have intertwined so quickly. And how entwined the vines are . . . no one can disentangle them. I won't allow it."

With a cry, Princess Ana leaped back into the sea for the maiden. She pulled the maiden in for a series of kisses that left Korrina dizzy and desirous to experience every iteration and retelling of their love story.

"See you tomorrow night."

When tomorrow arrived and the princess did not, worry stewed within the maiden as she scanned the desolate shore.

She could not venture onto the sand without a potion at her disposal, and there would not be one another for a decade.

For hours, the maiden watched the shore, her eyes and forehead exposed to the open air.

It became clear as water that Princess Anaphora would not visit her tonight. With the lonely moon high in the sky, Korinna disappeared below the water.

She found herself grateful that at least her tears were concealed by the quiet sea.

Yet Korinna did not give up. She showed up for her love, only to be greeted by an empty shore each time.

Her subjects and the royal family grew concerned when, on the fifth night that the maiden returned to the palace, she appeared crestfallen yet again. But when questioned, she shared no answers. Korrina knew without a doubt that if this rejection were to continue, she may perish from the heartache.

She promised that tonight would be the final night she would visit the shore.

No more.

To her disappointment, Princess Anaphora still did not come. As Korinna prepared to leave, the moon reflected off a bobbing bottle on the outskirts of her vision.

The maiden swam to the glass and snatched it below with sharp precision. She returned to the underwater dome, pulled out the cork, and upended the bottle. A parchment piece fell in her hand.

She unfurled the letter and devoured the words, for she had been starved for any correspondence from her lover.

PLEASE FORGIVE ME, PRINCESS KORRINA. I HAVE been called away, called back to my home. My father passed and my mother is too distressed. As I am the eldest sibling, I am next in line for the throne. I am sinking under the weight of my new crown, the responsibilities it carries. Yet all I can do is think of you and the promises I have broken.

I have been tasked with funeral arrangements, new trade agreements, and to my dismay, avoiding war with neighboring territories. There is so much to do that I've not been able to steal a moment for myself. Though I ache to return to the shore, I lack the time to do so.

I have entrusted this letter to a royal adviser, instructing him where to deliver it and when. I sincerely hope that you see it. I will be devastated should it float away from your line of sight, or into the wrong hands. But I trust that it will find you.

I want you to know that I haven't forgotten about you or thrown away our love. The feeling sticks to my heart with an intensity impossible to sever. I do hope that you receive this letter. I will send my adviser to return for a response in three days' time. If he does not deliver your letter to me, I can only assume that my absence is unforgivable. If this letter finds its way to you, know that you will always have my heart.

With all my love, forever and whatever existence after,

Queen Ana

Princess Korrina burst into tears. She clutched the letter to her chest. With the tears from her cheeks and a little mermaid magic, she turned the letter over and composed a response.

Once finished, she vowed to stash the letter in her brassiere and return it to the human world when the time arrived.

Yet when the time arrived, Princess Korrina was detained

to the confines of the palace. Overhead, a hulking ship passed slowly over the palace, over her entire world.

It would have been a death sentence to breach the surface. Once a decision was reached by the king that it was safe to leave, still the maiden could not.

She cried for days upon days . . . until she made herself sick. No one could soothe her. For three weeks, Princess Korrina refused to leave her room. She lost weight, lost hair, but worst of all, her smile vanished as well. The loss of her love drowned her, and she made no effort to swim above the heartbreak.

TEN YEARS LATER . . .

She removed the seaweed, wrapped like fabric on her ankles, one at a time. She stared at the sand, at the water and that lovely line where they had kissed so long ago.

She hadn't the heart to return here for a decade. She only hoped that these numerous years, many filled with war, were not etched into the lines that now decorated her face.

But something brought Queen Anaphora humming through the trees, back to this spot again.

The queen never married, no woman in her kingdom could ever hold a flame to Korrina. The ache grew smaller, but in its place was a loneliness that Ana knew she could never cure.

Queen Anaphora rolled the hem of her trousers up past her ankles until she thought better of it. Instead, she undressed fully, inhaled, then dove into the clear water. Ana knew where to go. She couldn't swim like she used to—especially without the guidance of a certain mermaid—but with a pinch of luck and burning lungs, she located the cove.

Ana waited.

And waited.

Not a soul arrived.

She refused to cry, though her body craved it. What did she expect?

Why did she think, after so many years later, that Princess Korrina, likely a queen herself now, would greet her?

The lack of a letter from all those years ago was answer enough.

Korrina did not want her.

She didn't love her.

The swim back to land was near impossible in the dark. Queen Ana didn't return to the surface so much as she had washed up on it, lungs filled with water. She coughed up salty fluid, which decorated the light sand with dark speckles.

Ana collapsed on her back, still coughing. She pushed herself up to a sitting position, head hung low between her knees. Then she heard footsteps.

Light and barefoot, the sounds seem to come from behind her, from the cottage. But Ana didn't have the strength to lift her head and see.

The footsteps halted, just inches before Ana's exhausted, naked figure. The scent of seaweed invaded her nose.

A soft hand ran its fingers down the length of her back. Wound itself into the roots of Ana's tarnished red hair.

Then they spoke, and the voice sent a shiver of hope through Queen Ana.

"Never in my wildest dreams did I think seeing you again would be possible. You seeped into my every thought, it was impossible to be rid of you."

Strength fueled Ana's limbs as she turned around to gaze into the eyes of her lover, the one she had been missing for what seemed like two centuries.

"Korrina, is that you?"

She needn't ask. It was obvious. Though age lined her

cheeks and streaks of gray colored her hair, the maiden, *her* maiden, was easily recognizable.

Her love smiled.

"Well, I have a new name now. Follow me to my cottage, and I might just reveal it."

Ana allowed herself to be guided to the cabin. And that night, and for many nights to come, she learned numerous ways to say Queen Korrina.

The End.

Acknowledgments

This book has been a labor of love. And I've only probably cried a little bit about it. (This is a lie) I want to give a shout out to our live action Ariel–Halle Bailey–because that's where this all started. I read a news article about *The Little Mermaid* and was so excited to see a Black actress on the screen. Even if the movie wouldn't release for another two years. Did I mention that the movie was released on my birthday?? If that's not a sign, I don't know what is.

Thank you to the people that took the time to read my novel–ARC readers, Betas, Editors. *SLS* would not be here today without your input. Specifically, cheers to Andrea, Tony, and Britney for reading early versions of *SLS*.

Thank you to Kaitlin Schmidt for dev editing. Remember when I thought this was just a 40k novella?! I want to give a HUGE thank you to Sebbie for all the wonderful edits that followed. I dare say, you might love my characters as much as I do, if not more lol. ***sidenote**, so, so very sorry about what happened to your faves 😬

Writing is often a solitary action but there are some people I'm glad to have met along the way, even if I rarely show up to our monthly meetings 😸 MVICW crew–ya'll are so, so talented and I'm excited for your books to be released in the future!

Shoutout to all the cool people I've gotten to engage with on Threads as well! I'm an introvert in real life, but you guys get the best extroverted me lol.

Lastly, I want to thank We Need Diverse Books for believing in me when I submitted my first ever finished manuscript to their Black Creatives program. That was the catalyst to this all. Writing was no longer a fun hobby. I wanted to do this frfr.

To the writers that want to be published—sometimes you have to do it yourself lol. Whether you're aspiring to be indie or trad, just keep writing and learning. That's what matters.

🩶

Please leave a review!

Thank you so much for taking the time to read
Siren's Last Song !!!

Reviews help Indie Authors out a ton, so please leave one
when you get a chance :)

Ashleigh Martin (she/her) is an occasionally proud Texan and an always proud cat mom. When she's not working as a librarian, you can find her reading, crafting, or writing something sapphic. She's also a Martha's Vineyard Institute of Creative Writing Fellow and a WNDB Black Creatives Workshop participant. You can find her online at ashleighmartin.com or @ashleighmwrites on various social media sites. *Siren's Last Song* is her debut novel.